the Archie® DIGEST LIBRARY

Jughead® with Archie®

– in –

Family Photos

Spotlight

visit us at
www.abdopublishing.com

Exclusive Spotlight library bound edition published in 2007 by Spotlight, a division of ABDO Publishing Group, Edina, Minnesota. Spotlight produces high quality reinforced library bound editions for schools and libraries. Published by agreement with Archie Comic Publications, Inc.

Library of Congress Cataloging-in-Publication Data

Jughead with Archie in Family photos / edited by Nelson Ribeiro & Victor Gorelick.
    p. cm. -- (The Archie digest library)
    Revision of issue no. 188 (Jan. 2004) of Jughead with Archie digest magazine.
    ISBN-13: 978-1-59961-273-7
    ISBN-10: 1-59961-273-9
    1. Comic books, strips, etc. I. Ribeiro, Nelson. II. Gorelick, Victor. III. Jughead with Archie digest magazine. 188. IV. Title: Family photos.

PN6728.A72J86 2007
741.5'973--dc22

2006050550

All Spotlight books are reinforced library binding
and manufactured in the United States of America.

Contents

Jughead® with Archie®

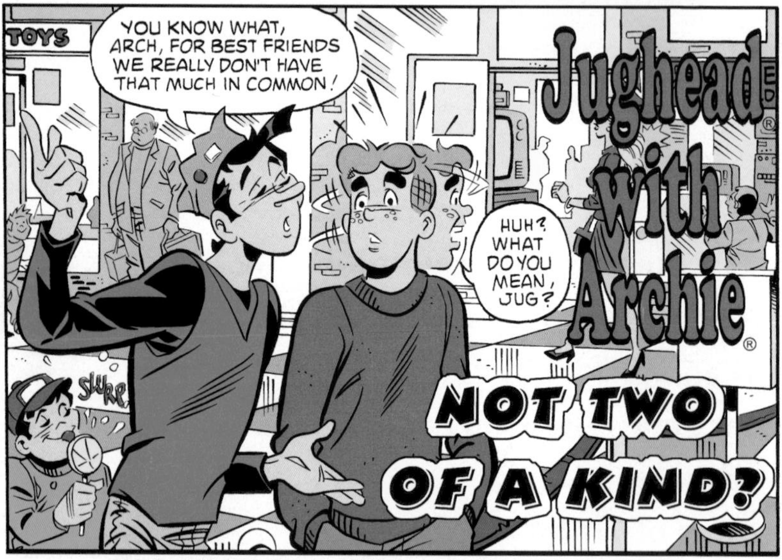

TOYS
YOU KNOW WHAT, ARCH, FOR BEST FRIENDS WE REALLY DON'T HAVE THAT MUCH IN COMMON!
HUH? WHAT DO YOU MEAN, JUG?
Jughead® with Archie®
NOT TWO OF A KIND?

SCRIPT: MIKE PELLOWKI PENCILS: AL BIGLEY INKS: AL MILGROM
COLORS: BARRY GROSSMAN LETTERS: BILL YOSHIDA
EDITORS: NELSON RIBEIRO & VICTOR GORELICK EDITOR-IN-CHIEF: RICHARD GOLDWATER

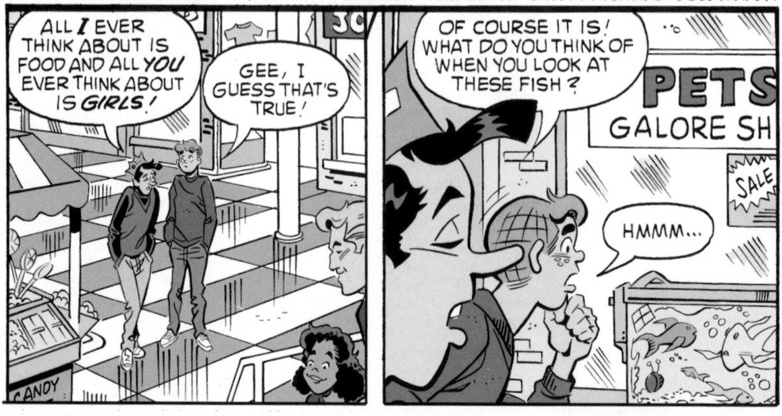

ALL I EVER THINK ABOUT IS FOOD AND ALL YOU EVER THINK ABOUT IS GIRLS!
GEE, I GUESS THAT'S TRUE!
CANDY
OF COURSE IT IS! WHAT DO YOU THINK OF WHEN YOU LOOK AT THESE FISH?
PETS
GALORE SH
SALE
HMMM...

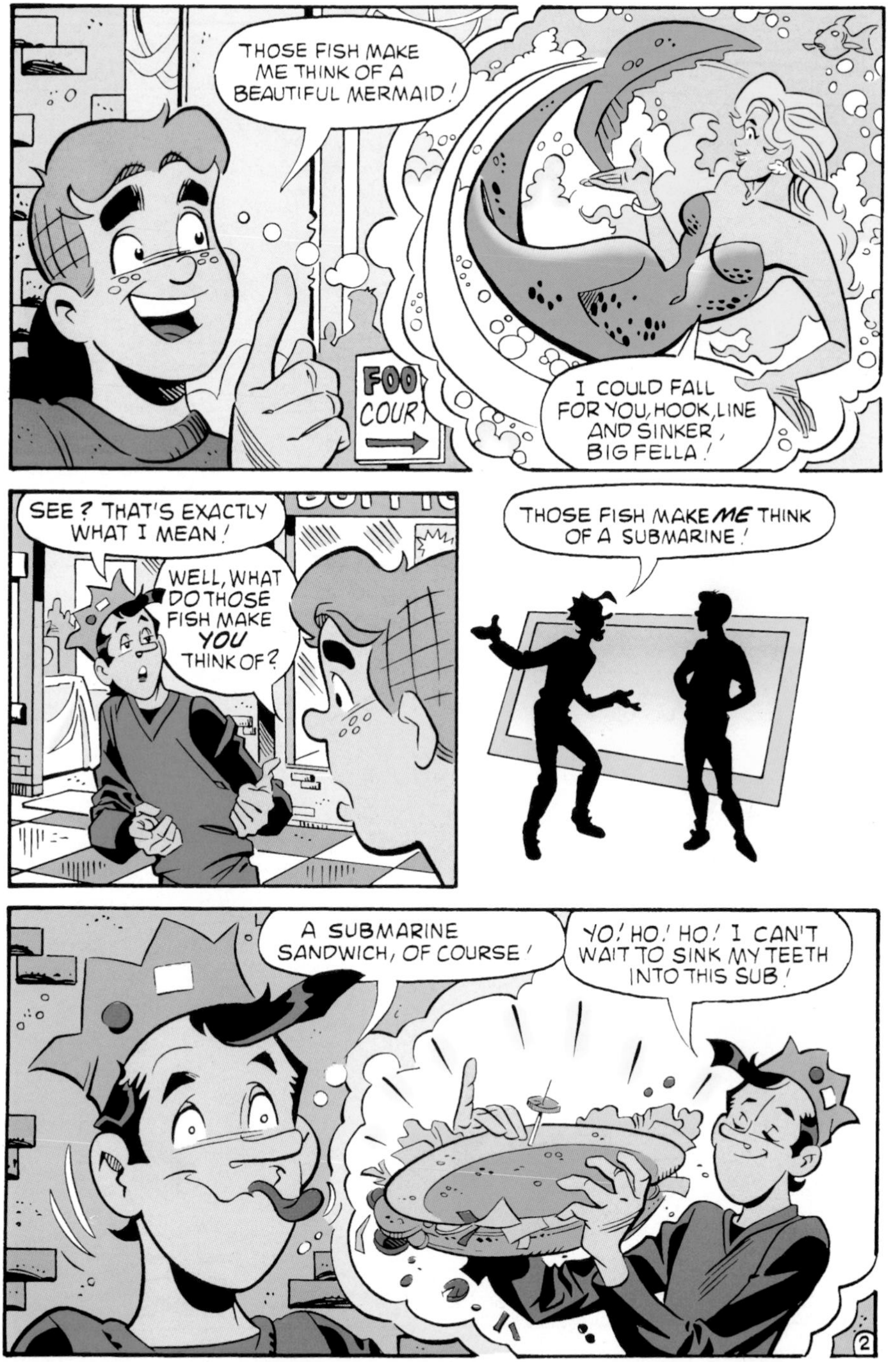
THOSE FISH MAKE ME THINK OF A BEAUTIFUL MERMAID!
I COULD FALL FOR YOU, HOOK, LINE AND SINKER, BIG FELLA!
FOO COURT
SEE? THAT'S EXACTLY WHAT I MEAN!
WELL, WHAT DO THOSE FISH MAKE YOU THINK OF?
THOSE FISH MAKE ME THINK OF A SUBMARINE!
A SUBMARINE SANDWICH, OF COURSE!
YO! HO! HO! I CAN'T WAIT TO SINK MY TEETH INTO THIS SUB!
2

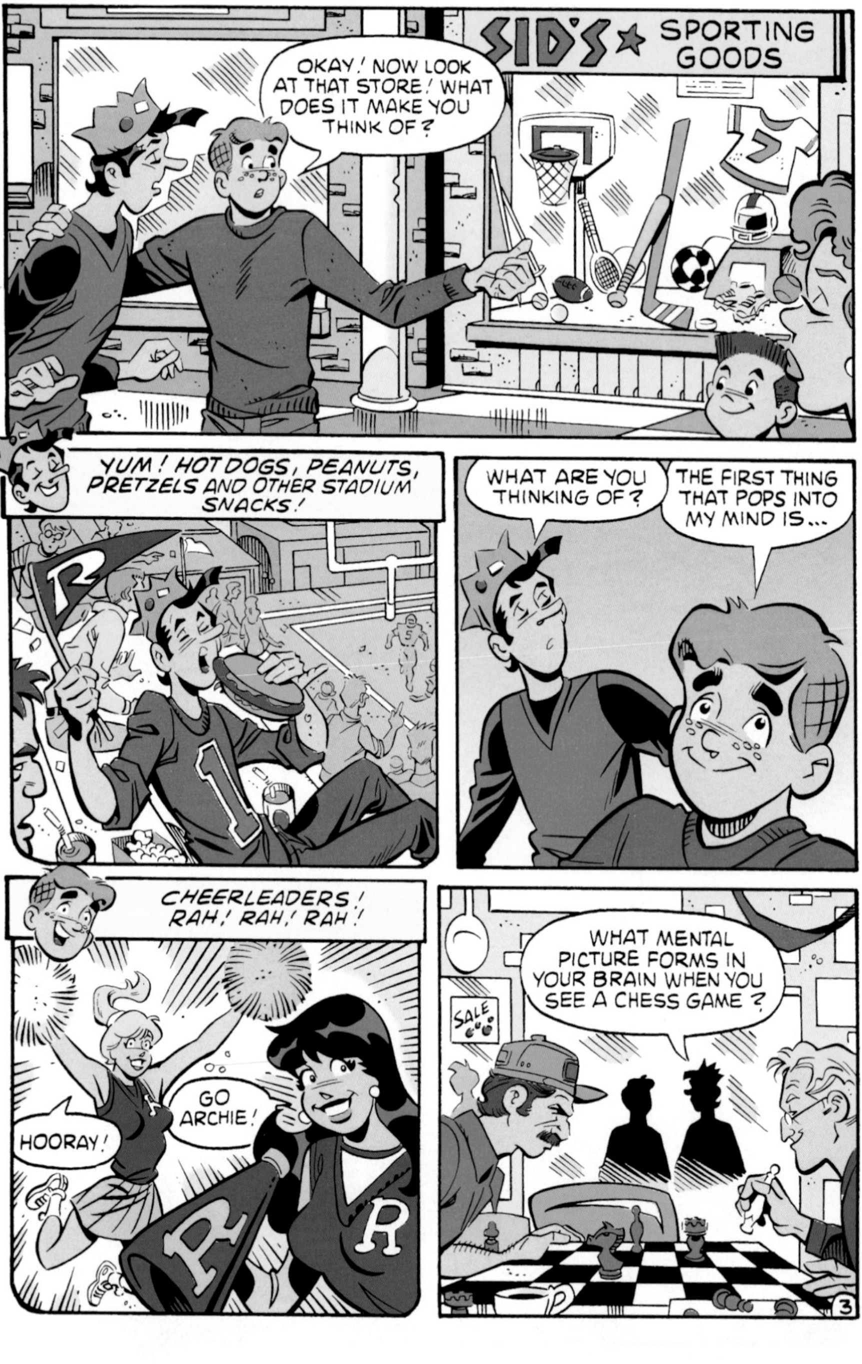
SID'S SPORTING GOODS
OKAY! NOW LOOK AT THAT STORE! WHAT DOES IT MAKE YOU THINK OF?
YUM! HOT DOGS, PEANUTS, PRETZELS AND OTHER STADIUM SNACKS!
WHAT ARE YOU THINKING OF?
THE FIRST THING THAT POPS INTO MY MIND IS...
CHEERLEADERS! RAH! RAH! RAH!
HOORAY!
GO ARCHIE!
WHAT MENTAL PICTURE FORMS IN YOUR BRAIN WHEN YOU SEE A CHESS GAME?
SALE
3

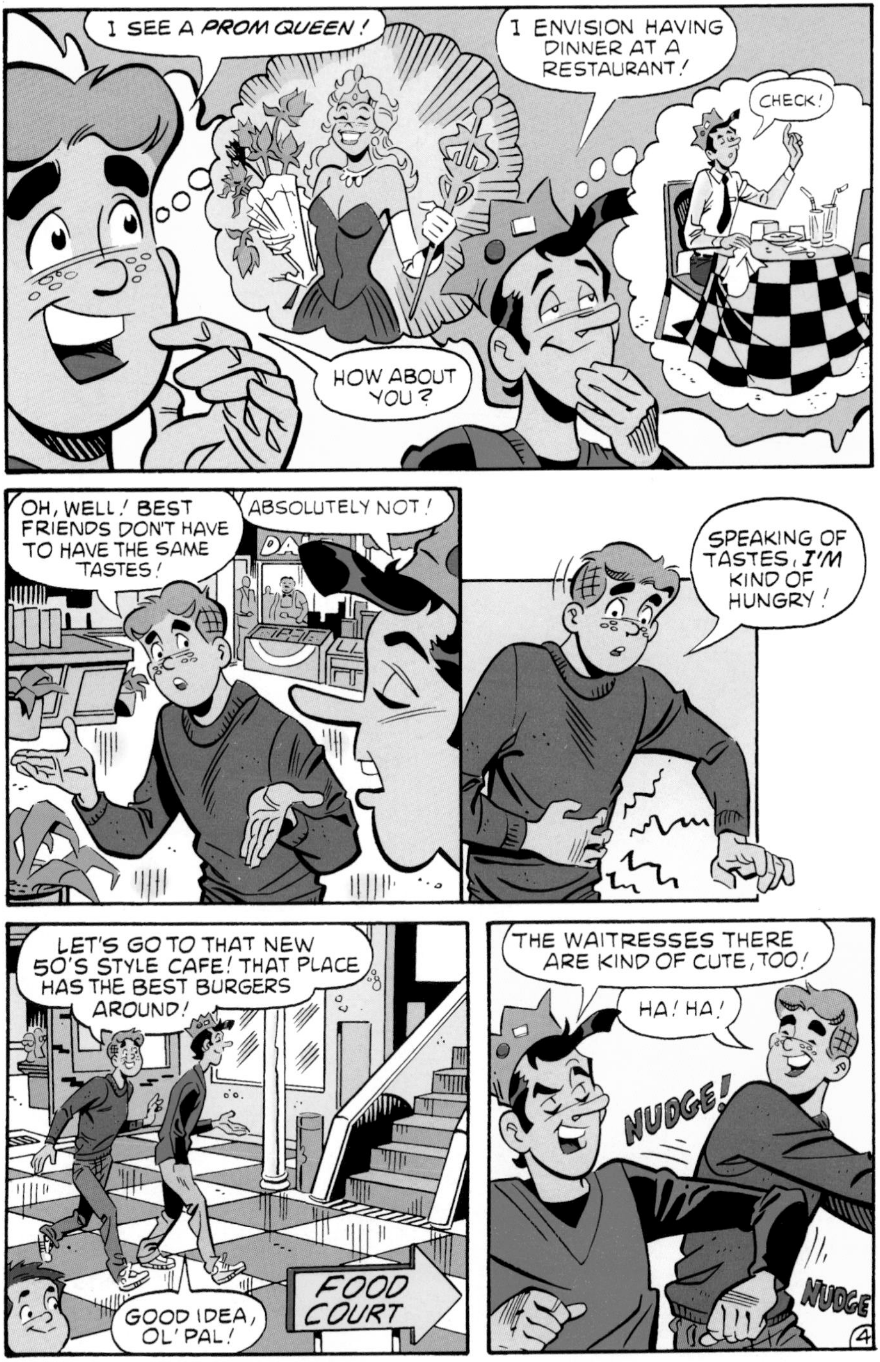
I SEE A *PROM QUEEN*!
HOW ABOUT YOU?
I ENVISION HAVING DINNER AT A RESTAURANT!
CHECK!
OH, WELL! BEST FRIENDS DON'T HAVE TO HAVE THE SAME TASTES!
ABSOLUTELY NOT!
SPEAKING OF TASTES, *I'M* KIND OF HUNGRY!
LET'S GO TO THAT NEW 50'S STYLE CAFE! THAT PLACE HAS THE BEST BURGERS AROUND!
GOOD IDEA, OL' PAL!
FOOD COURT
THE WAITRESSES THERE ARE KIND OF CUTE, TOO!
HA! HA!
NUDGE!
NUDGE
4

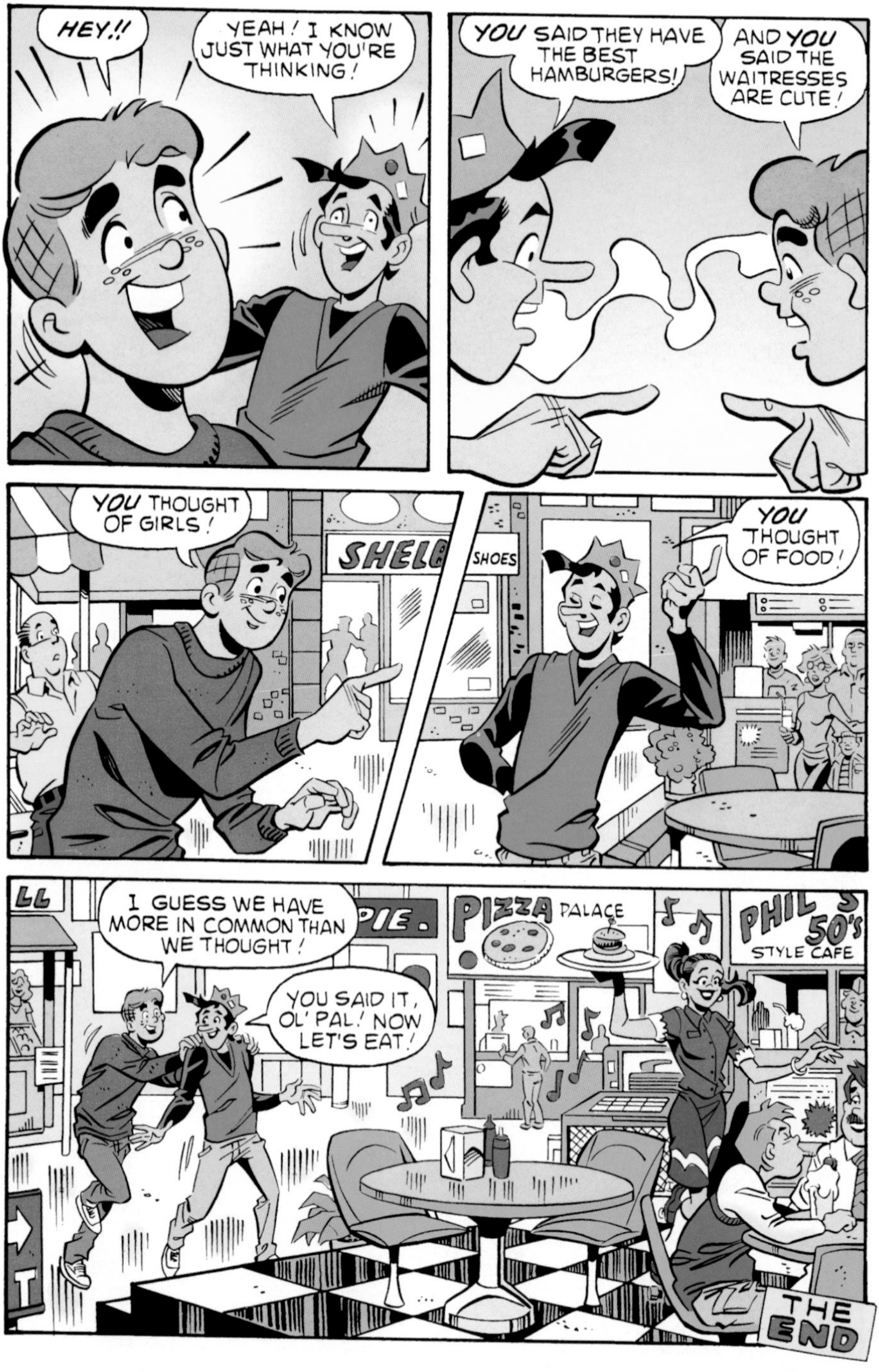
HEY!!
YEAH! I KNOW JUST WHAT YOU'RE THINKING!
YOU SAID THEY HAVE THE BEST HAMBURGERS!
AND YOU SAID THE WAITRESSES ARE CUTE!
YOU THOUGHT OF GIRLS!
SHOES
YOU THOUGHT OF FOOD!
I GUESS WE HAVE MORE IN COMMON THAN WE THOUGHT!
PIE.
PIZZA PALACE
PHIL'S 50's STYLE CAFE
YOU SAID IT, OL' PAL! NOW LET'S EAT!
THE END

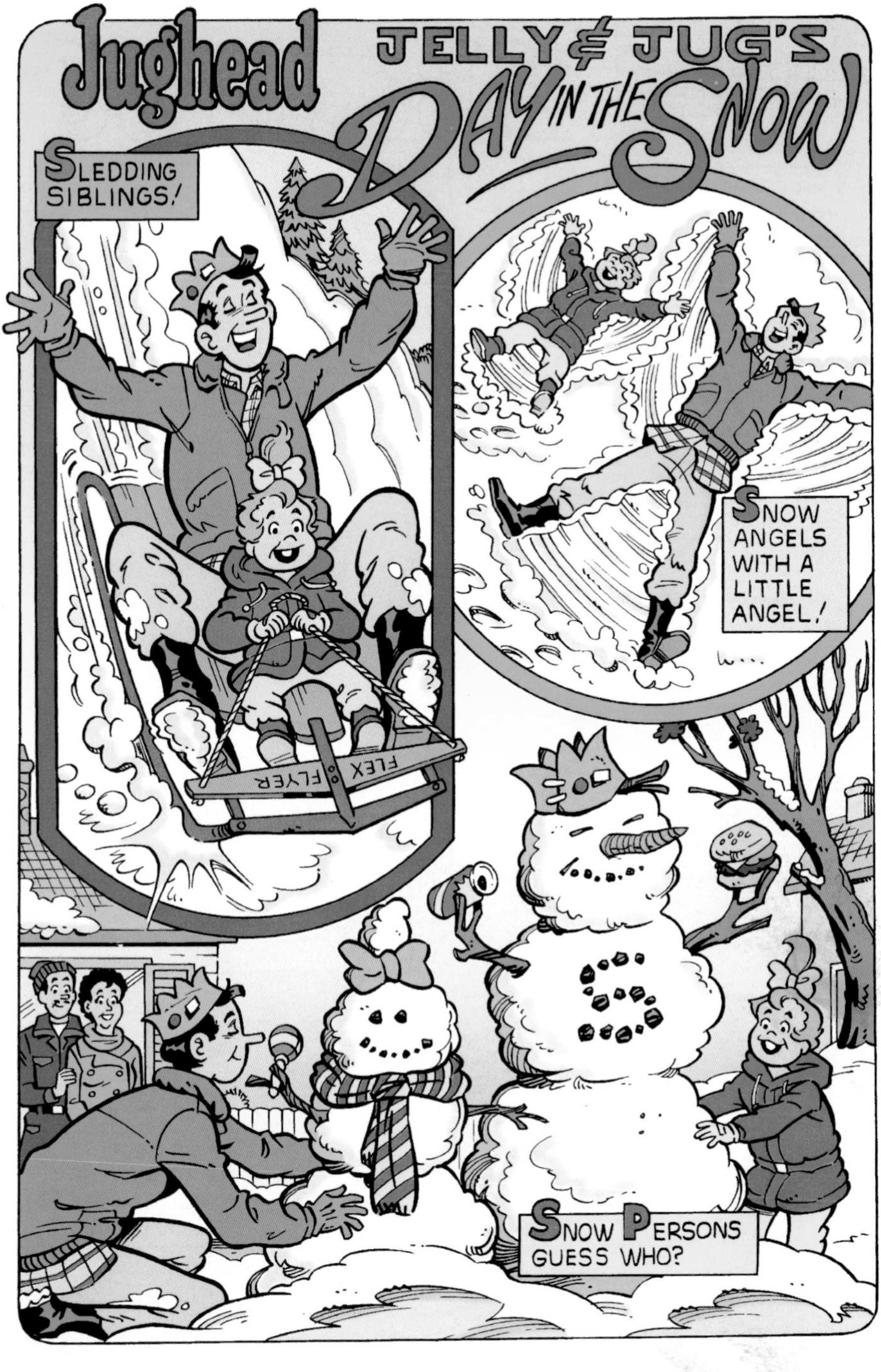
Jughead
JELLY & JUG'S DAY IN THE SNOW
SLEDDING SIBLINGS!
FLEX FLYER
SNOW ANGELS WITH A LITTLE ANGEL!
SNOW PERSONS GUESS WHO?

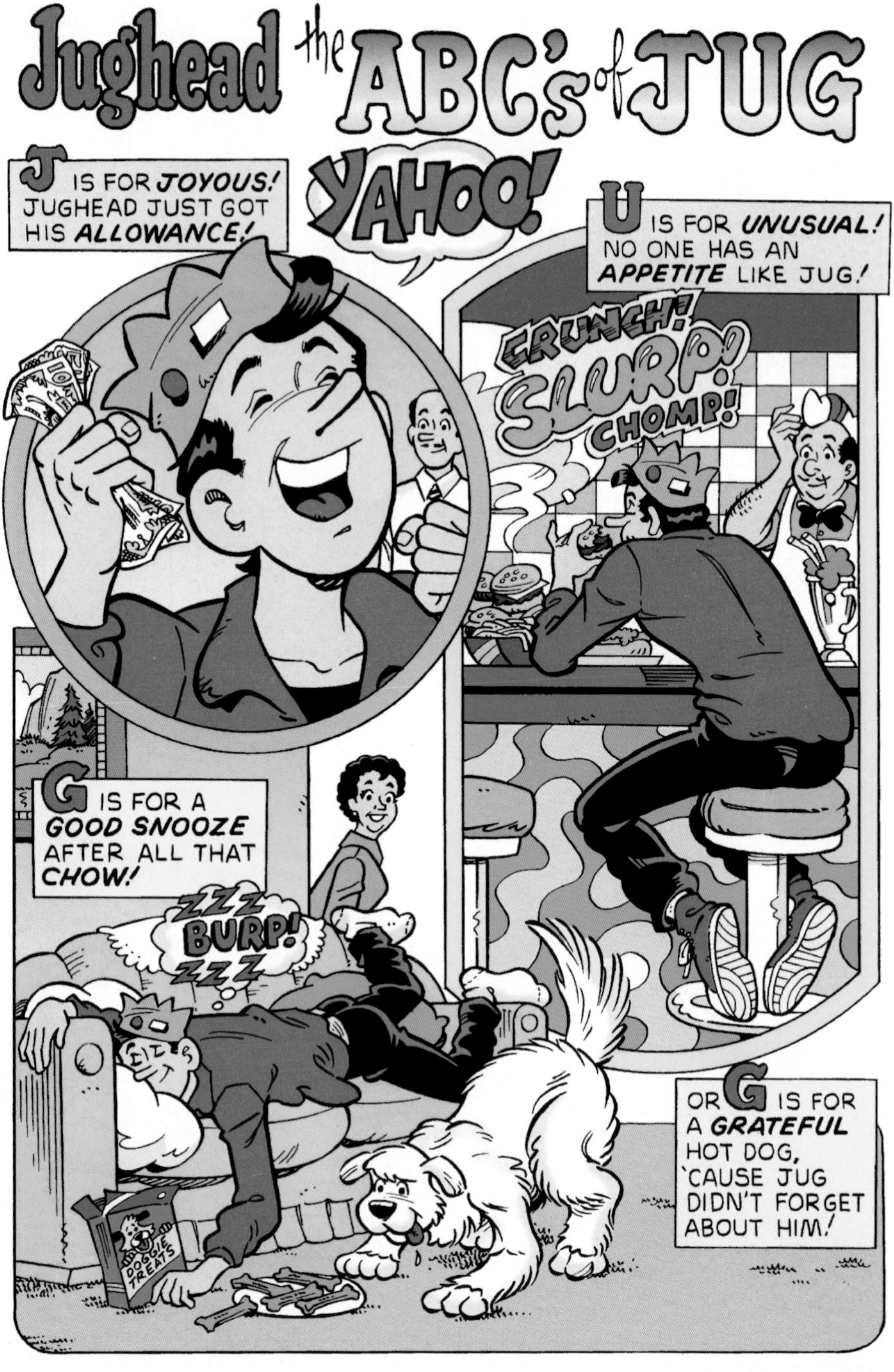
Jughead
the ABC's of JUG
J IS FOR JOYOUS! JUGHEAD JUST GOT HIS ALLOWANCE!
YAHOO!
U IS FOR UNUSUAL! NO ONE HAS AN APPETITE LIKE JUG!
CRUNCH! SLURP! CHOMP!
G IS FOR A GOOD SNOOZE AFTER ALL THAT CHOW!
ZZZ BURP! ZZZ
OR G IS FOR A GRATEFUL HOT DOG, 'CAUSE JUG DIDN'T FORGET ABOUT HIM!
DOGGIE TREATS

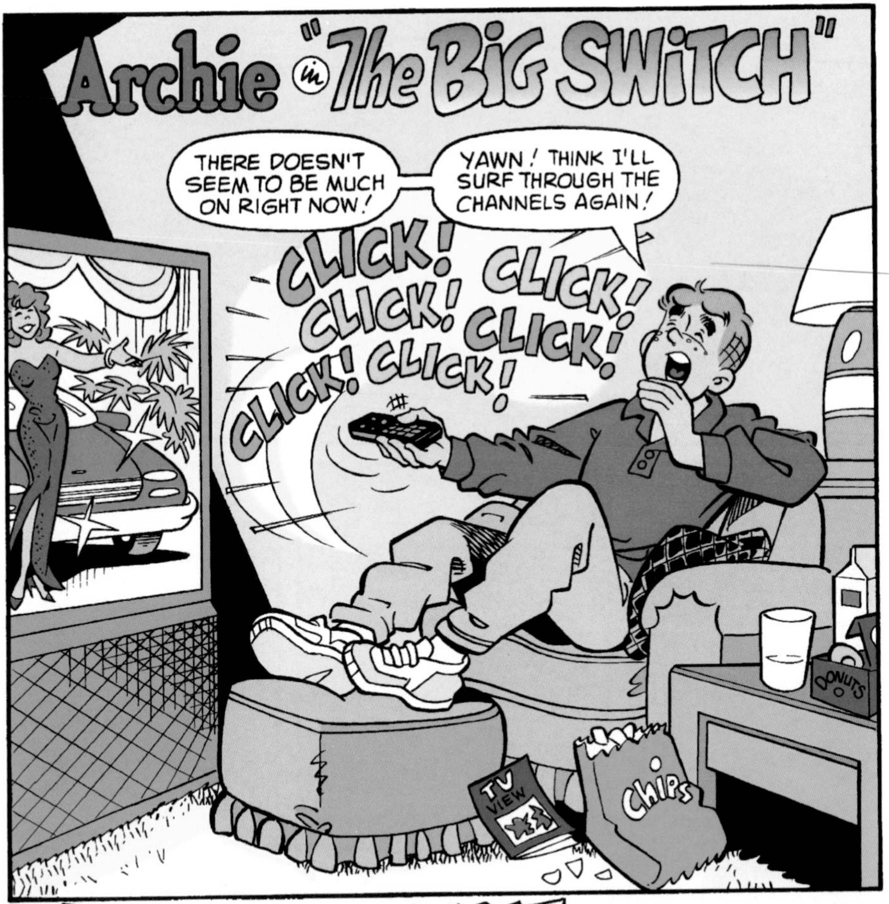
Archie in "The BIG SWITCH"
THERE DOESN'T SEEM TO BE MUCH ON RIGHT NOW!
YAWN! THINK I'LL SURF THROUGH THE CHANNELS AGAIN!
CLICK! CLICK! CLICK! CLICK! CLICK! CLICK!
TV VIEW
CHIPS
DONUTS

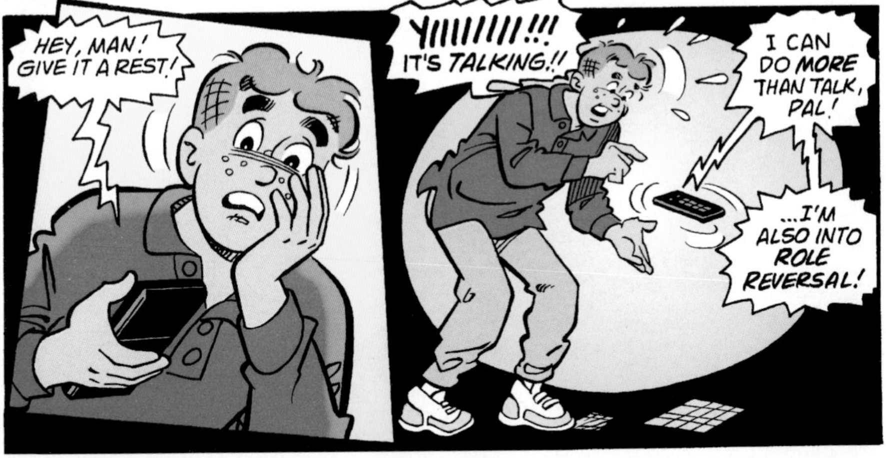
HEY, MAN! GIVE IT A REST!
YIIIIIIII!!! IT'S TALKING!!
I CAN DO MORE THAN TALK, PAL!
...I'M ALSO INTO ROLE REVERSAL!

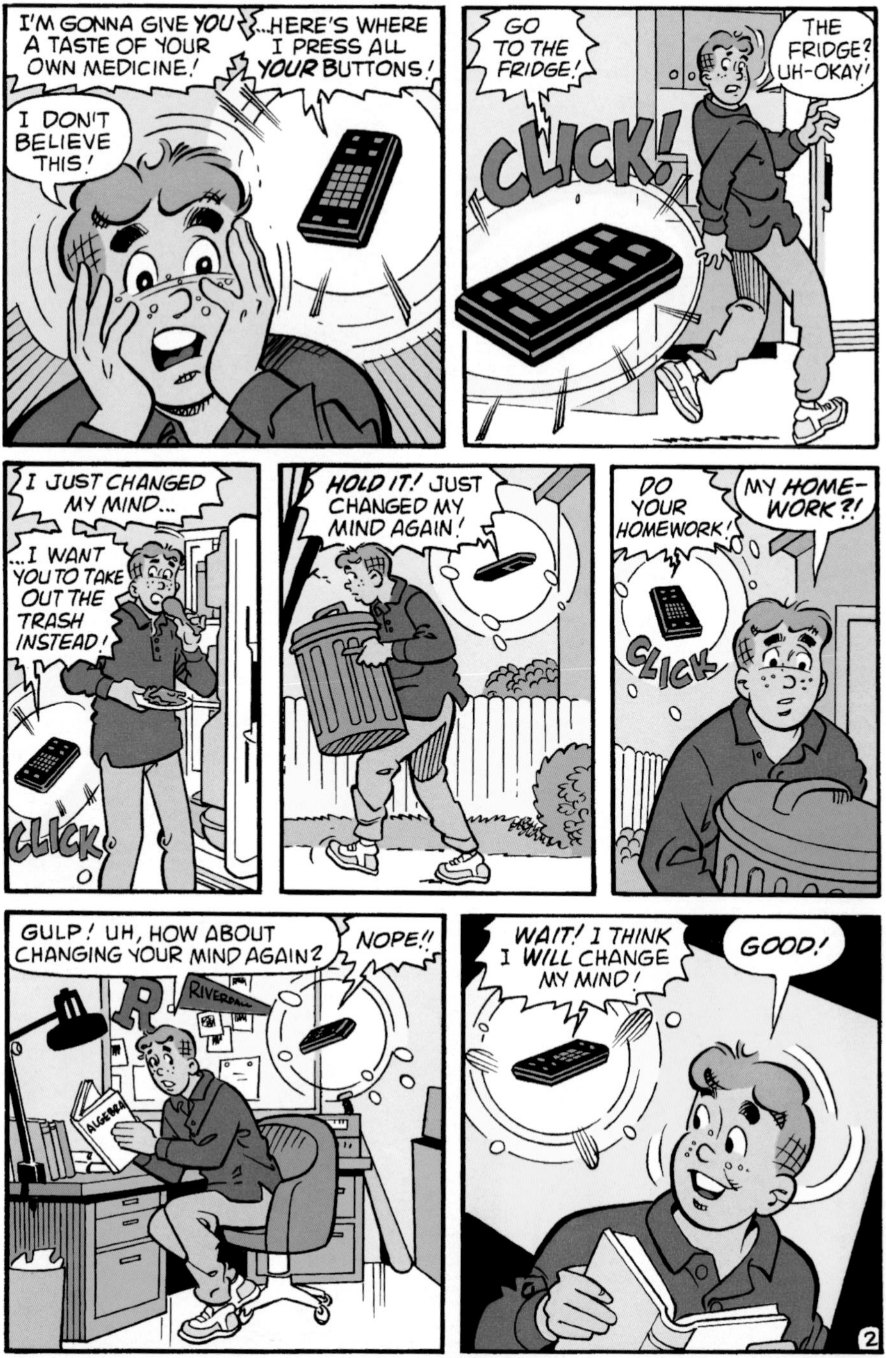
I'M GONNA GIVE YOU A TASTE OF YOUR OWN MEDICINE!
...HERE'S WHERE I PRESS ALL YOUR BUTTONS!
I DON'T BELIEVE THIS!
GO TO THE FRIDGE!
CLICK!
THE FRIDGE? UH-OKAY!
I JUST CHANGED MY MIND...
...I WANT YOU TO TAKE OUT THE TRASH INSTEAD!
CLICK
HOLD IT! JUST CHANGED MY MIND AGAIN!
DO YOUR HOMEWORK!
CLICK
MY HOMEWORK?!
GULP! UH, HOW ABOUT CHANGING YOUR MIND AGAIN?
NOPE!!
R
RIVERDALE
ALGEBRA
WAIT! I THINK I WILL CHANGE MY MIND!
GOOD!
2

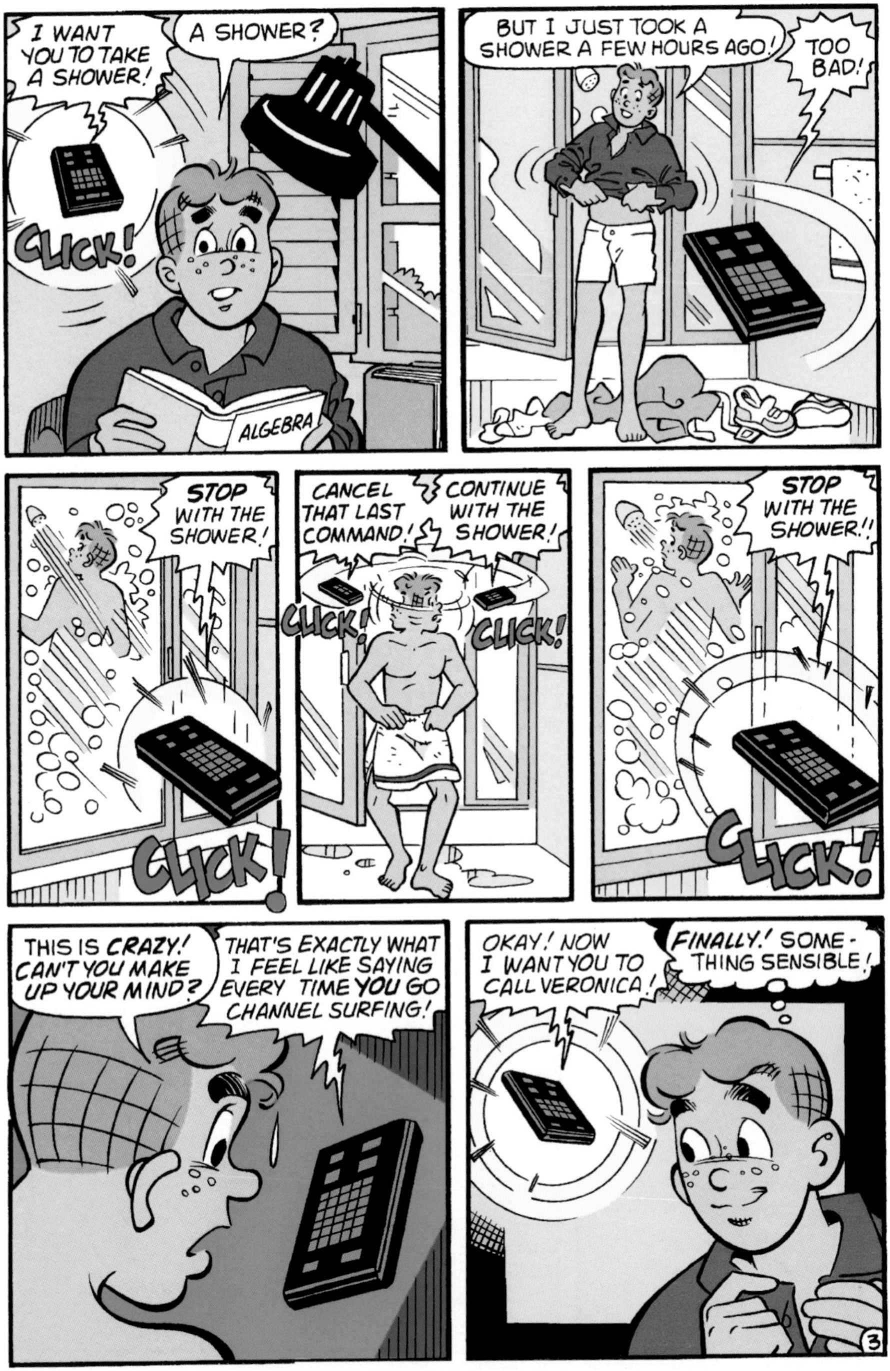
I WANT YOU TO TAKE A SHOWER!
CLICK!
A SHOWER?
ALGEBRA
BUT I JUST TOOK A SHOWER A FEW HOURS AGO!
TOO BAD!
STOP WITH THE SHOWER!
CLICK!
CANCEL THAT LAST COMMAND!
CONTINUE WITH THE SHOWER!
CLICK!
CLICK!
STOP WITH THE SHOWER!!
CLICK!
THIS IS CRAZY! CAN'T YOU MAKE UP YOUR MIND?
THAT'S EXACTLY WHAT I FEEL LIKE SAYING EVERY TIME YOU GO CHANNEL SURFING!
OKAY! NOW I WANT YOU TO CALL VERONICA!
FINALLY! SOME-THING SENSIBLE!
3

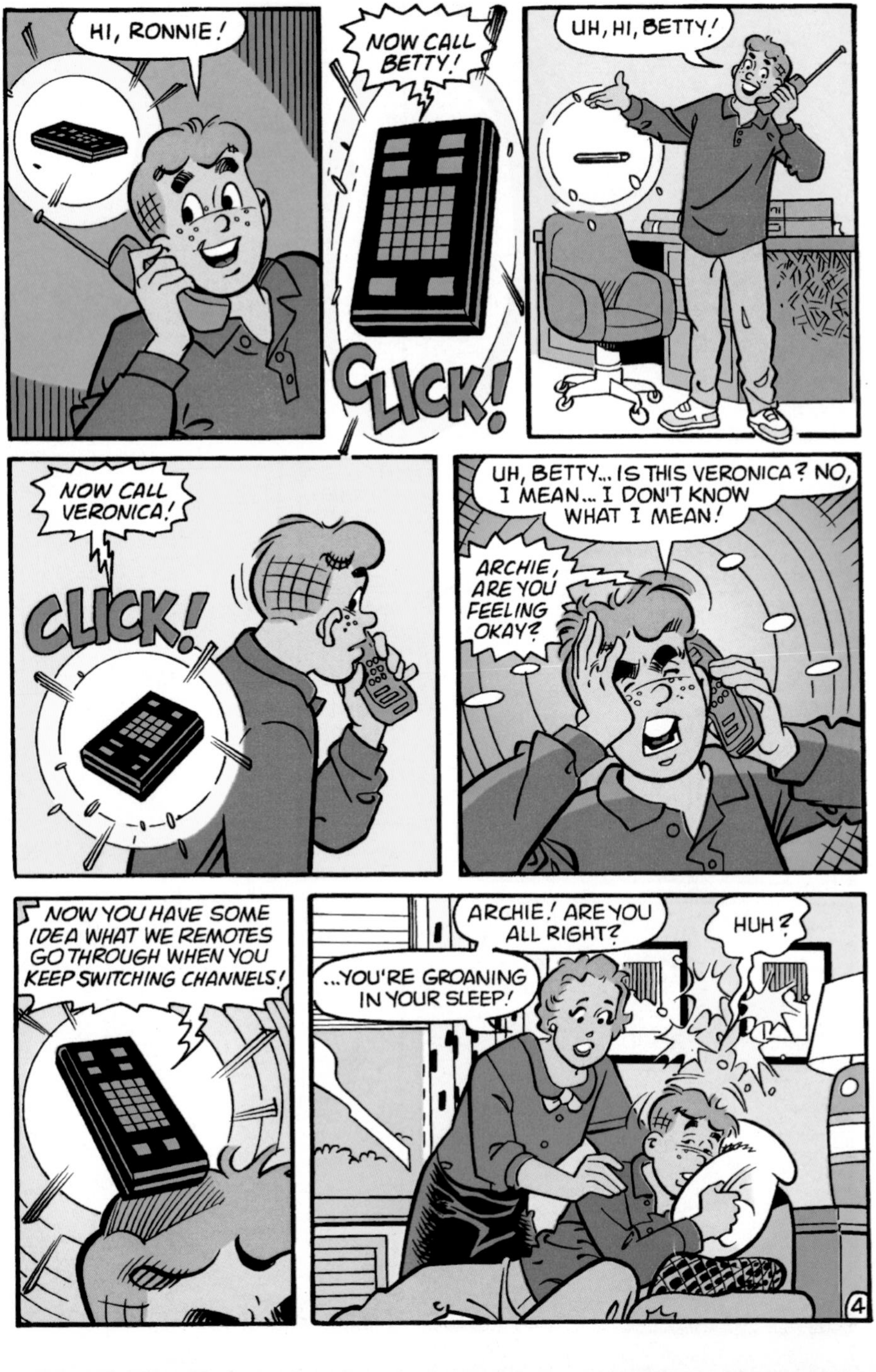
HI, RONNIE!
NOW CALL BETTY!
CLICK!
UH, HI, BETTY!
NOW CALL VERONICA!
CLICK!
UH, BETTY... IS THIS VERONICA? NO, I MEAN... I DON'T KNOW WHAT I MEAN!
ARCHIE, ARE YOU FEELING OKAY?
NOW YOU HAVE SOME IDEA WHAT WE REMOTES GO THROUGH WHEN YOU KEEP SWITCHING CHANNELS!
ARCHIE! ARE YOU ALL RIGHT?
...YOU'RE GROANING IN YOUR SLEEP!
HUH?
4

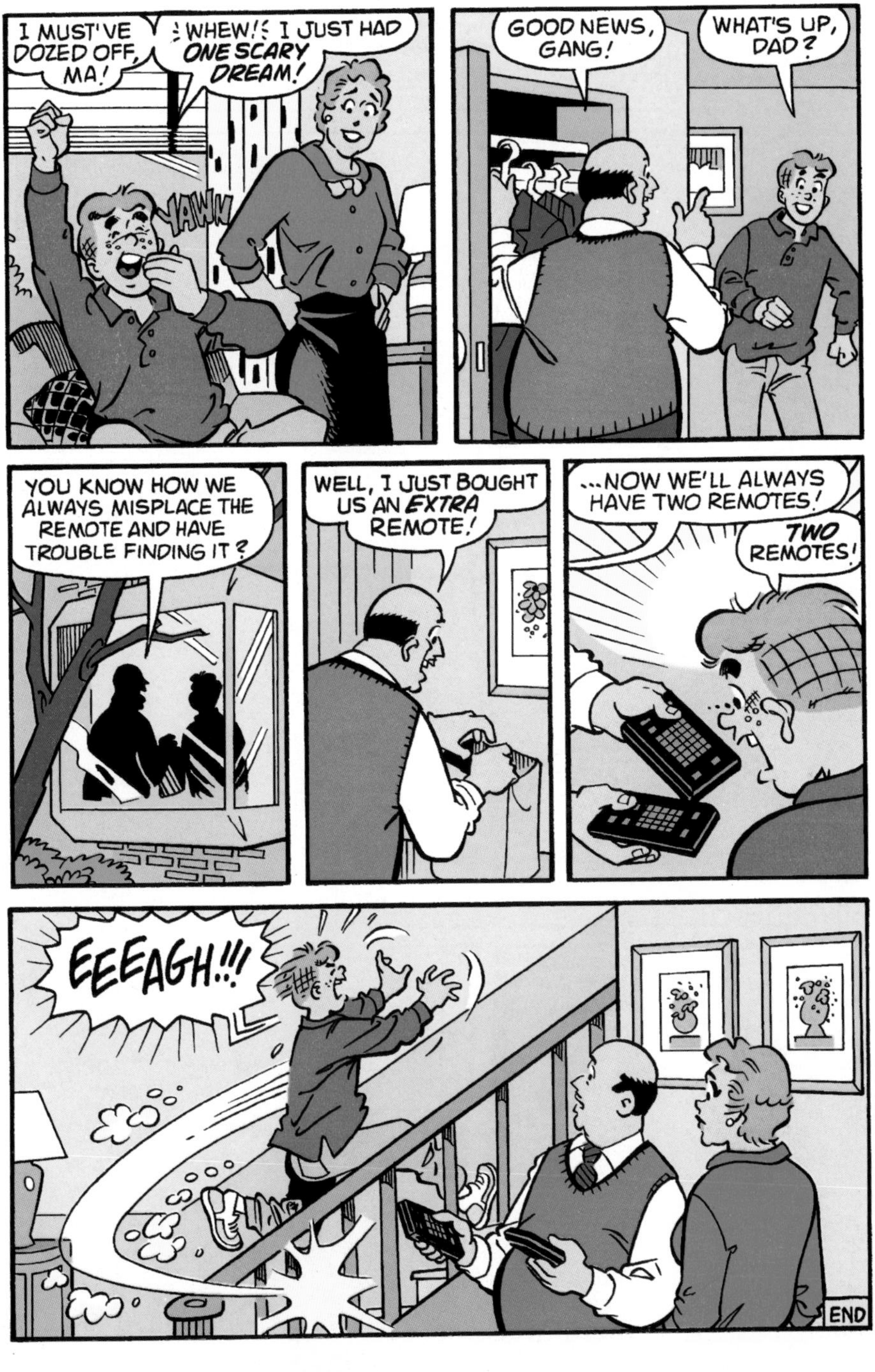
I MUST'VE DOZED OFF, MA!
WHEW! I JUST HAD ONE SCARY DREAM!
YAWN
GOOD NEWS, GANG!
WHAT'S UP, DAD?
YOU KNOW HOW WE ALWAYS MISPLACE THE REMOTE AND HAVE TROUBLE FINDING IT?
WELL, I JUST BOUGHT US AN EXTRA REMOTE!
...NOW WE'LL ALWAYS HAVE TWO REMOTES!
TWO REMOTES!
EEEAGH!!!
END

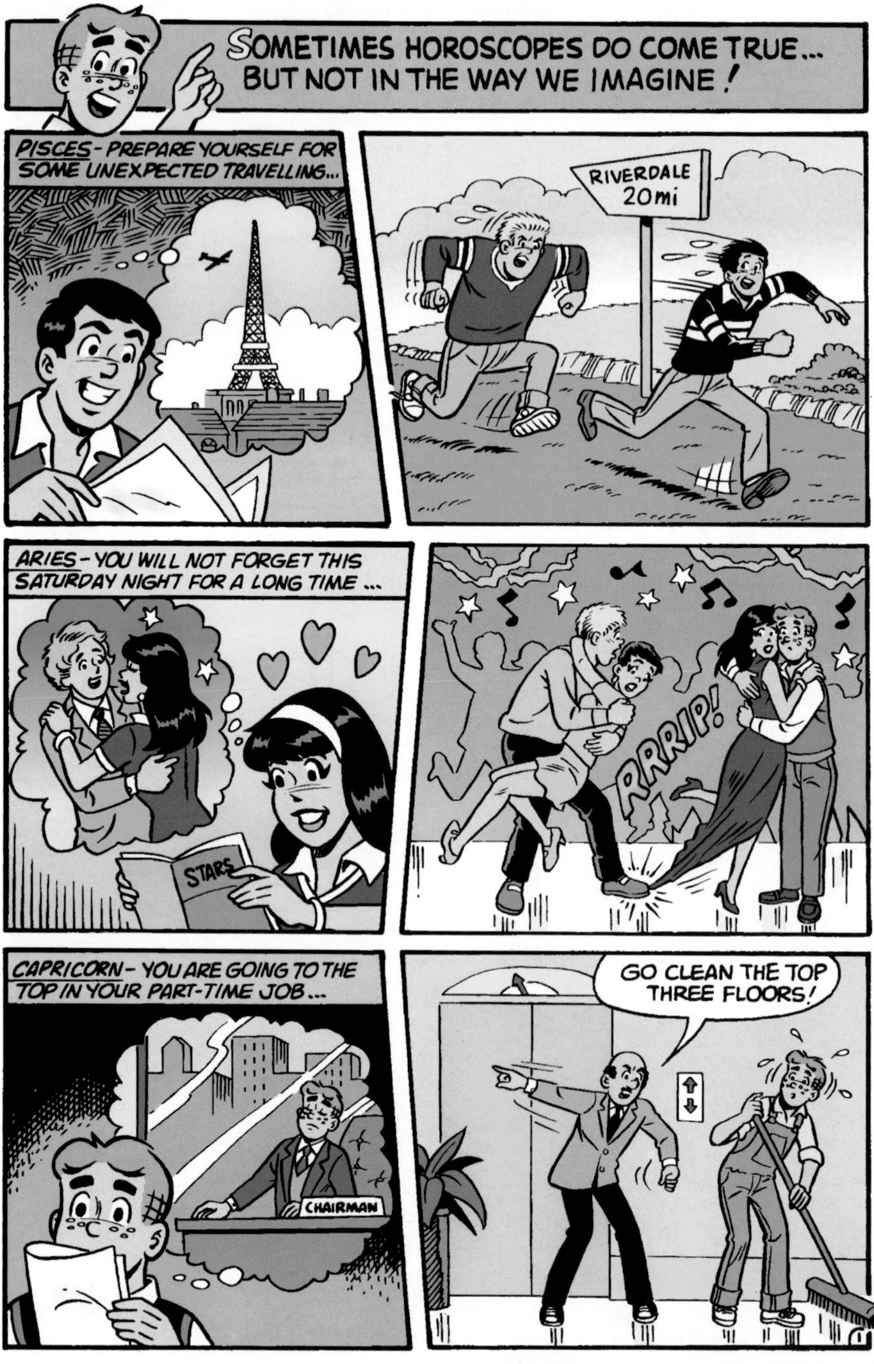
SOMETIMES HOROSCOPES DO COME TRUE... BUT NOT IN THE WAY WE IMAGINE!
PISCES - PREPARE YOURSELF FOR SOME UNEXPECTED TRAVELLING...
RIVERDALE 20mi
ARIES - YOU WILL NOT FORGET THIS SATURDAY NIGHT FOR A LONG TIME ...
STARS
RRRIP!
CAPRICORN - YOU ARE GOING TO THE TOP IN YOUR PART-TIME JOB...
CHAIRMAN
GO CLEAN THE TOP THREE FLOORS!

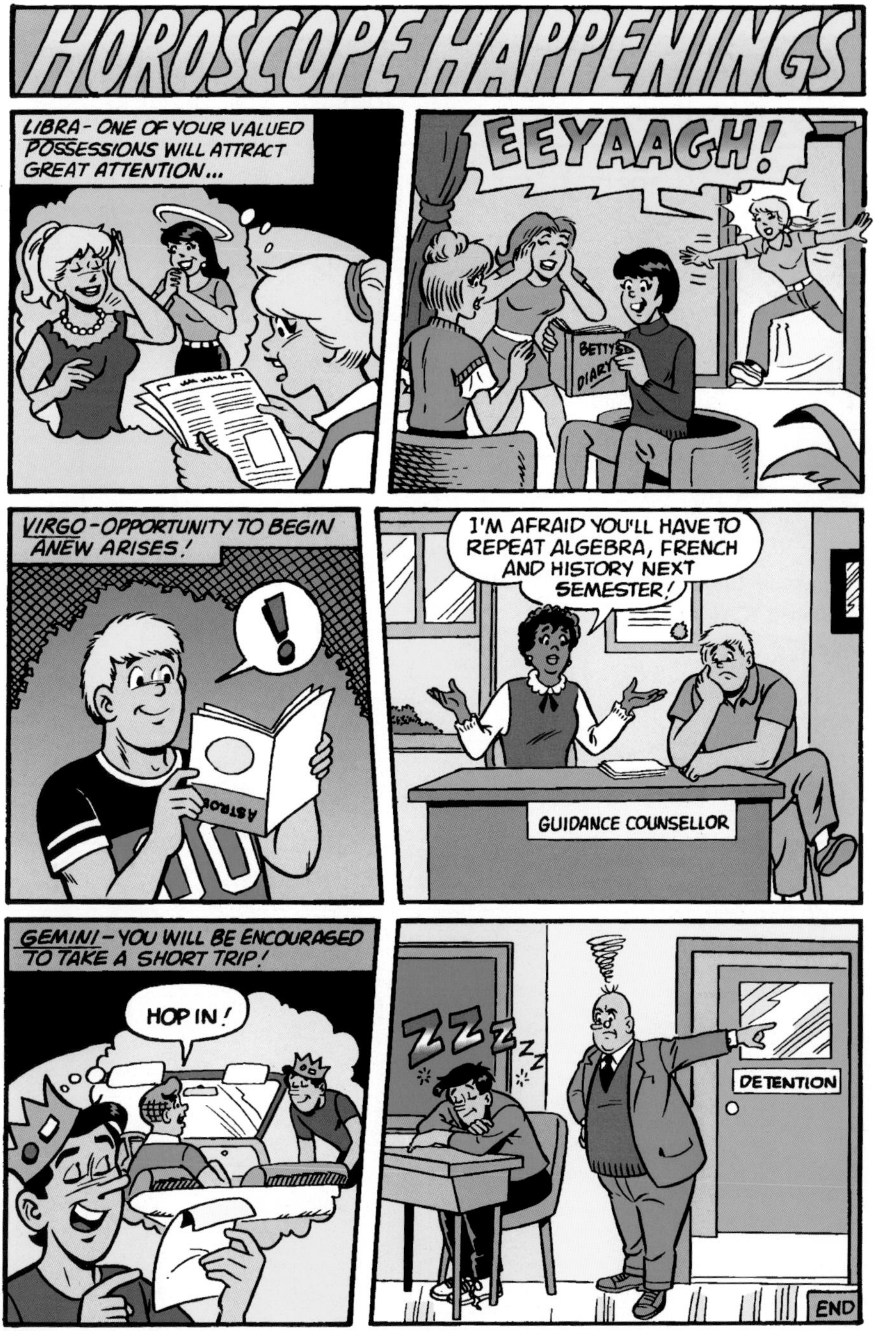
HOROSCOPE HAPPENINGS
LIBRA- ONE OF YOUR VALUED POSSESSIONS WILL ATTRACT GREAT ATTENTION...
EEYAAGH!
BETTY'S DIARY
VIRGO-OPPORTUNITY TO BEGIN ANEW ARISES!
!
ASTRO
I'M AFRAID YOU'LL HAVE TO REPEAT ALGEBRA, FRENCH AND HISTORY NEXT SEMESTER!
GUIDANCE COUNSELLOR
GEMINI-YOU WILL BE ENCOURAGED TO TAKE A SHORT TRIP!
HOP IN!
ZZZ
ZZ
DETENTION
END

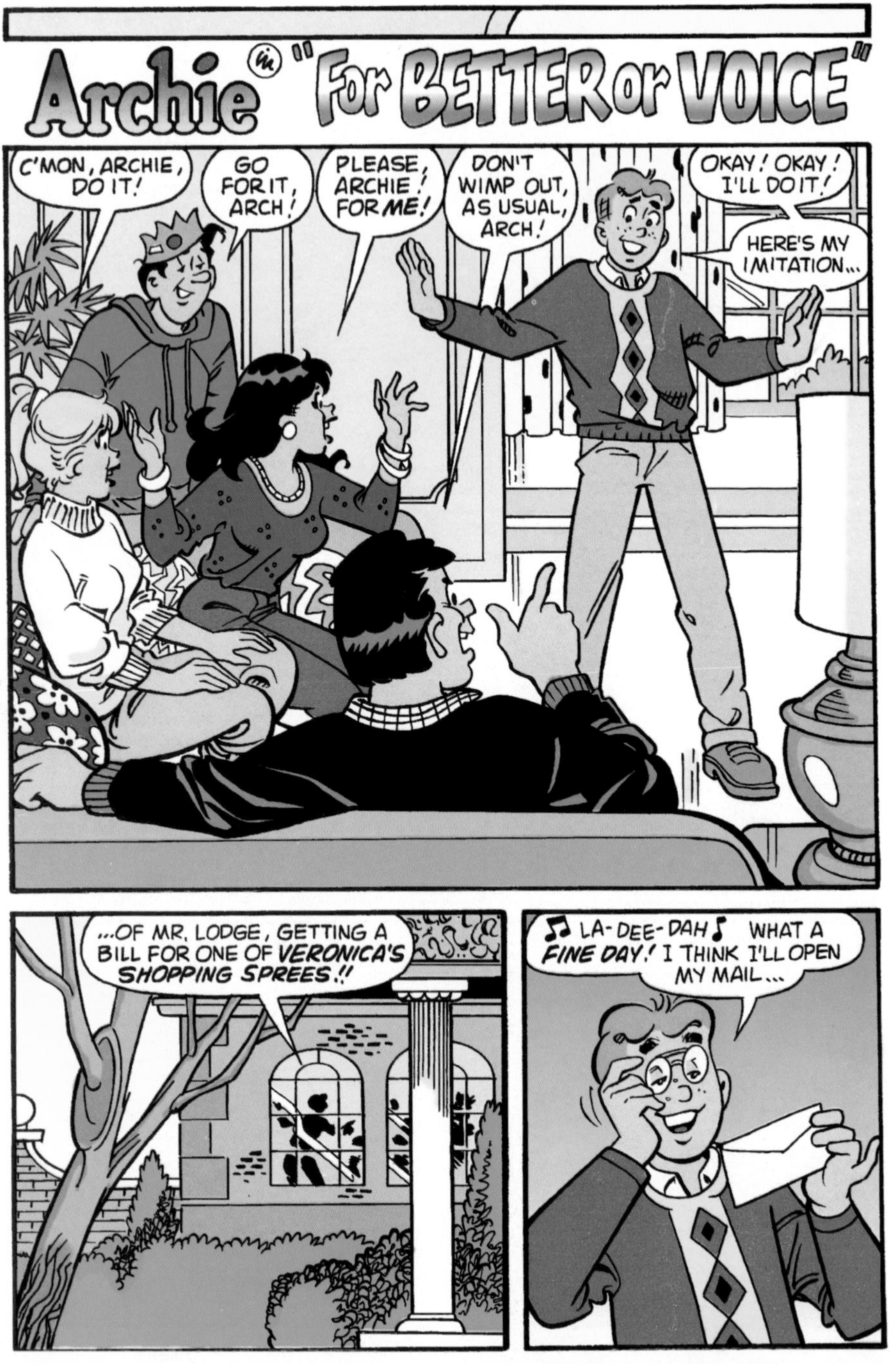
Archie in "For BETTER or VOICE"
C'MON, ARCHIE, DO IT!
GO FOR IT, ARCH!
PLEASE, ARCHIE! FOR ME!
DON'T WIMP OUT, AS USUAL, ARCH!
OKAY! OKAY! I'LL DO IT!
HERE'S MY IMITATION...
...OF MR. LODGE, GETTING A BILL FOR ONE OF VERONICA'S SHOPPING SPREES!!
LA-DEE-DAH WHAT A FINE DAY! I THINK I'LL OPEN MY MAIL...

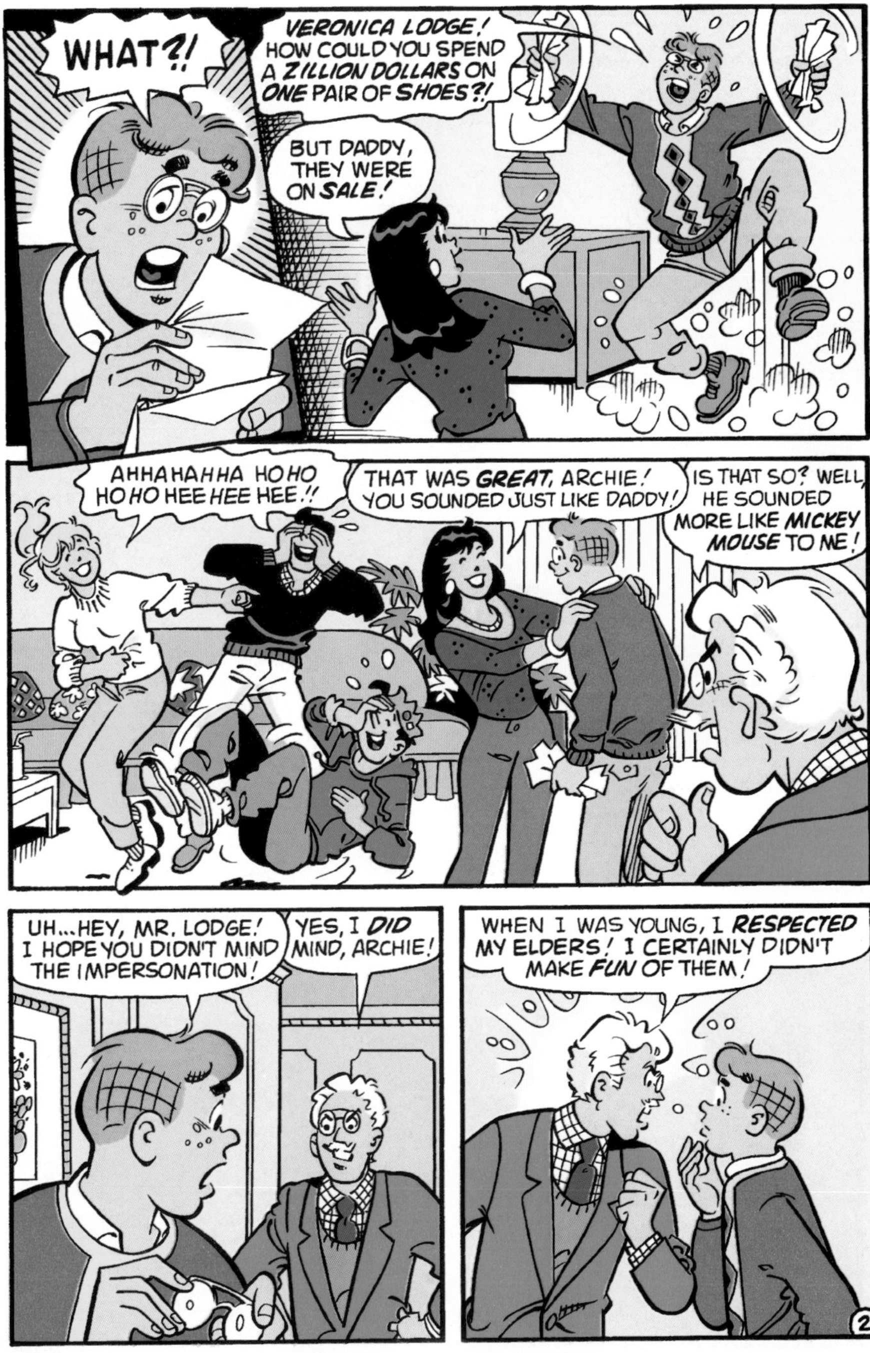
WHAT?!
VERONICA LODGE! HOW COULD YOU SPEND A ZILLION DOLLARS ON ONE PAIR OF SHOES?!
BUT DADDY, THEY WERE ON SALE!
AHHAHAHHA HOHO HOHO HEEHEE HEE!!
THAT WAS GREAT, ARCHIE! YOU SOUNDED JUST LIKE DADDY!
IS THAT SO? WELL, HE SOUNDED MORE LIKE MICKEY MOUSE TO ME!
UH...HEY, MR. LODGE! I HOPE YOU DIDN'T MIND THE IMPERSONATION!
YES, I DID MIND, ARCHIE!
WHEN I WAS YOUNG, I RESPECTED MY ELDERS! I CERTAINLY DIDN'T MAKE FUN OF THEM!
2

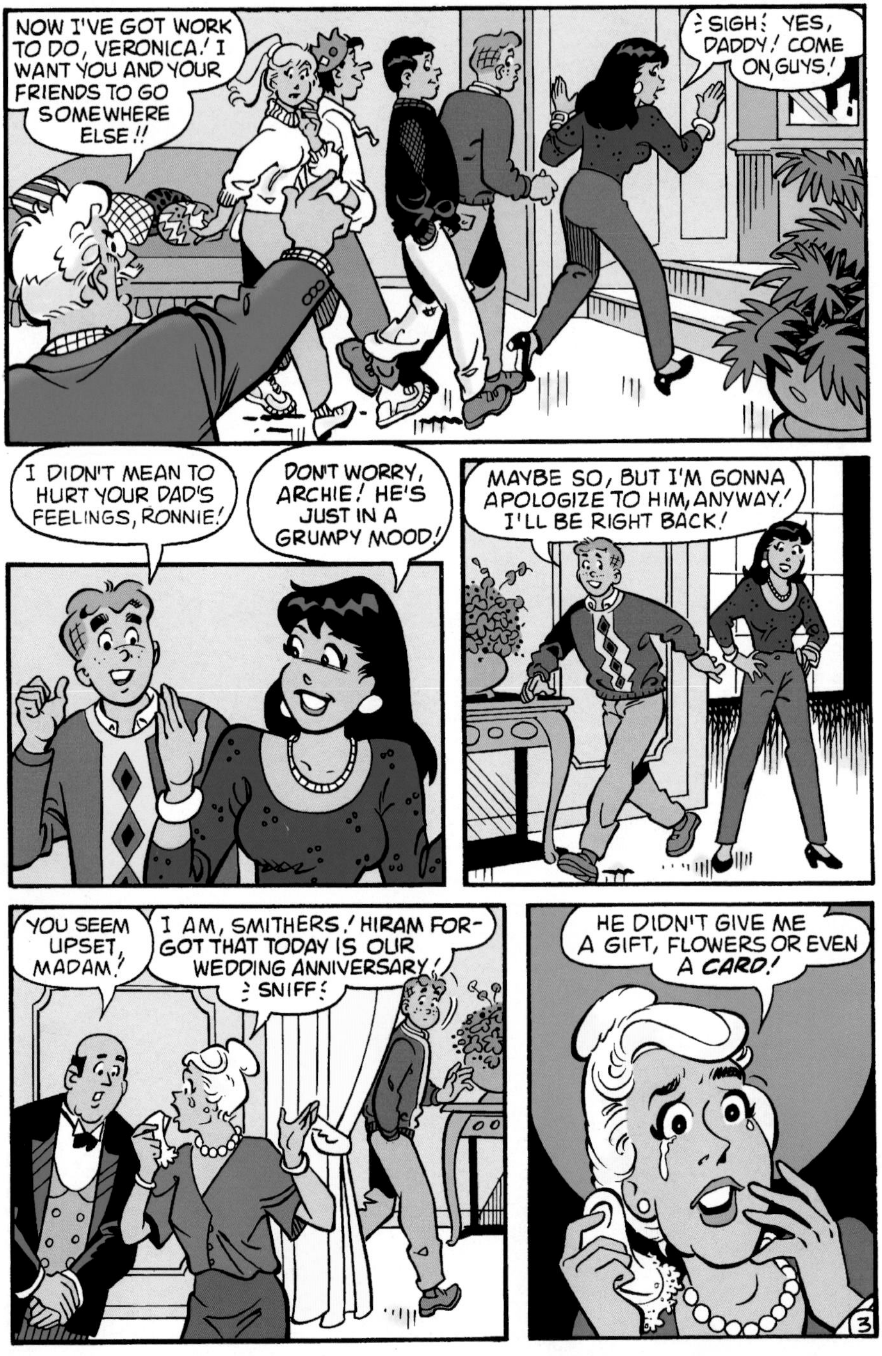
NOW I'VE GOT WORK TO DO, VERONICA! I WANT YOU AND YOUR FRIENDS TO GO SOMEWHERE ELSE!!
SIGH! YES, DADDY! COME ON, GUYS!
I DIDN'T MEAN TO HURT YOUR DAD'S FEELINGS, RONNIE!
DON'T WORRY, ARCHIE! HE'S JUST IN A GRUMPY MOOD!
MAYBE SO, BUT I'M GONNA APOLOGIZE TO HIM, ANYWAY! I'LL BE RIGHT BACK!
YOU SEEM UPSET, MADAM!
I AM, SMITHERS! HIRAM FORGOT THAT TODAY IS OUR WEDDING ANNIVERSARY!
SNIFF!
HE DIDN'T GIVE ME A GIFT, FLOWERS OR EVEN A CARD!
3

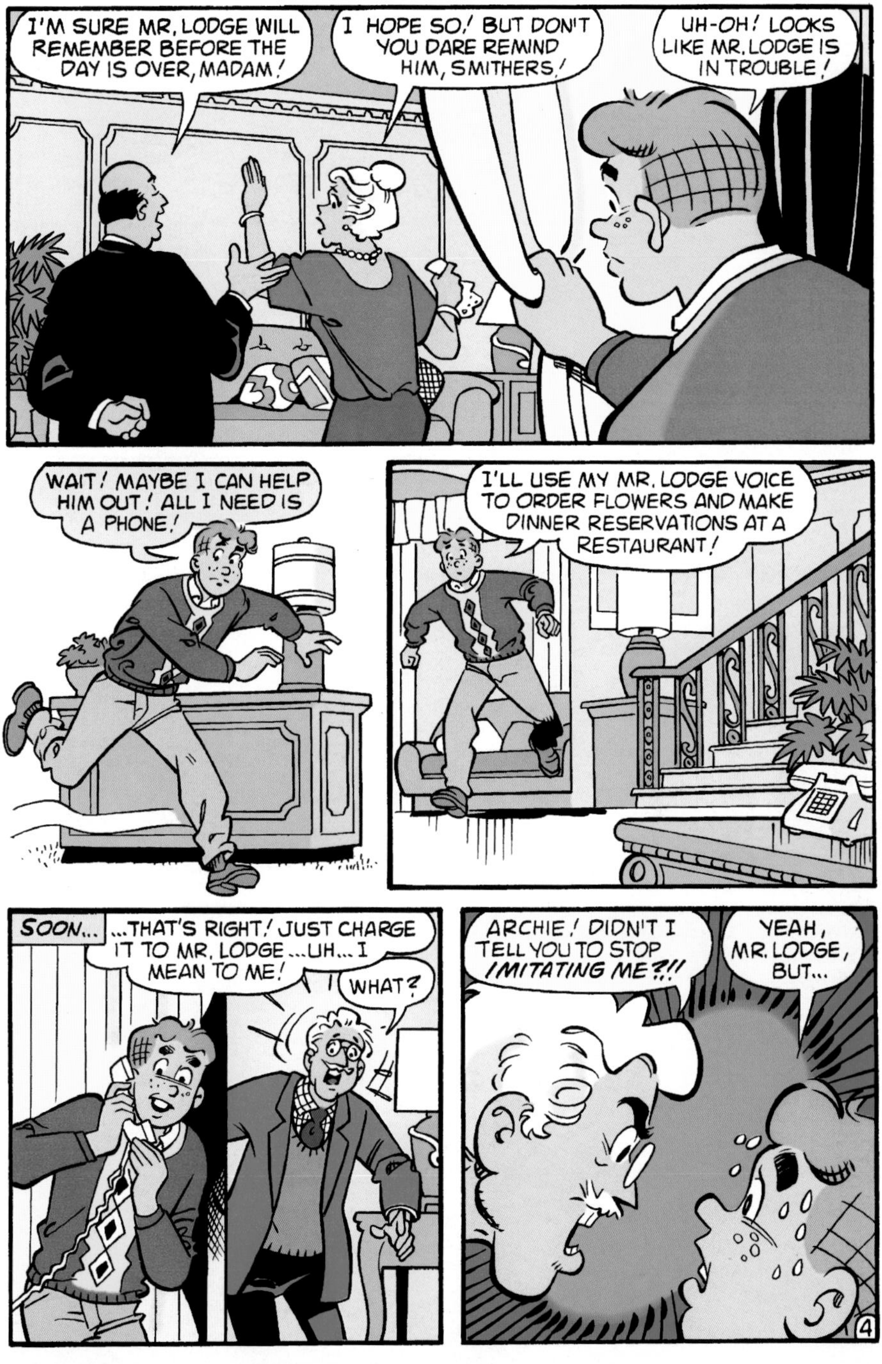
I'M SURE MR. LODGE WILL REMEMBER BEFORE THE DAY IS OVER, MADAM!
I HOPE SO! BUT DON'T YOU DARE REMIND HIM, SMITHERS!
UH-OH! LOOKS LIKE MR. LODGE IS IN TROUBLE!
WAIT! MAYBE I CAN HELP HIM OUT! ALL I NEED IS A PHONE!
I'LL USE MY MR. LODGE VOICE TO ORDER FLOWERS AND MAKE DINNER RESERVATIONS AT A RESTAURANT!
SOON...
...THAT'S RIGHT! JUST CHARGE IT TO MR. LODGE ...UH... I MEAN TO ME!
WHAT?
ARCHIE! DIDN'T I TELL YOU TO STOP *IMITATING ME?!!*
YEAH, MR. LODGE, BUT...
4

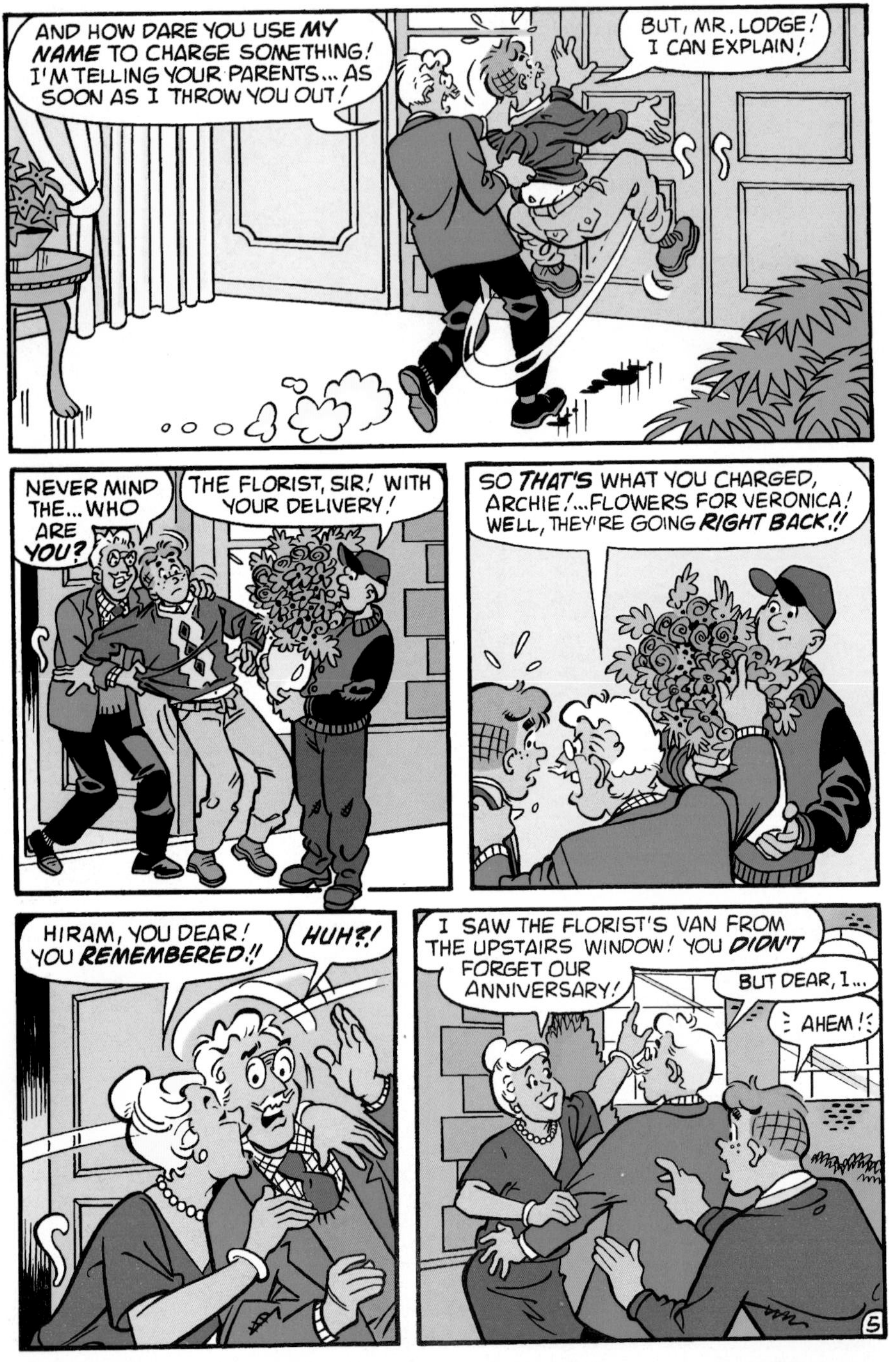
AND HOW DARE YOU USE MY NAME TO CHARGE SOMETHING! I'M TELLING YOUR PARENTS... AS SOON AS I THROW YOU OUT!
BUT, MR. LODGE! I CAN EXPLAIN!
NEVER MIND THE... WHO ARE YOU?
THE FLORIST, SIR! WITH YOUR DELIVERY!
SO THAT'S WHAT YOU CHARGED, ARCHIE!...FLOWERS FOR VERONICA! WELL, THEY'RE GOING RIGHT BACK!!
HIRAM, YOU DEAR! YOU REMEMBERED!!
HUH?!
I SAW THE FLORIST'S VAN FROM THE UPSTAIRS WINDOW! YOU DIDN'T FORGET OUR ANNIVERSARY!
BUT DEAR, I...
AHEM!
5

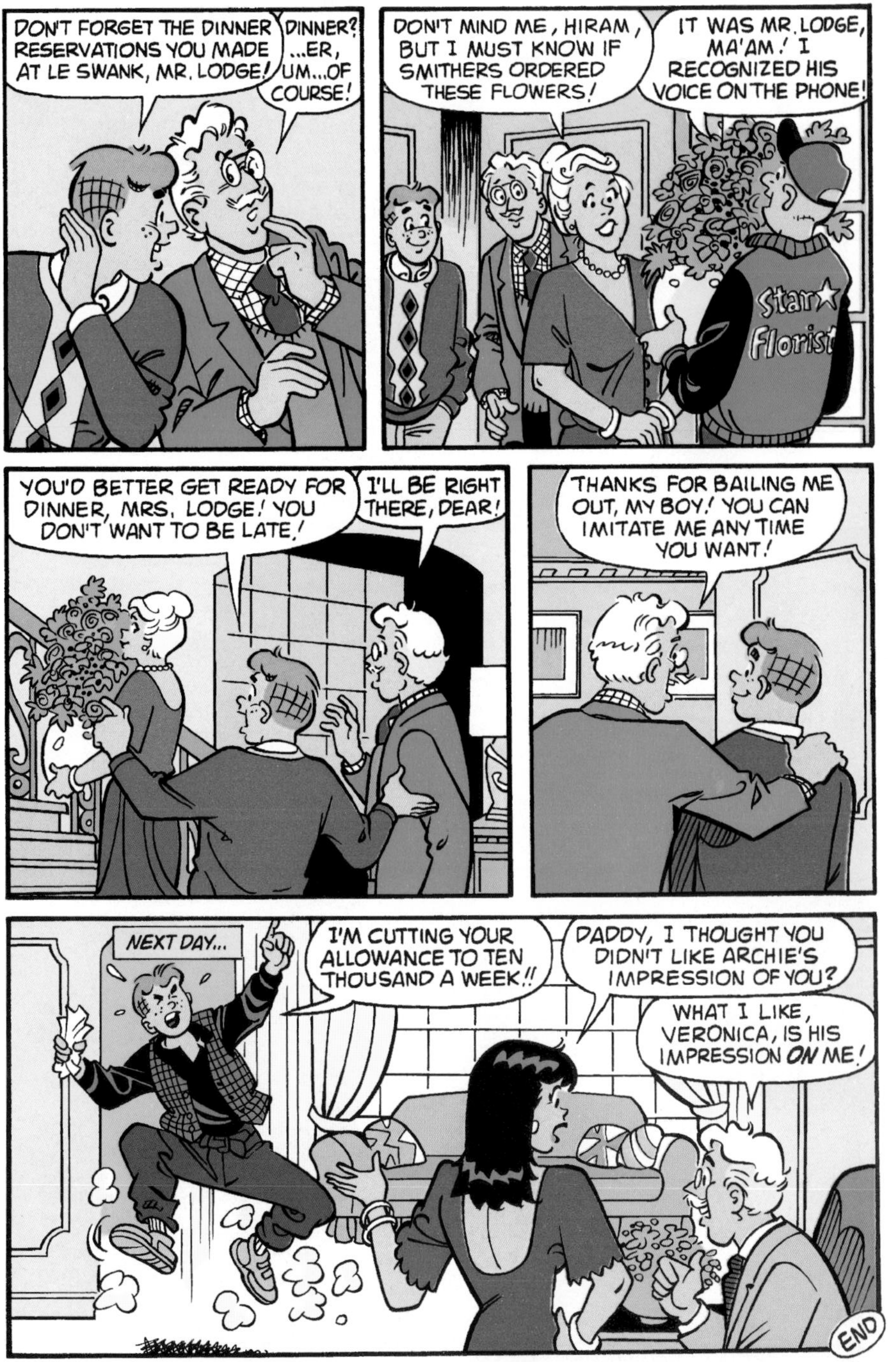
DON'T FORGET THE DINNER RESERVATIONS YOU MADE AT LE SWANK, MR. LODGE!
DINNER? ...ER, UM...OF COURSE!
DON'T MIND ME, HIRAM, BUT I MUST KNOW IF SMITHERS ORDERED THESE FLOWERS!
IT WAS MR. LODGE, MA'AM! I RECOGNIZED HIS VOICE ON THE PHONE!
Star Florist
YOU'D BETTER GET READY FOR DINNER, MRS. LODGE! YOU DON'T WANT TO BE LATE!
I'LL BE RIGHT THERE, DEAR!
THANKS FOR BAILING ME OUT, MY BOY! YOU CAN IMITATE ME ANY TIME YOU WANT!
NEXT DAY...
I'M CUTTING YOUR ALLOWANCE TO TEN THOUSAND A WEEK!!
DADDY, I THOUGHT YOU DIDN'T LIKE ARCHIE'S IMPRESSION OF YOU?
WHAT I LIKE, VERONICA, IS HIS IMPRESSION ON ME!
END

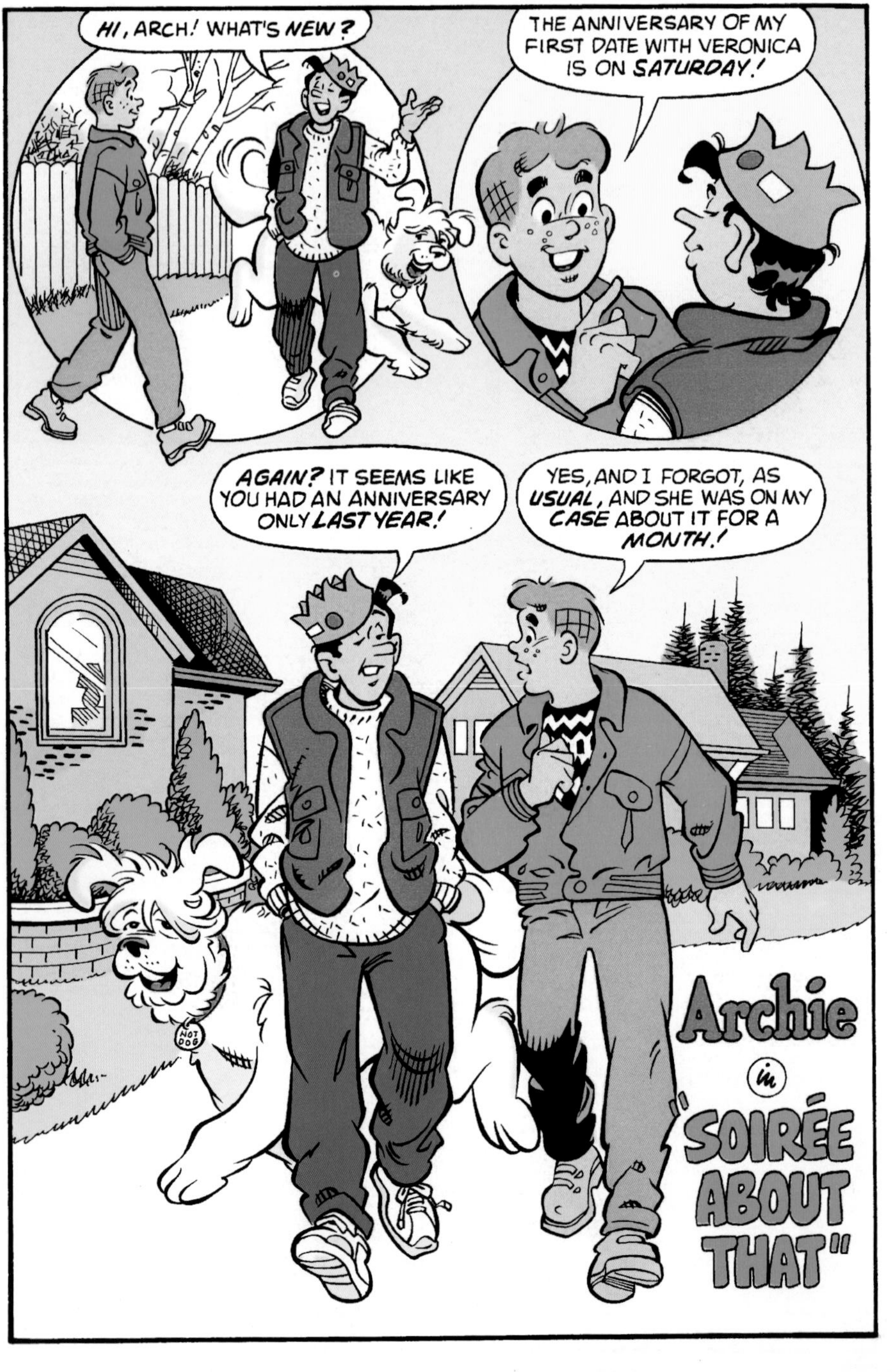
HI, ARCH! WHAT'S NEW?
THE ANNIVERSARY OF MY FIRST DATE WITH VERONICA IS ON SATURDAY!
AGAIN? IT SEEMS LIKE YOU HAD AN ANNIVERSARY ONLY LAST YEAR!
YES, AND I FORGOT, AS USUAL, AND SHE WAS ON MY CASE ABOUT IT FOR A MONTH!
HOT DOG
Archie
in
"SOIRÉE ABOUT THAT"

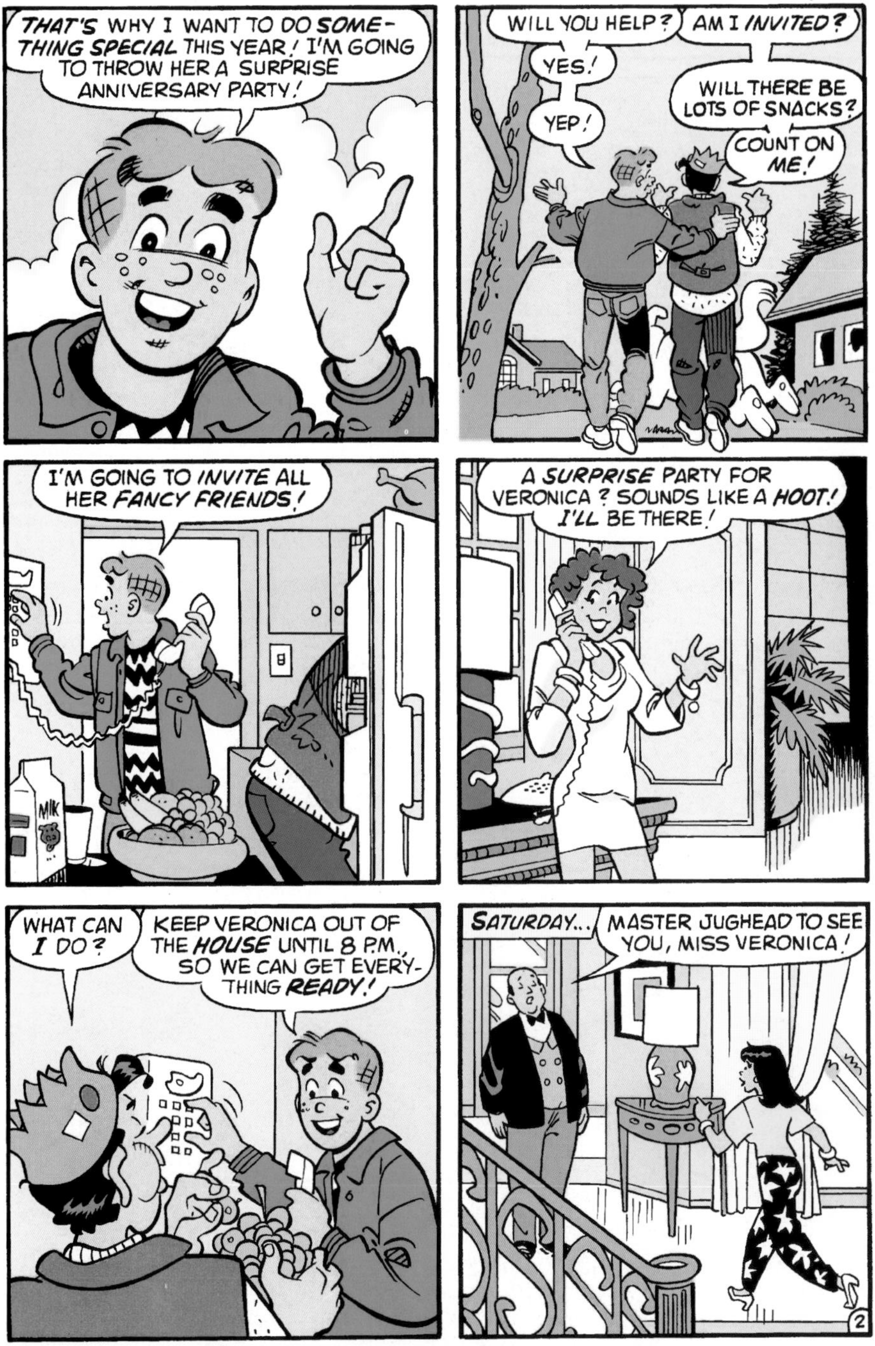
THAT'S WHY I WANT TO DO SOMETHING SPECIAL THIS YEAR! I'M GOING TO THROW HER A SURPRISE ANNIVERSARY PARTY!
WILL YOU HELP?
YES!
YEP!
AM I INVITED?
WILL THERE BE LOTS OF SNACKS?
COUNT ON ME!
I'M GOING TO INVITE ALL HER FANCY FRIENDS!
MILK
A SURPRISE PARTY FOR VERONICA? SOUNDS LIKE A HOOT! I'LL BE THERE!
WHAT CAN I DO?
KEEP VERONICA OUT OF THE HOUSE UNTIL 8 P.M., SO WE CAN GET EVERYTHING READY!
SATURDAY...
MASTER JUGHEAD TO SEE YOU, MISS VERONICA!
2

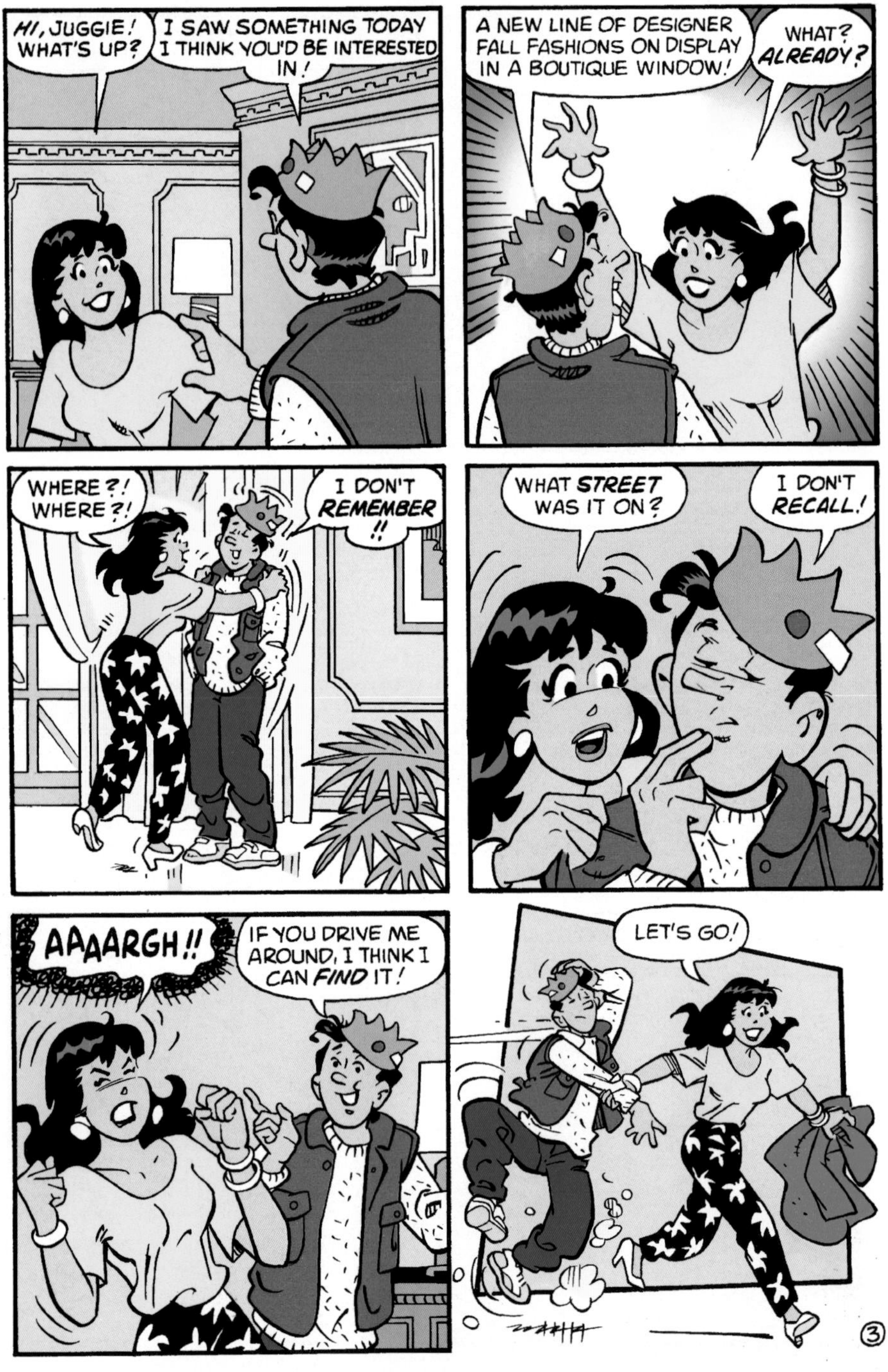
HI, JUGGIE! WHAT'S UP?
I SAW SOMETHING TODAY I THINK YOU'D BE INTERESTED IN!
A NEW LINE OF DESIGNER FALL FASHIONS ON DISPLAY IN A BOUTIQUE WINDOW!
WHAT? ALREADY?
WHERE?! WHERE?!
I DON'T REMEMBER!!
WHAT STREET WAS IT ON?
I DON'T RECALL!
AAAARGH!!
IF YOU DRIVE ME AROUND, I THINK I CAN FIND IT!
LET'S GO!
3

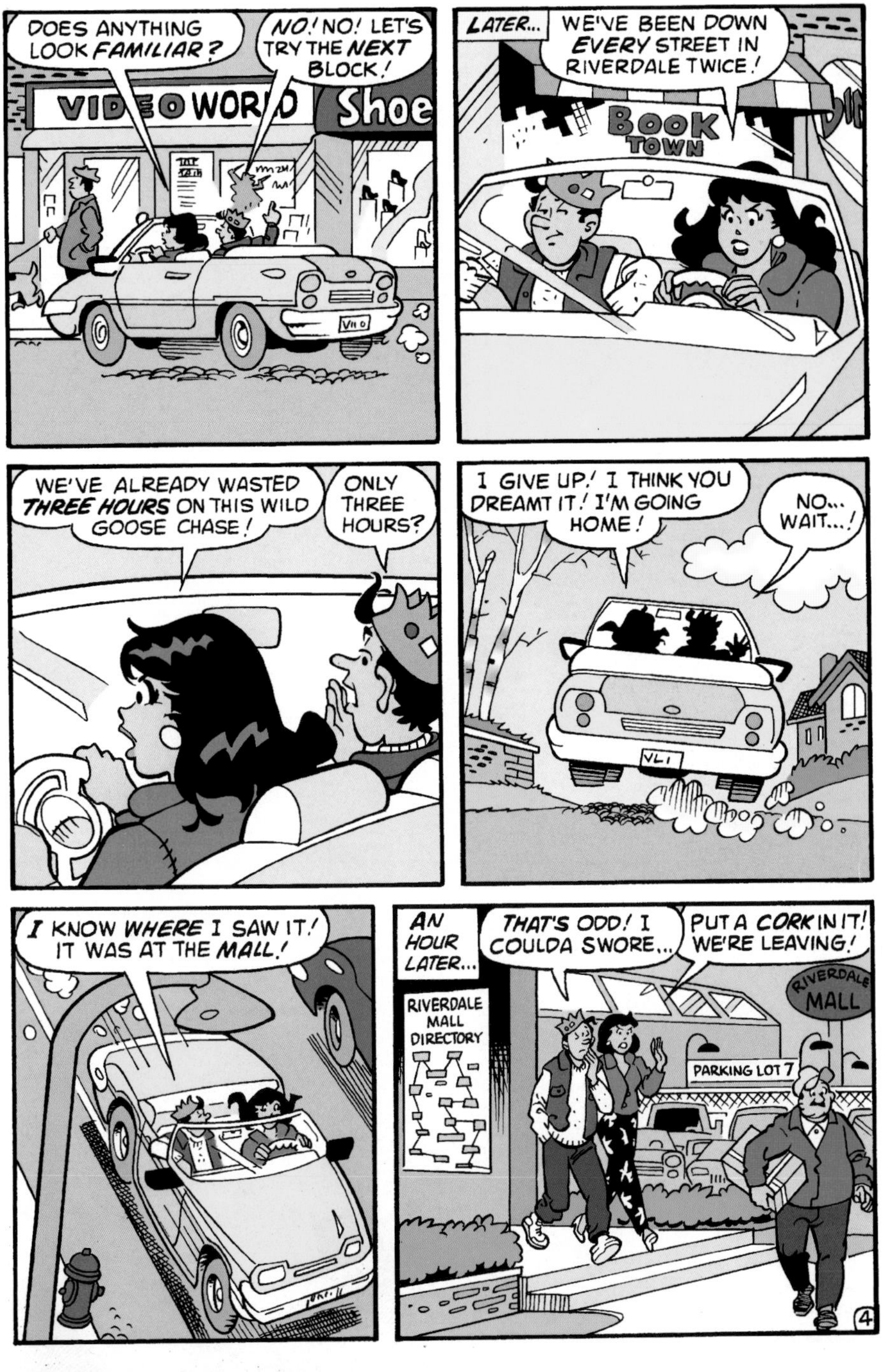
DOES ANYTHING LOOK FAMILIAR?
NO! NO! LET'S TRY THE NEXT BLOCK!
VIDEO WORLD
Shoe
LATER...
WE'VE BEEN DOWN EVERY STREET IN RIVERDALE TWICE!
BOOK TOWN
WE'VE ALREADY WASTED THREE HOURS ON THIS WILD GOOSE CHASE!
ONLY THREE HOURS?
I GIVE UP! I THINK YOU DREAMT IT! I'M GOING HOME!
NO... WAIT...!
I KNOW WHERE I SAW IT! IT WAS AT THE MALL!
AN HOUR LATER...
THAT'S ODD! I COULDA SWORE...
PUT A CORK IN IT! WE'RE LEAVING!
RIVERDALE MALL
RIVERDALE MALL DIRECTORY
PARKING LOT 7
4

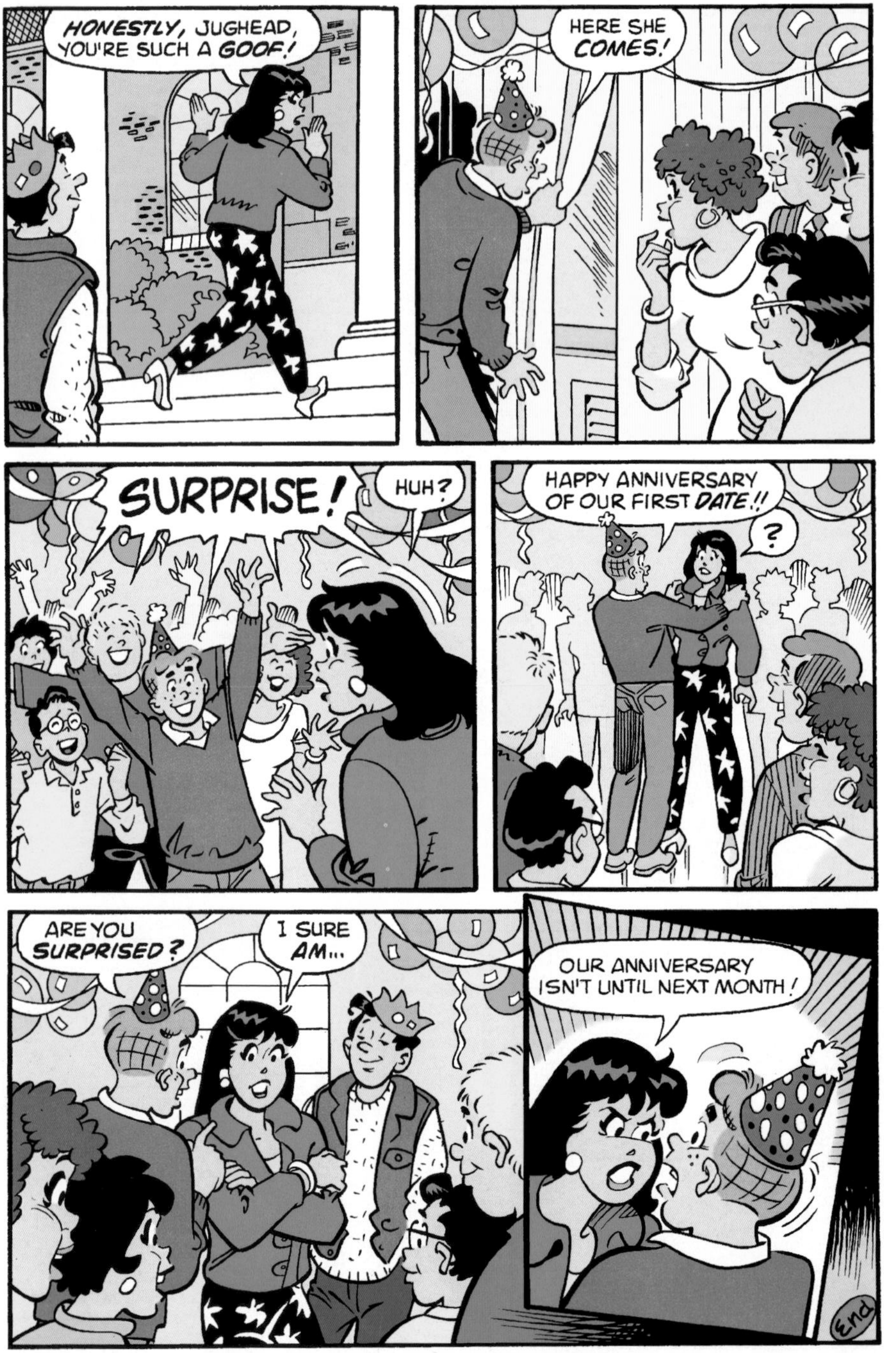
HONESTLY, JUGHEAD, YOU'RE SUCH A GOOF!
HERE SHE COMES!
SURPRISE!
HUH?
HAPPY ANNIVERSARY OF OUR FIRST DATE!!
?
ARE YOU SURPRISED?
I SURE AM...
OUR ANNIVERSARY ISN'T UNTIL NEXT MONTH!
End

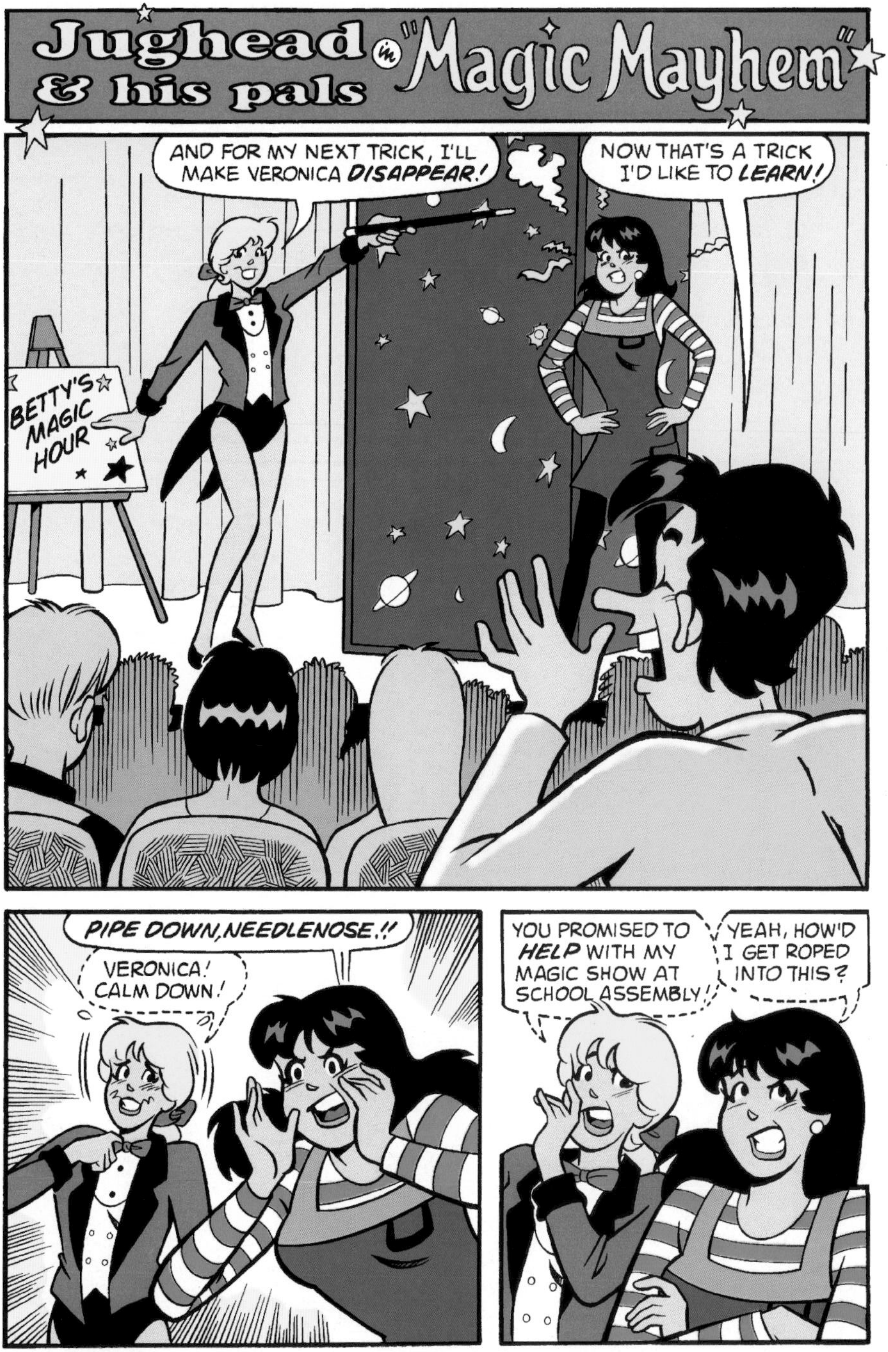
Jughead & his pals in "Magic Mayhem"
AND FOR MY NEXT TRICK, I'LL MAKE VERONICA DISAPPEAR!
NOW THAT'S A TRICK I'D LIKE TO LEARN!
BETTY'S MAGIC HOUR
PIPE DOWN, NEEDLENOSE!!
VERONICA! CALM DOWN!
YOU PROMISED TO HELP WITH MY MAGIC SHOW AT SCHOOL ASSEMBLY!
YEAH, HOW'D I GET ROPED INTO THIS?

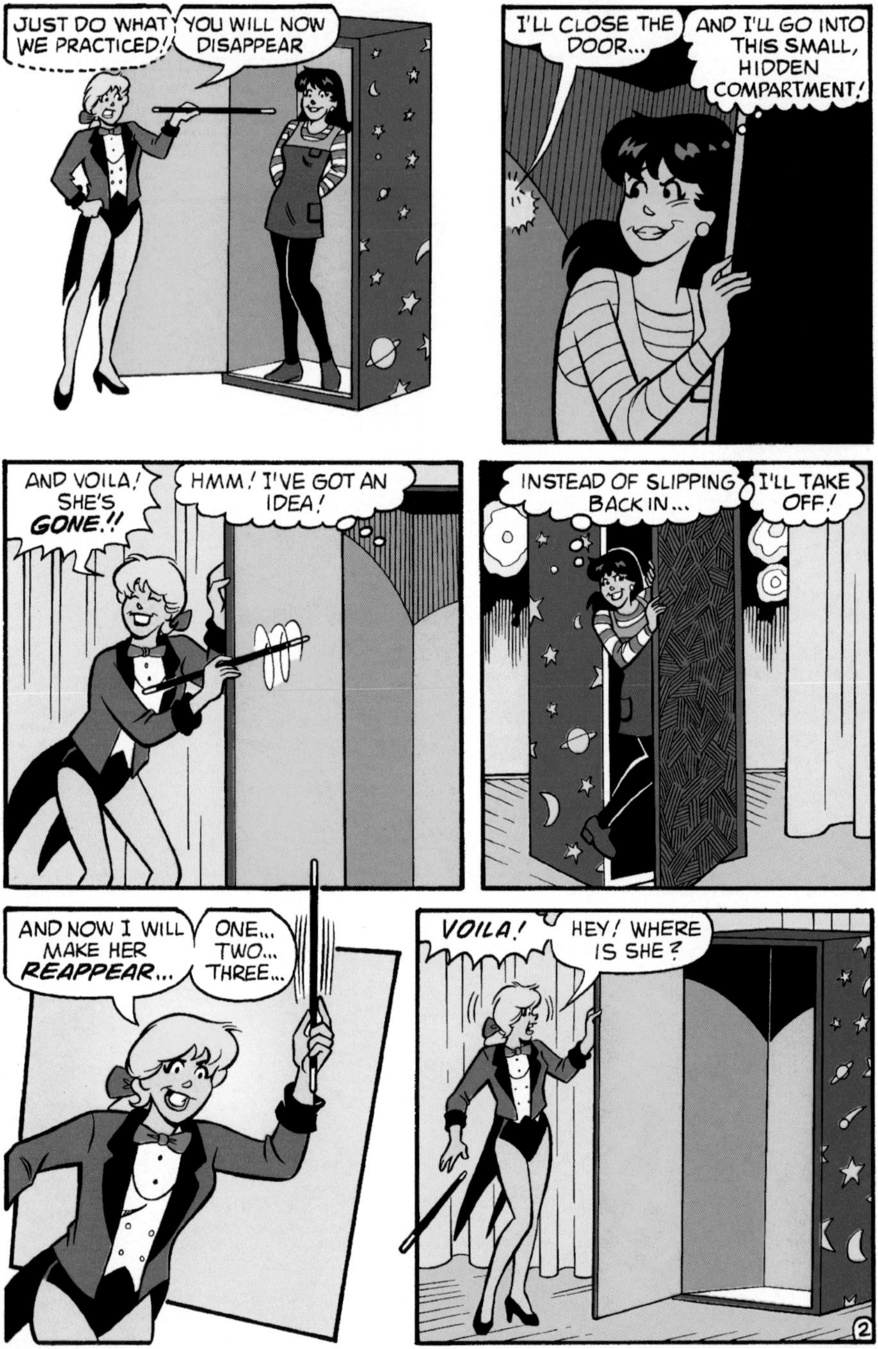
JUST DO WHAT WE PRACTICED!
YOU WILL NOW DISAPPEAR
I'LL CLOSE THE DOOR...
AND I'LL GO INTO THIS SMALL, HIDDEN COMPARTMENT!
AND VOILA! SHE'S GONE!!
HMM! I'VE GOT AN IDEA!
INSTEAD OF SLIPPING BACK IN...
I'LL TAKE OFF!
AND NOW I WILL MAKE HER REAPPEAR...
ONE... TWO... THREE...
VOILA!
HEY! WHERE IS SHE?
2

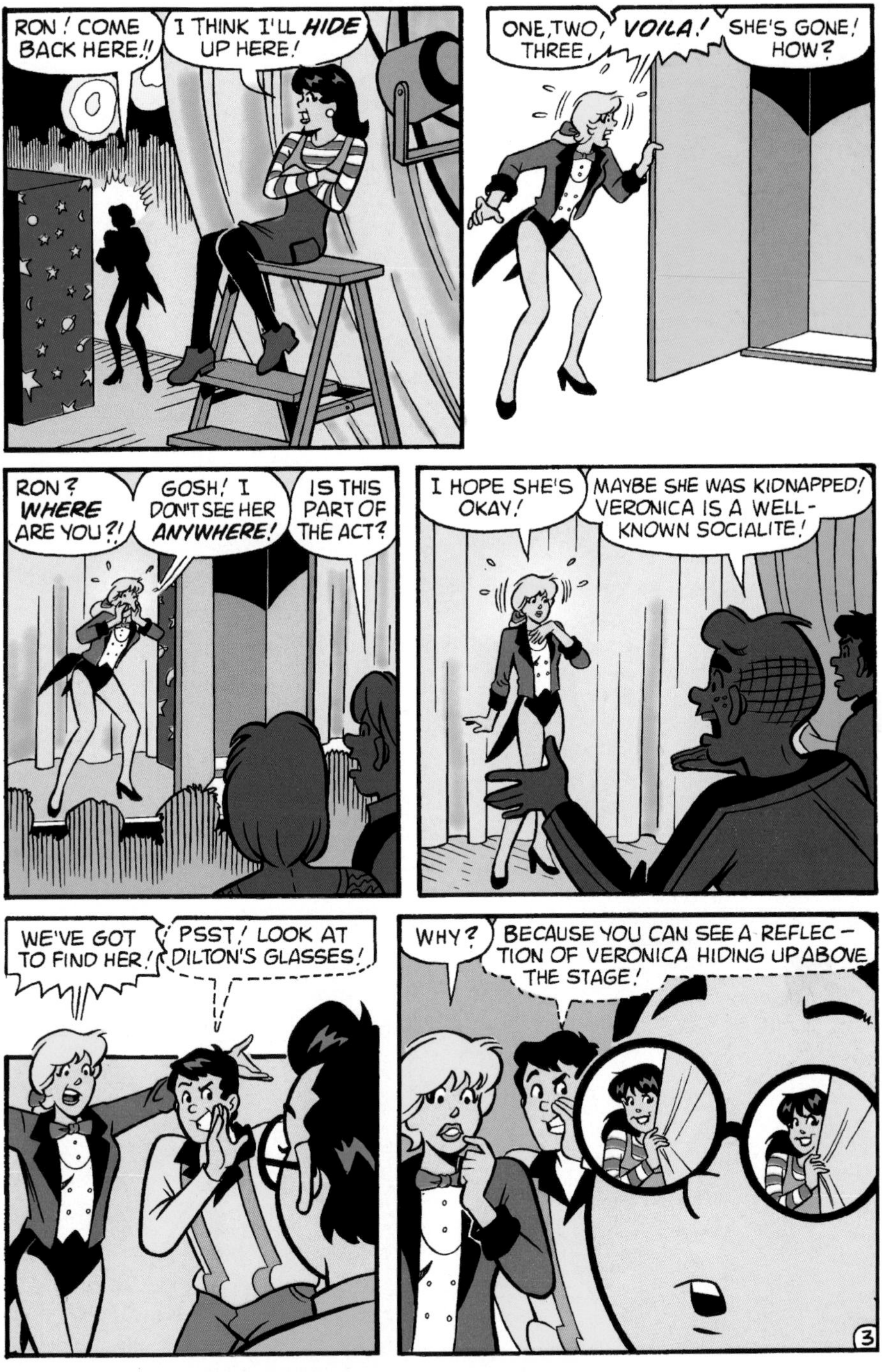
RON! COME BACK HERE!!
I THINK I'LL HIDE UP HERE!
ONE, TWO, THREE,
VOILA!
SHE'S GONE! HOW?
RON? WHERE ARE YOU?!
GOSH! I DON'T SEE HER ANYWHERE!
IS THIS PART OF THE ACT?
I HOPE SHE'S OKAY!
MAYBE SHE WAS KIDNAPPED! VERONICA IS A WELL-KNOWN SOCIALITE!
WE'VE GOT TO FIND HER!
PSST! LOOK AT DILTON'S GLASSES!
WHY?
BECAUSE YOU CAN SEE A REFLECTION OF VERONICA HIDING UP ABOVE THE STAGE!
3

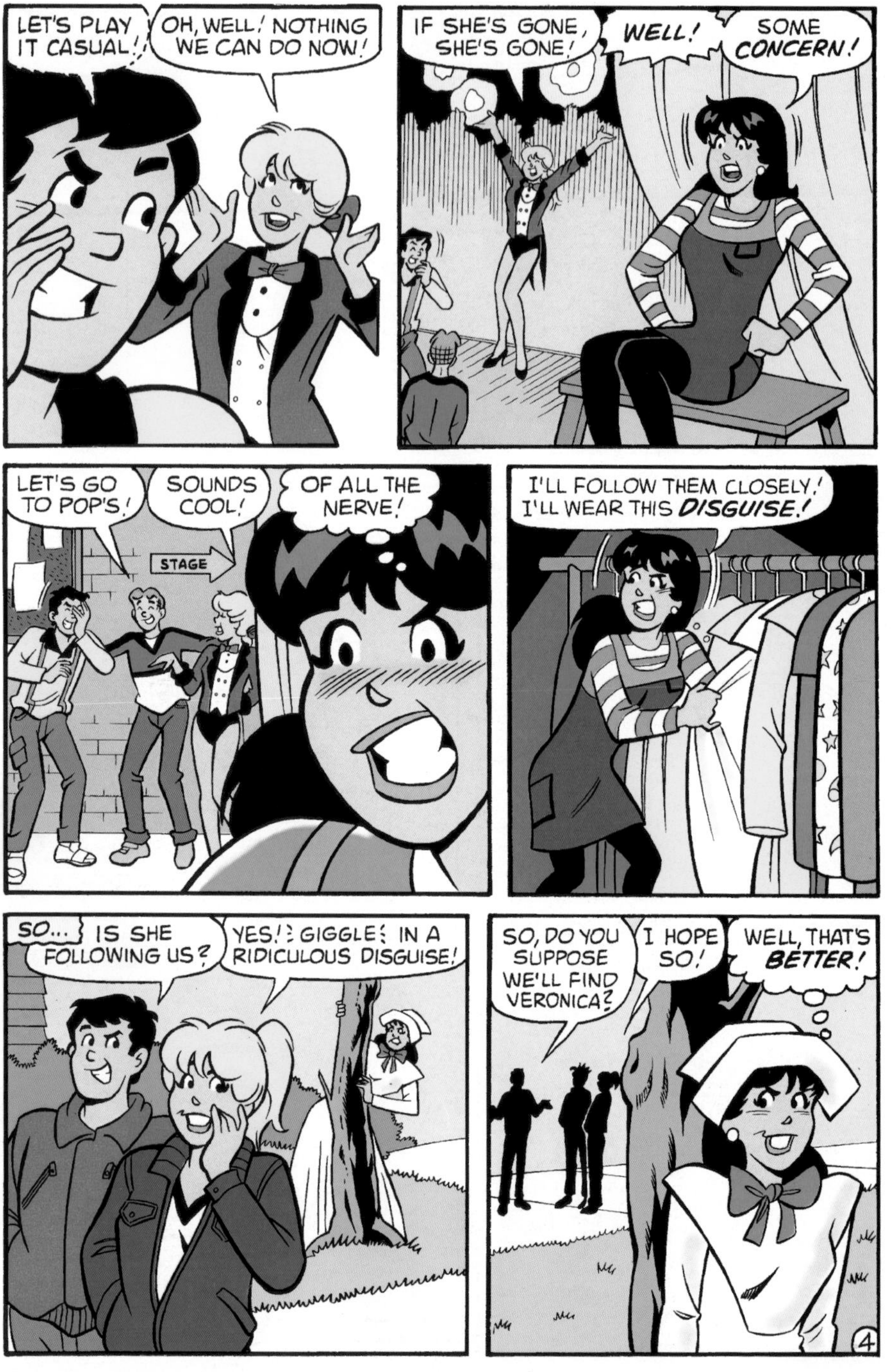
LET'S PLAY IT CASUAL!
OH, WELL! NOTHING WE CAN DO NOW!
IF SHE'S GONE, SHE'S GONE!
WELL!
SOME CONCERN!
LET'S GO TO POP'S!
SOUNDS COOL!
OF ALL THE NERVE!
STAGE
I'LL FOLLOW THEM CLOSELY! I'LL WEAR THIS DISGUISE!
SO...
IS SHE FOLLOWING US?
YES! GIGGLE! IN A RIDICULOUS DISGUISE!
SO, DO YOU SUPPOSE WE'LL FIND VERONICA?
I HOPE SO!
WELL, THAT'S BETTER!
4

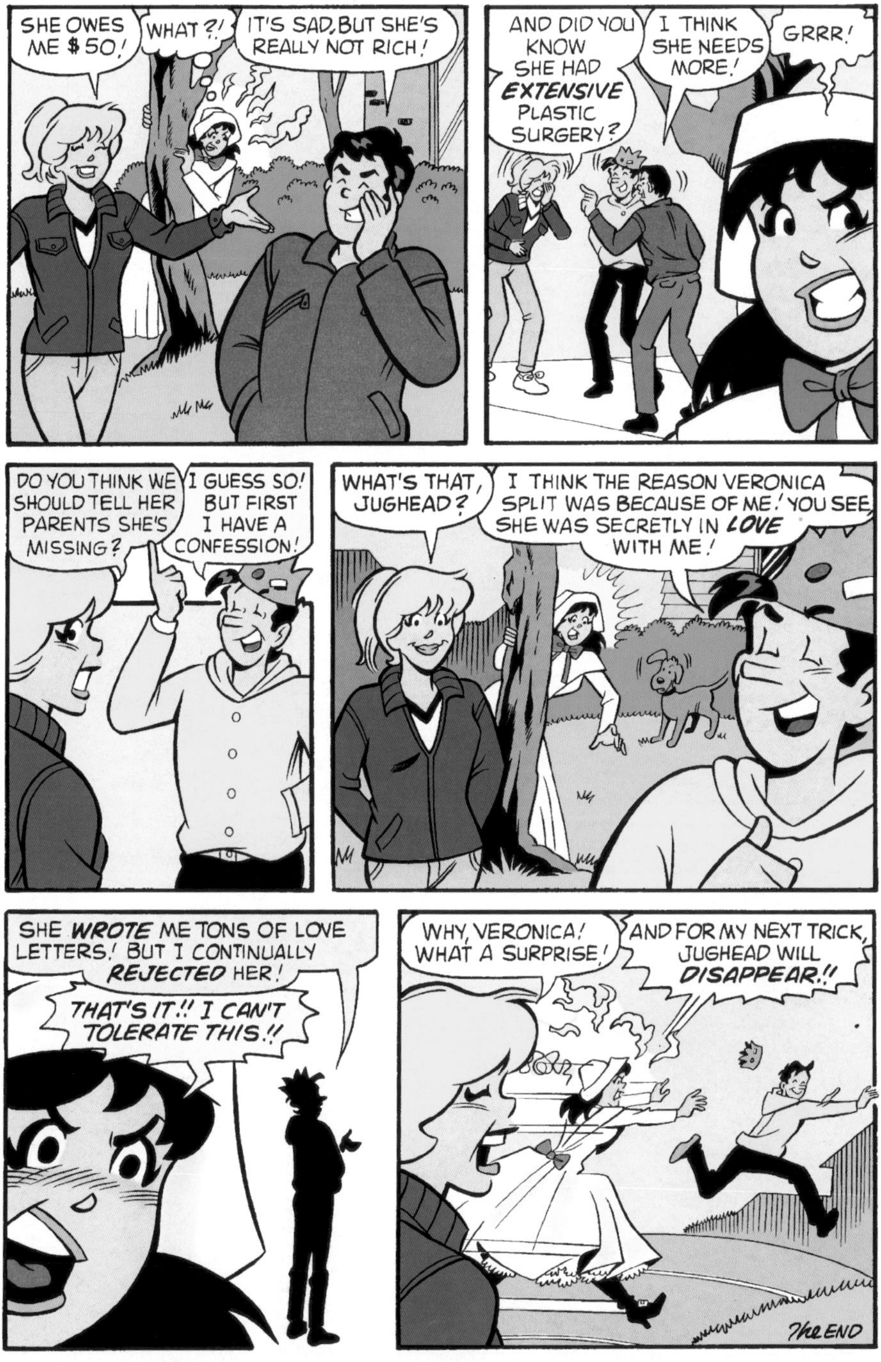
SHE OWES ME $ 50!
WHAT ?!
IT'S SAD, BUT SHE'S REALLY NOT RICH!
AND DID YOU KNOW SHE HAD EXTENSIVE PLASTIC SURGERY?
I THINK SHE NEEDS MORE!
GRRR!
DO YOU THINK WE SHOULD TELL HER PARENTS SHE'S MISSING?
I GUESS SO! BUT FIRST I HAVE A CONFESSION!
WHAT'S THAT, JUGHEAD?
I THINK THE REASON VERONICA SPLIT WAS BECAUSE OF ME! YOU SEE, SHE WAS SECRETLY IN LOVE WITH ME!
SHE WROTE ME TONS OF LOVE LETTERS! BUT I CONTINUALLY REJECTED HER!
THAT'S IT!! I CAN'T TOLERATE THIS!!
WHY, VERONICA! WHAT A SURPRISE!
AND FOR MY NEXT TRICK, JUGHEAD WILL DISAPPEAR!!
The END

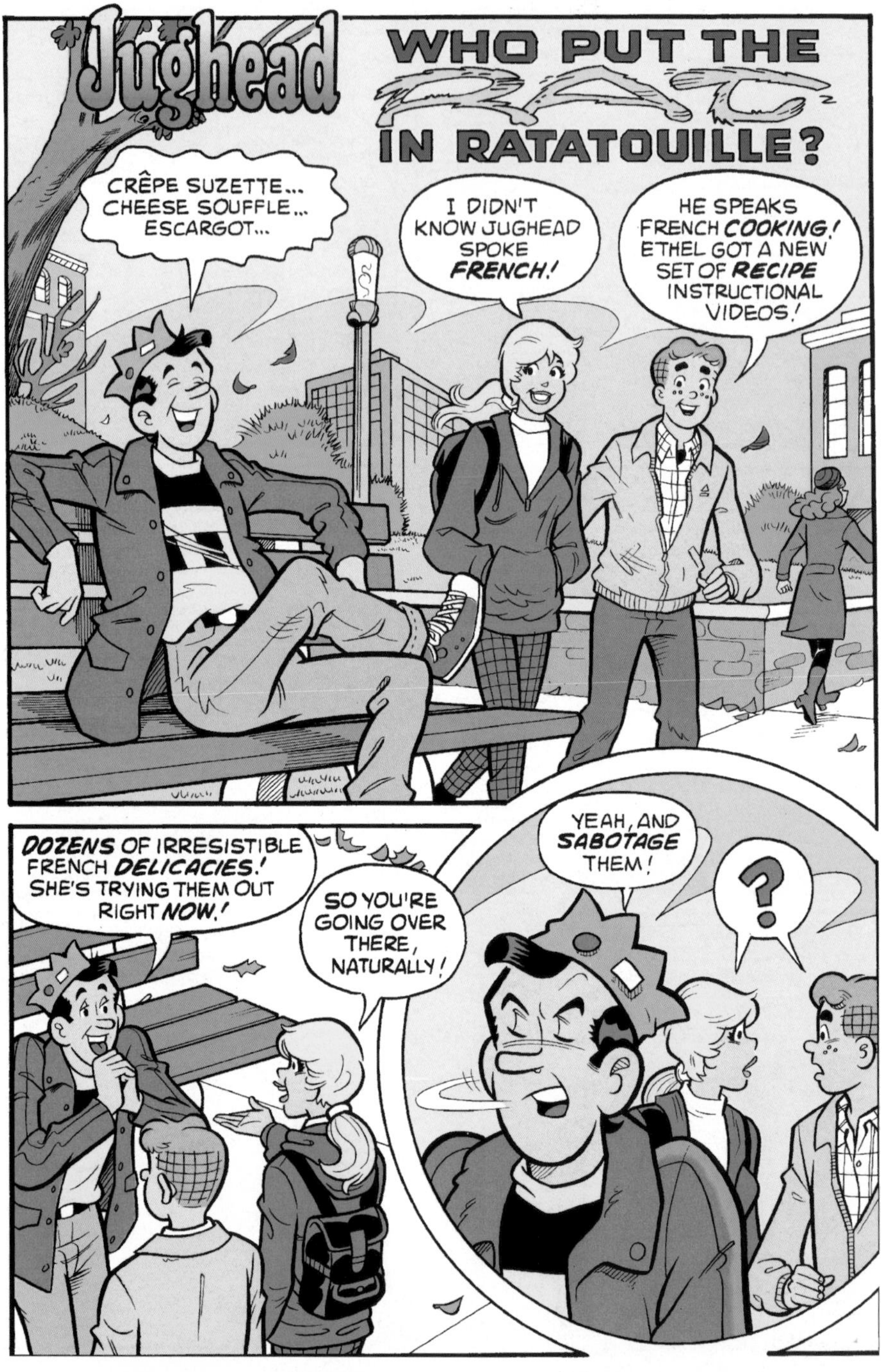
Jughead
WHO PUT THE RAT IN RATATOUILLE?
CRÊPE SUZETTE... CHEESE SOUFFLE... ESCARGOT...
I DIDN'T KNOW JUGHEAD SPOKE FRENCH!
HE SPEAKS FRENCH COOKING! ETHEL GOT A NEW SET OF RECIPE INSTRUCTIONAL VIDEOS!
DOZENS OF IRRESISTIBLE FRENCH DELICACIES! SHE'S TRYING THEM OUT RIGHT NOW!
SO YOU'RE GOING OVER THERE, NATURALLY!
YEAH, AND SABOTAGE THEM!
?

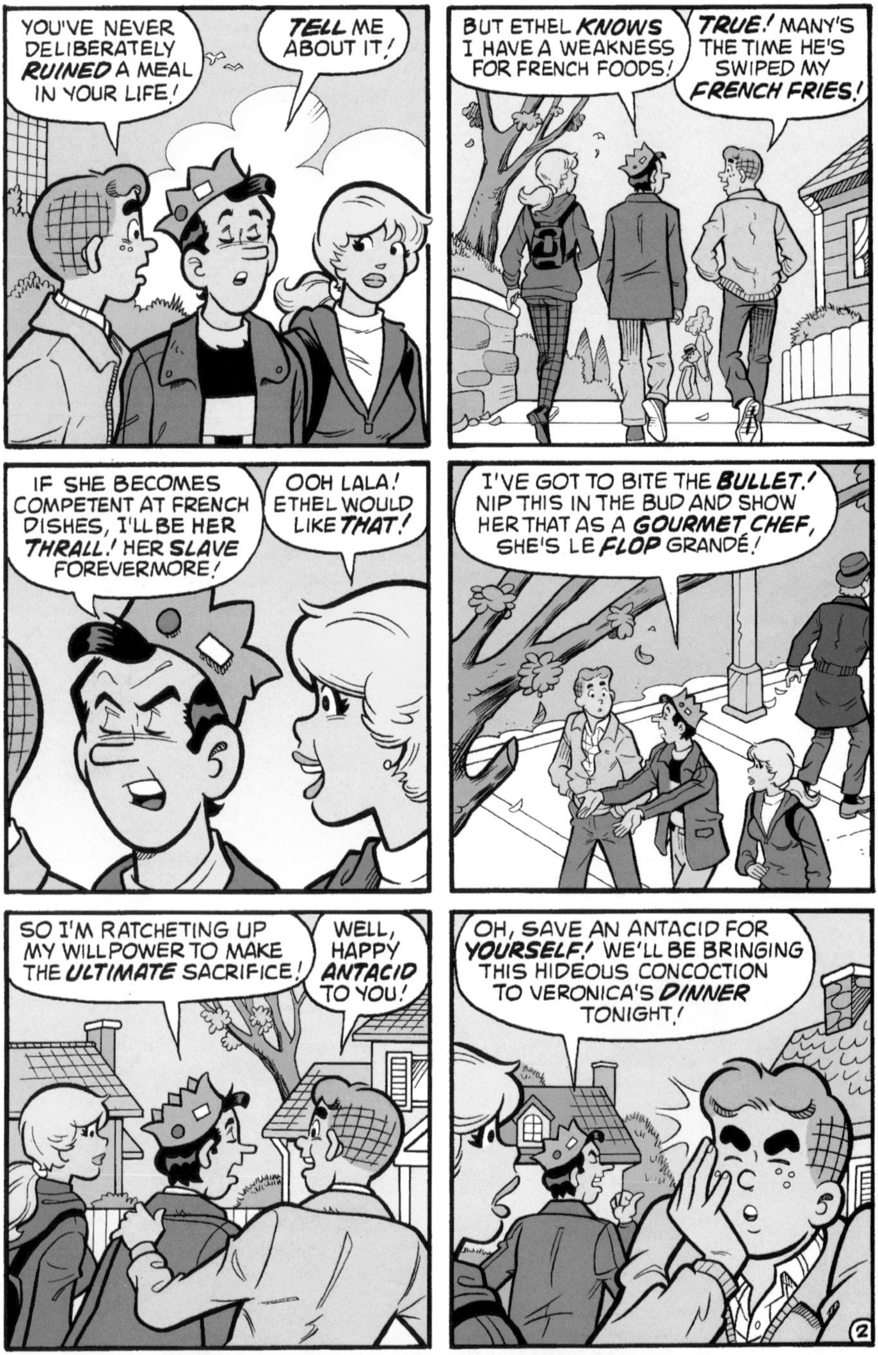
YOU'VE NEVER DELIBERATELY RUINED A MEAL IN YOUR LIFE!
TELL ME ABOUT IT!
BUT ETHEL KNOWS I HAVE A WEAKNESS FOR FRENCH FOODS!
TRUE! MANY'S THE TIME HE'S SWIPED MY FRENCH FRIES!
IF SHE BECOMES COMPETENT AT FRENCH DISHES, I'LL BE HER THRALL! HER SLAVE FOREVERMORE!
OOH LALA! ETHEL WOULD LIKE THAT!
I'VE GOT TO BITE THE BULLET! NIP THIS IN THE BUD AND SHOW HER THAT AS A GOURMET CHEF, SHE'S LE FLOP GRANDÉ!
SO I'M RATCHETING UP MY WILLPOWER TO MAKE THE ULTIMATE SACRIFICE!
WELL, HAPPY ANTACID TO YOU!
OH, SAVE AN ANTACID FOR YOURSELF! WE'LL BE BRINGING THIS HIDEOUS CONCOCTION TO VERONICA'S DINNER TONIGHT!
2

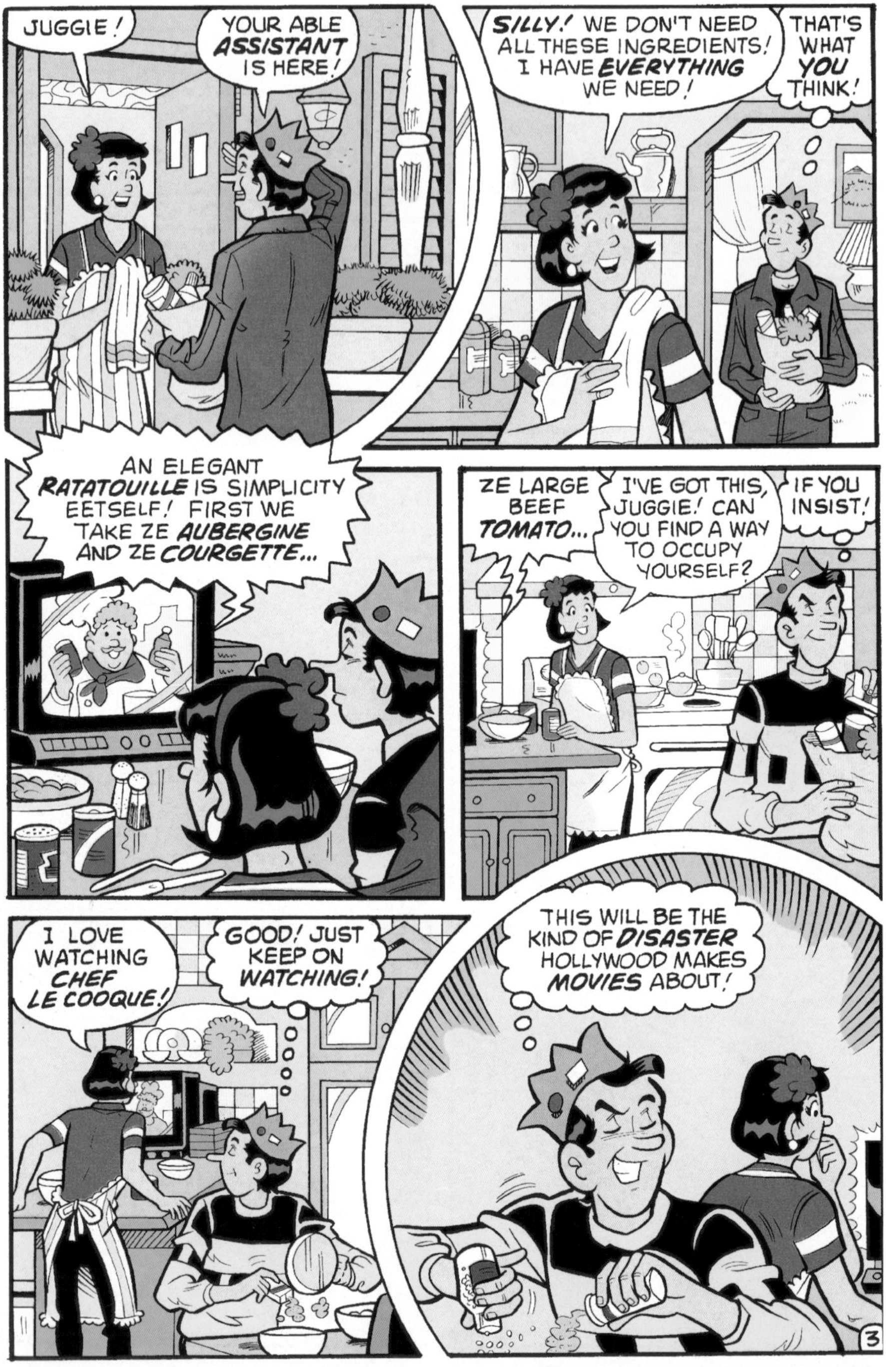
JUGGIE!
YOUR ABLE ASSISTANT IS HERE!
SILLY! WE DON'T NEED ALL THESE INGREDIENTS! I HAVE EVERYTHING WE NEED!
THAT'S WHAT YOU THINK!
AN ELEGANT RATATOUILLE IS SIMPLICITY EETSELF! FIRST WE TAKE ZE AUBERGINE AND ZE COURGETTE...
ZE LARGE BEEF TOMATO...
I'VE GOT THIS, JUGGIE! CAN YOU FIND A WAY TO OCCUPY YOURSELF?
IF YOU INSIST!
I LOVE WATCHING CHEF LE COOQUE!
GOOD! JUST KEEP ON WATCHING!
THIS WILL BE THE KIND OF DISASTER HOLLYWOOD MAKES MOVIES ABOUT!
3

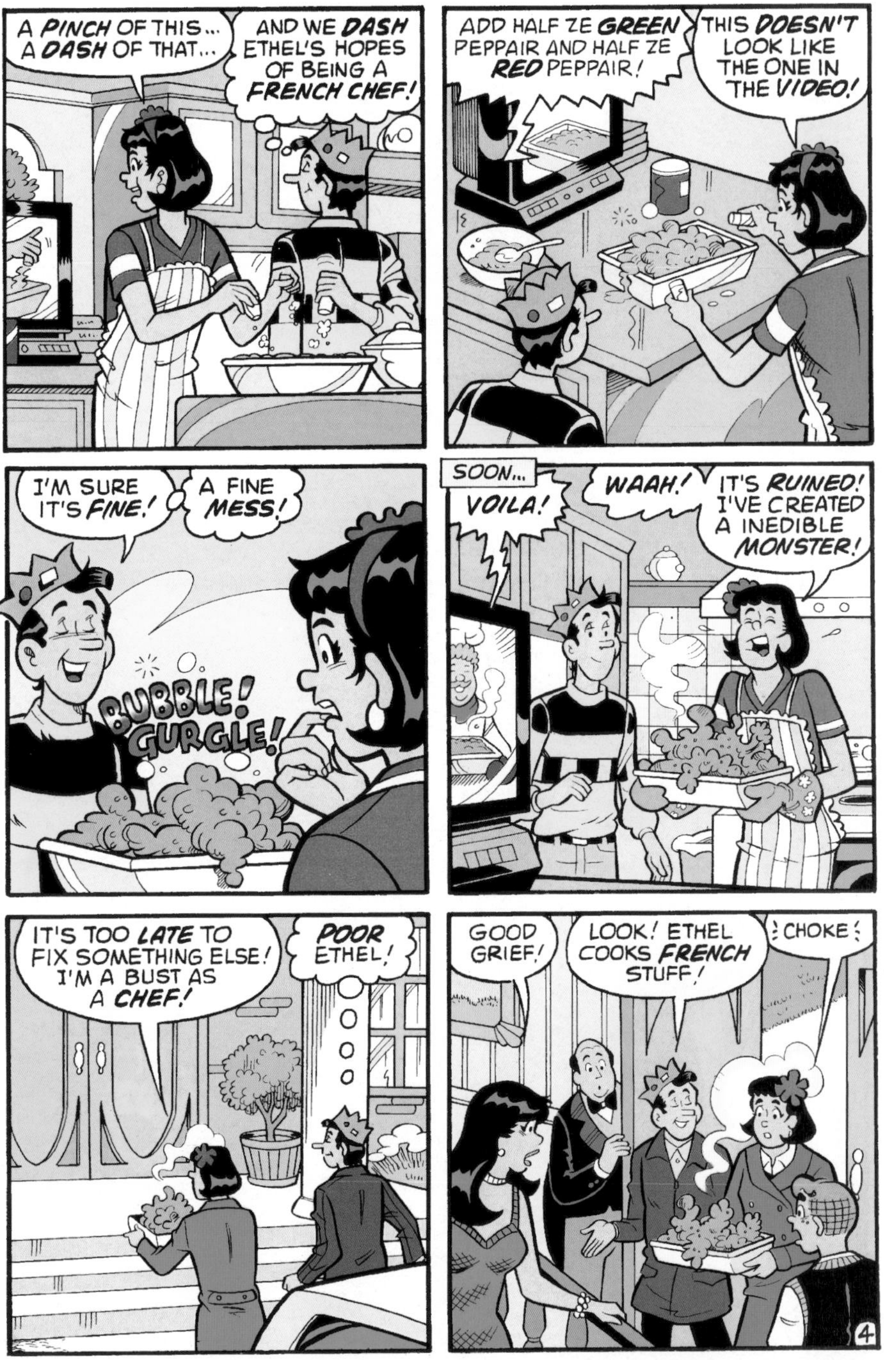
A PINCH OF THIS... A DASH OF THAT...
AND WE DASH ETHEL'S HOPES OF BEING A FRENCH CHEF!
ADD HALF ZE GREEN PEPPAIR AND HALF ZE RED PEPPAIR!
THIS DOESN'T LOOK LIKE THE ONE IN THE VIDEO!
I'M SURE IT'S FINE!
A FINE MESS!
BUBBLE! GURGLE!
SOON...
VOILA!
WAAH!
IT'S RUINED! I'VE CREATED A INEDIBLE MONSTER!
IT'S TOO LATE TO FIX SOMETHING ELSE! I'M A BUST AS A CHEF!
POOR ETHEL!
GOOD GRIEF!
LOOK! ETHEL COOKS FRENCH STUFF!
CHOKE
4

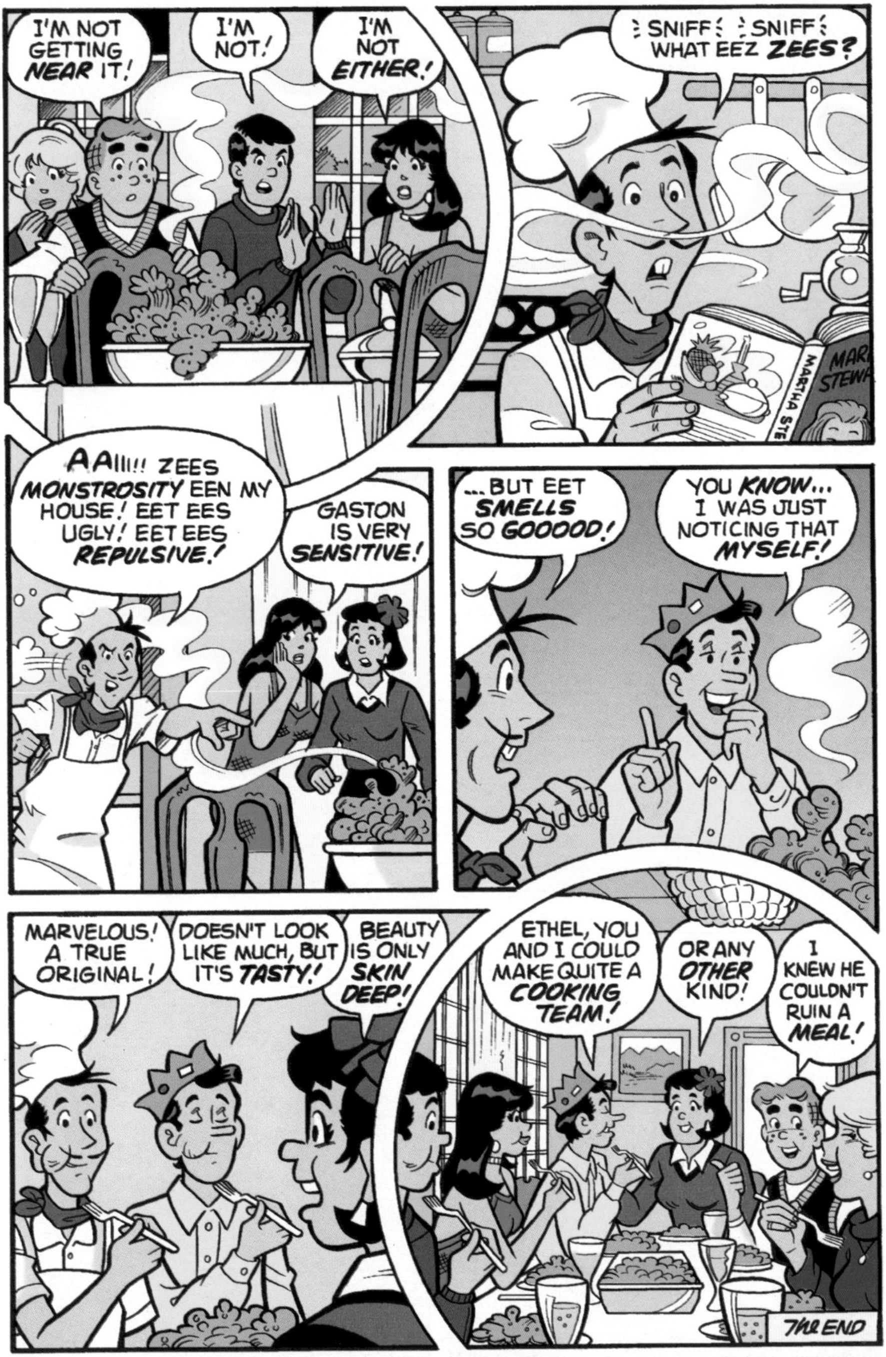
I'M NOT GETTING NEAR IT!
I'M NOT!
I'M NOT EITHER!
SNIFF SNIFF WHAT EEZ ZEES?
MARTHA STEWART
AAIII!!! ZEES MONSTROSITY EEN MY HOUSE! EET EES UGLY! EET EES REPULSIVE!
GASTON IS VERY SENSITIVE!
...BUT EET SMELLS SO GOOOOD!
YOU KNOW... I WAS JUST NOTICING THAT MYSELF!
MARVELOUS! A TRUE ORIGINAL!
DOESN'T LOOK LIKE MUCH, BUT IT'S TASTY!
BEAUTY IS ONLY SKIN DEEP!
ETHEL, YOU AND I COULD MAKE QUITE A COOKING TEAM!
OR ANY OTHER KIND!
I KNEW HE COULDN'T RUIN A MEAL!
THE END

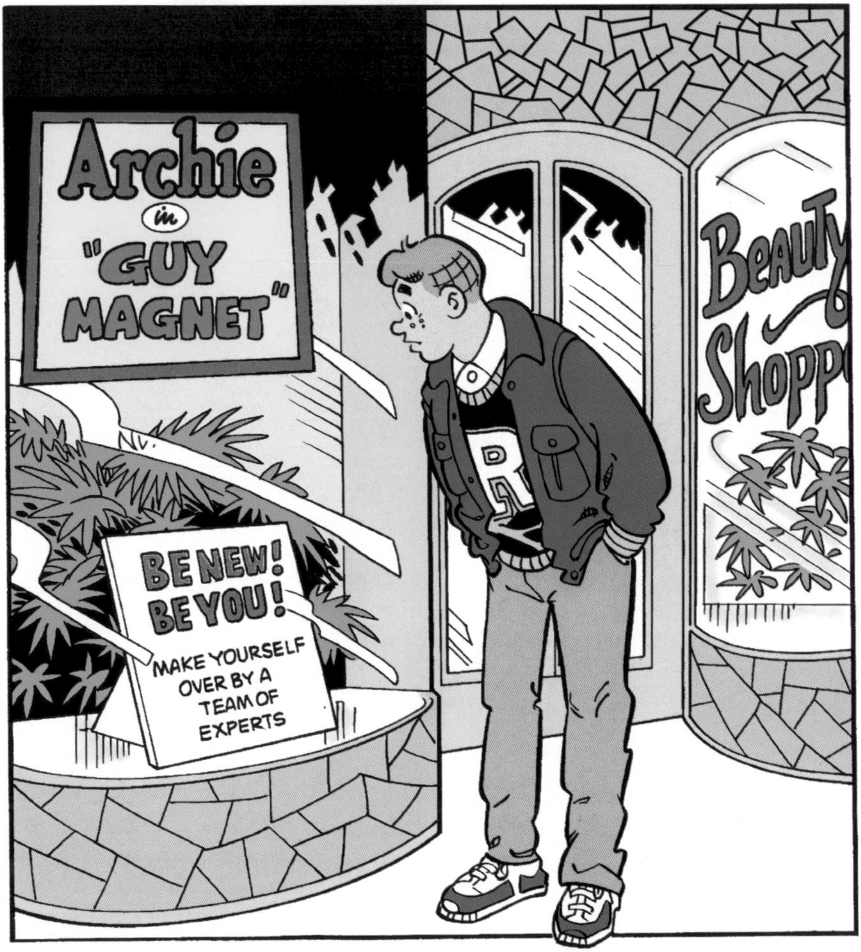
Archie in "GUY MAGNET"
Beauty Shoppe
BE NEW! BE YOU!
MAKE YOURSELF OVER BY A TEAM OF EXPERTS

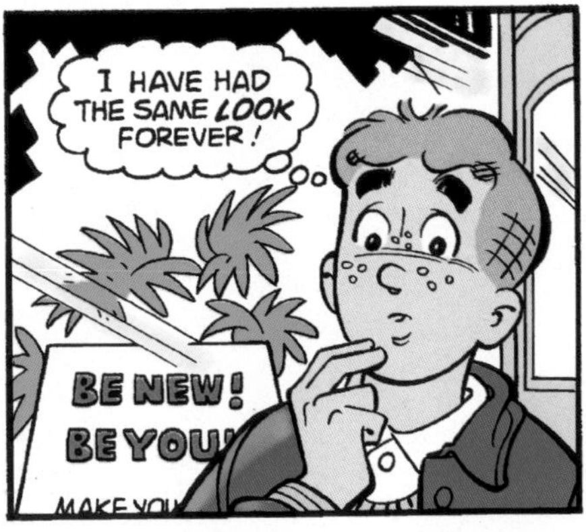
I HAVE HAD THE SAME LOOK FOREVER!
BE NEW! BE YOU

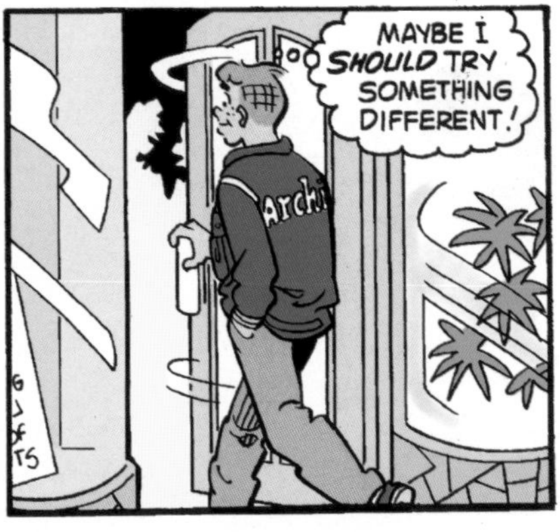
MAYBE I SHOULD TRY SOMETHING DIFFERENT!
Archie

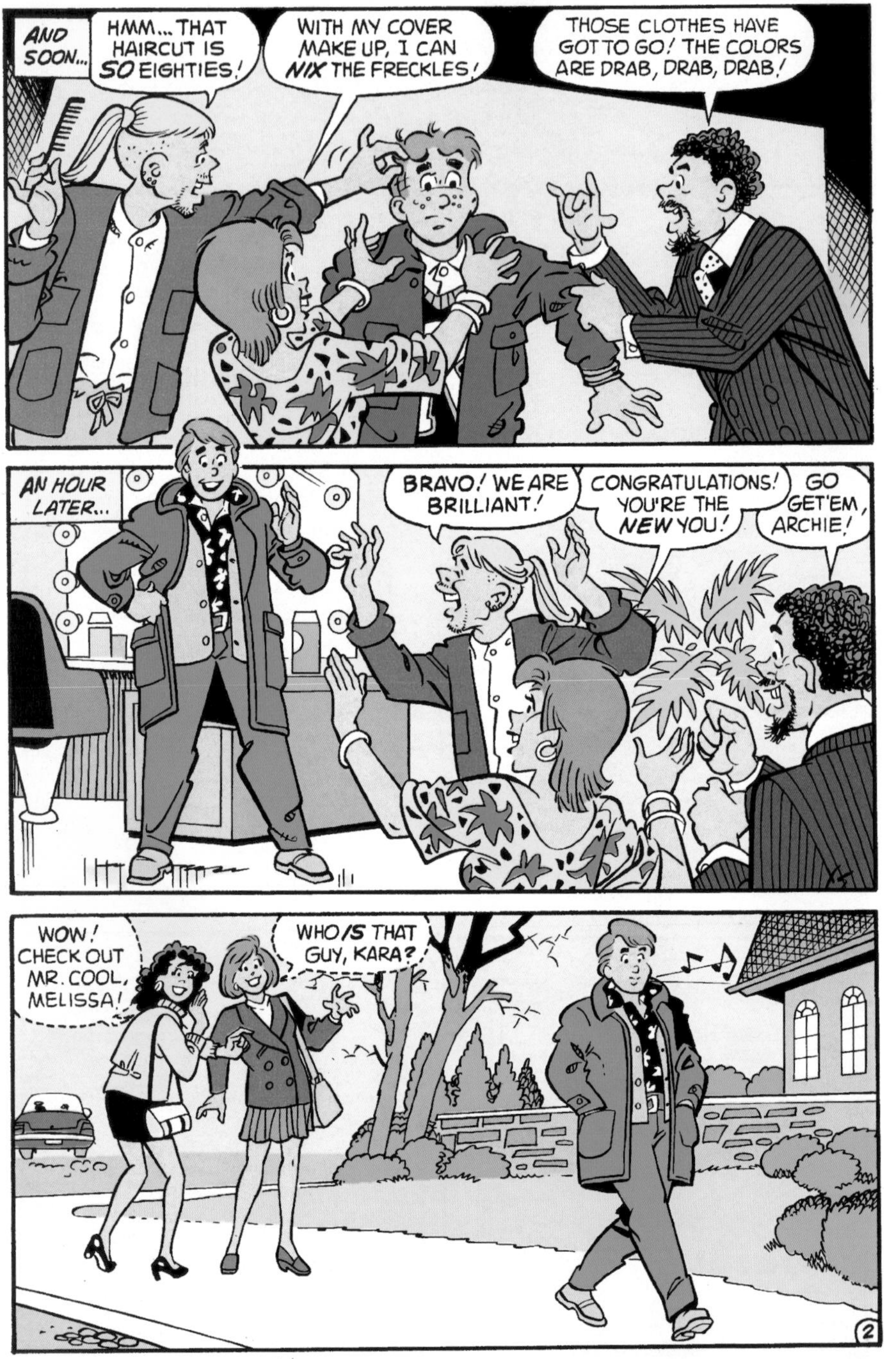
AND SOON...
HMM... THAT HAIRCUT IS SO EIGHTIES!
WITH MY COVER MAKE UP, I CAN NIX THE FRECKLES!
THOSE CLOTHES HAVE GOT TO GO! THE COLORS ARE DRAB, DRAB, DRAB!
AN HOUR LATER...
BRAVO! WE ARE BRILLIANT!
CONGRATULATIONS! YOU'RE THE NEW YOU!
GO GET'EM, ARCHIE!
WOW! CHECK OUT MR. COOL, MELISSA!
WHO IS THAT GUY, KARA?
2

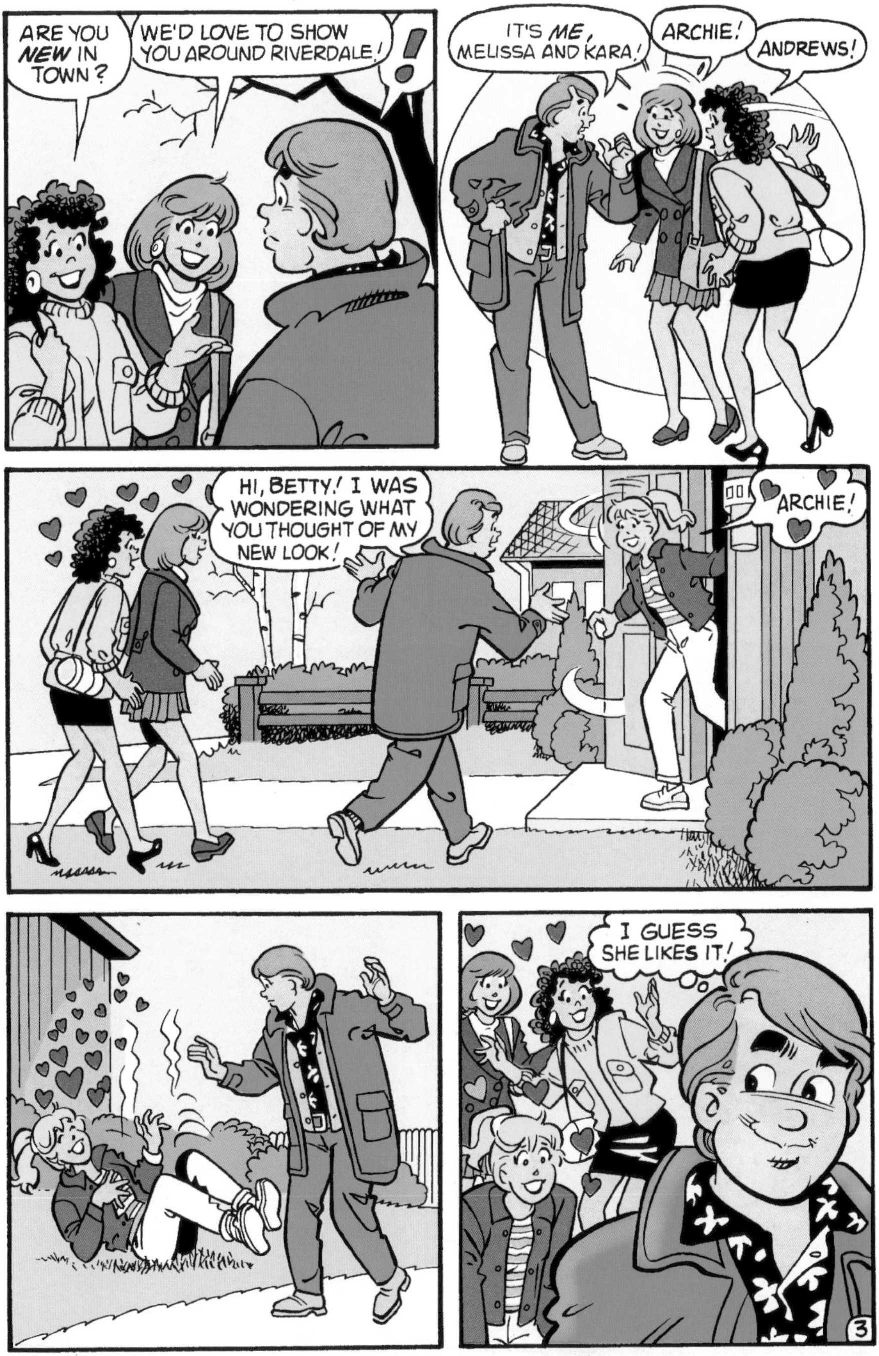
ARE YOU NEW IN TOWN?
WE'D LOVE TO SHOW YOU AROUND RIVERDALE!
!
IT'S ME, MELISSA AND KARA!
ARCHIE!
ANDREWS!
HI, BETTY! I WAS WONDERING WHAT YOU THOUGHT OF MY NEW LOOK!
ARCHIE!
I GUESS SHE LIKES IT!
3

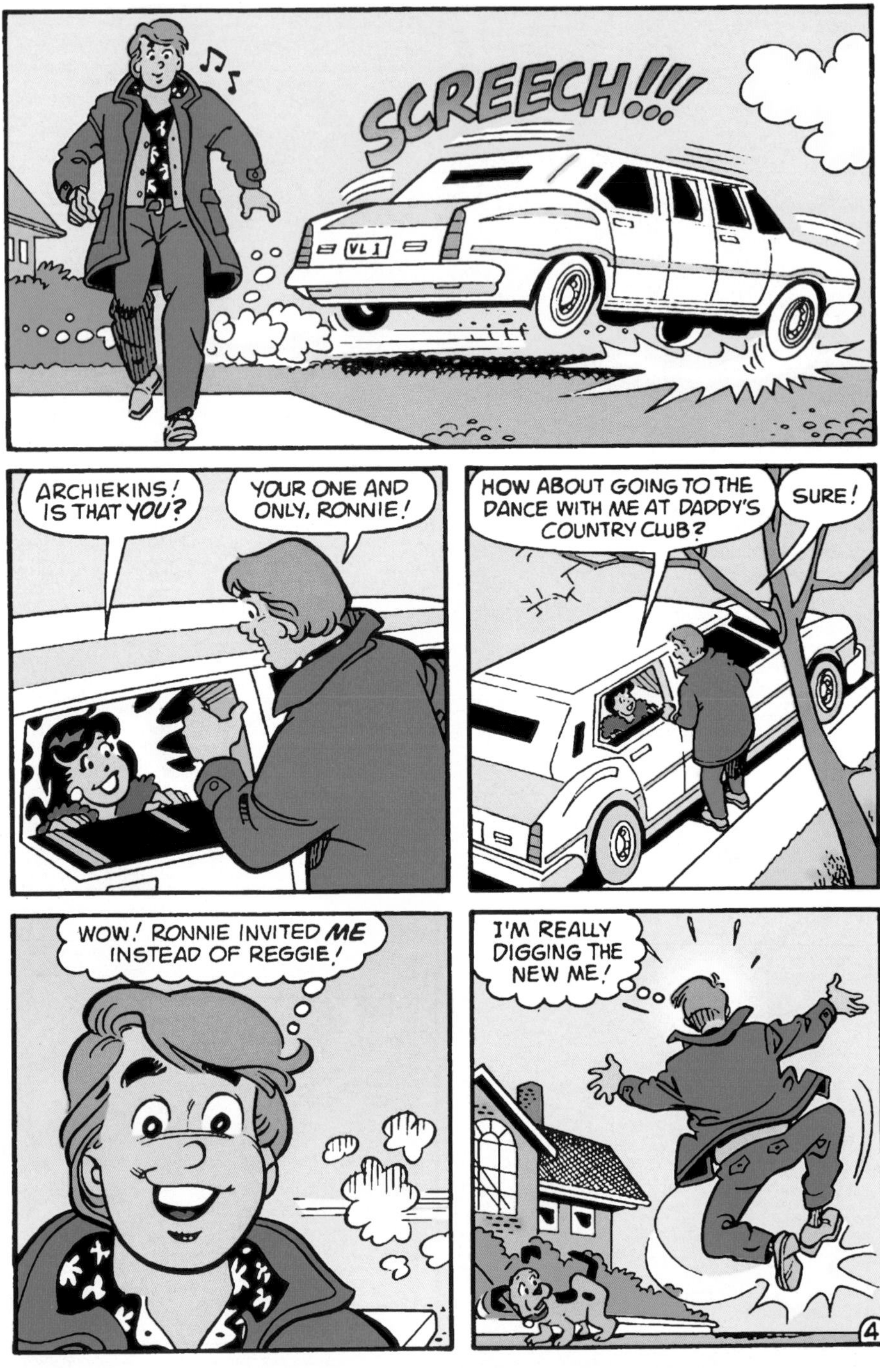
SCREECH!!!
VL 1
ARCHIEKINS! IS THAT YOU?
YOUR ONE AND ONLY, RONNIE!
HOW ABOUT GOING TO THE DANCE WITH ME AT DADDY'S COUNTRY CLUB?
SURE!
WOW! RONNIE INVITED ME INSTEAD OF REGGIE!
I'M REALLY DIGGING THE NEW ME!
4

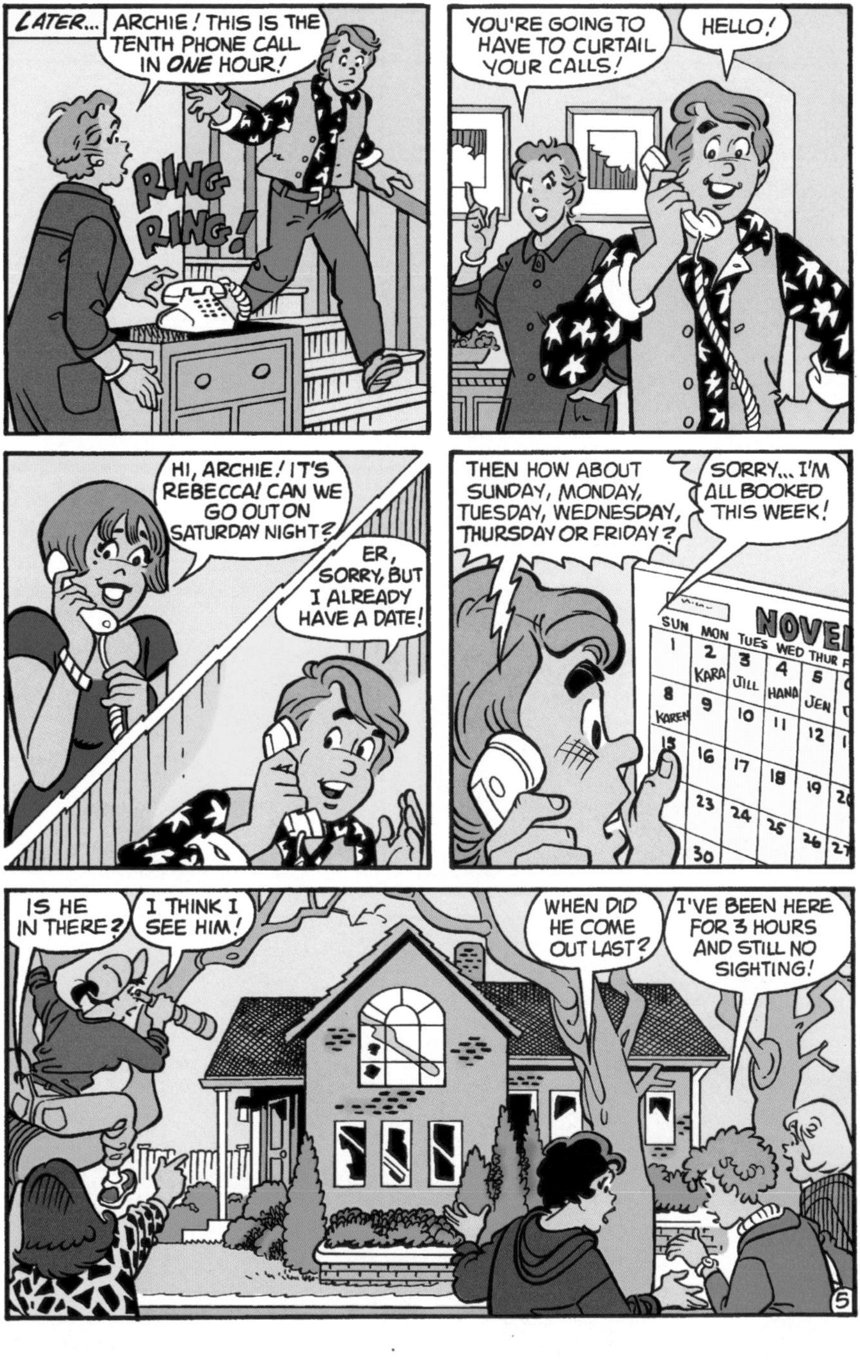
LATER...
ARCHIE! THIS IS THE TENTH PHONE CALL IN ONE HOUR!
RING RING!
YOU'RE GOING TO HAVE TO CURTAIL YOUR CALLS!
HELLO!
HI, ARCHIE! IT'S REBECCA! CAN WE GO OUT ON SATURDAY NIGHT?
ER, SORRY, BUT I ALREADY HAVE A DATE!
THEN HOW ABOUT SUNDAY, MONDAY, TUESDAY, WEDNESDAY, THURSDAY OR FRIDAY?
SORRY... I'M ALL BOOKED THIS WEEK!
IS HE IN THERE?
I THINK I SEE HIM!
WHEN DID HE COME OUT LAST?
I'VE BEEN HERE FOR 3 HOURS AND STILL NO SIGHTING!
5

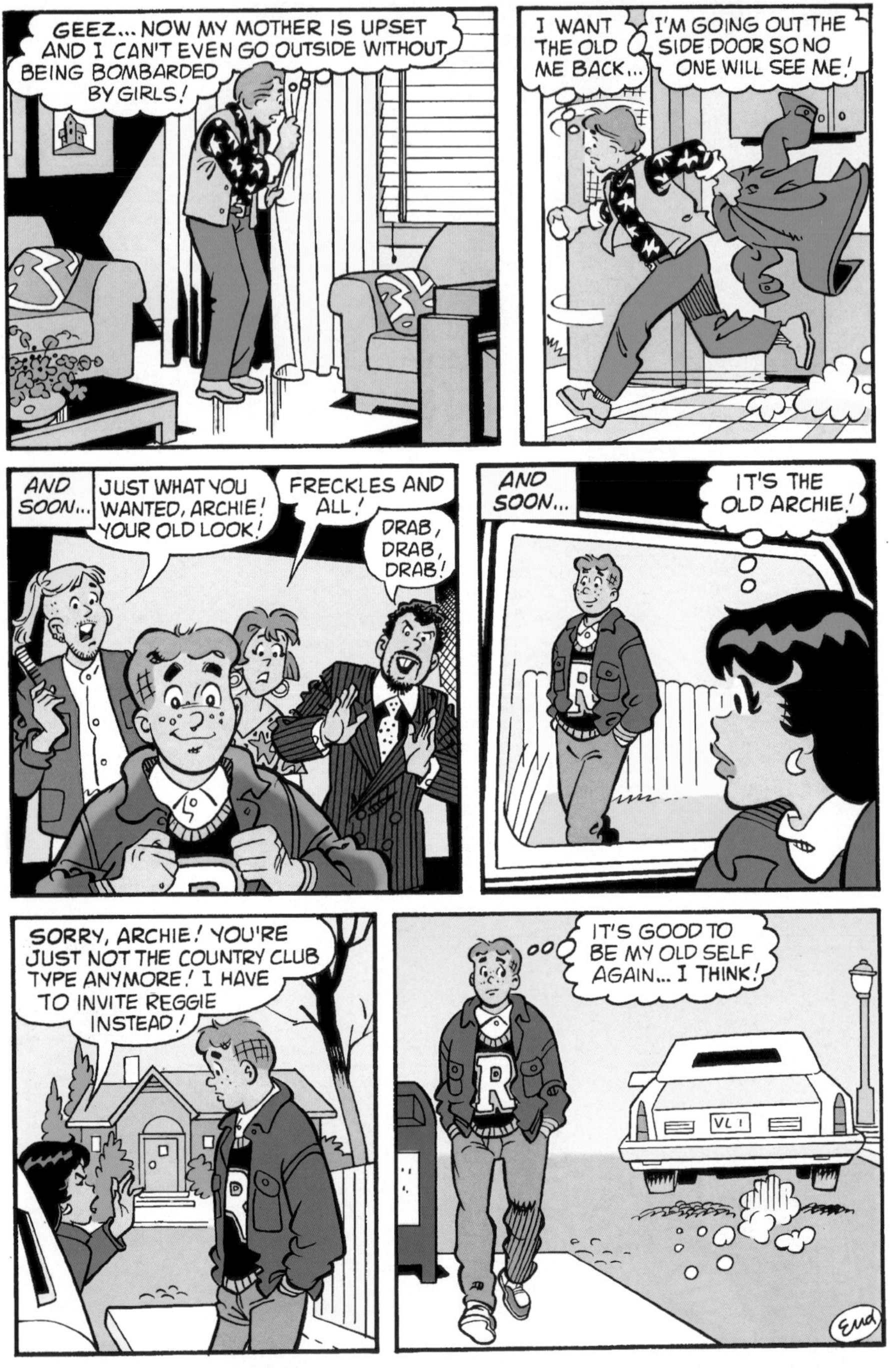
GEEZ... NOW MY MOTHER IS UPSET AND I CAN'T EVEN GO OUTSIDE WITHOUT BEING BOMBARDED BY GIRLS!
I WANT THE OLD ME BACK...
I'M GOING OUT THE SIDE DOOR SO NO ONE WILL SEE ME!
AND SOON...
JUST WHAT YOU WANTED, ARCHIE! YOUR OLD LOOK!
FRECKLES AND ALL!
DRAB, DRAB, DRAB!
AND SOON...
IT'S THE OLD ARCHIE!
SORRY, ARCHIE! YOU'RE JUST NOT THE COUNTRY CLUB TYPE ANYMORE! I HAVE TO INVITE REGGIE INSTEAD!
IT'S GOOD TO BE MY OLD SELF AGAIN... I THINK!
VL 1
End

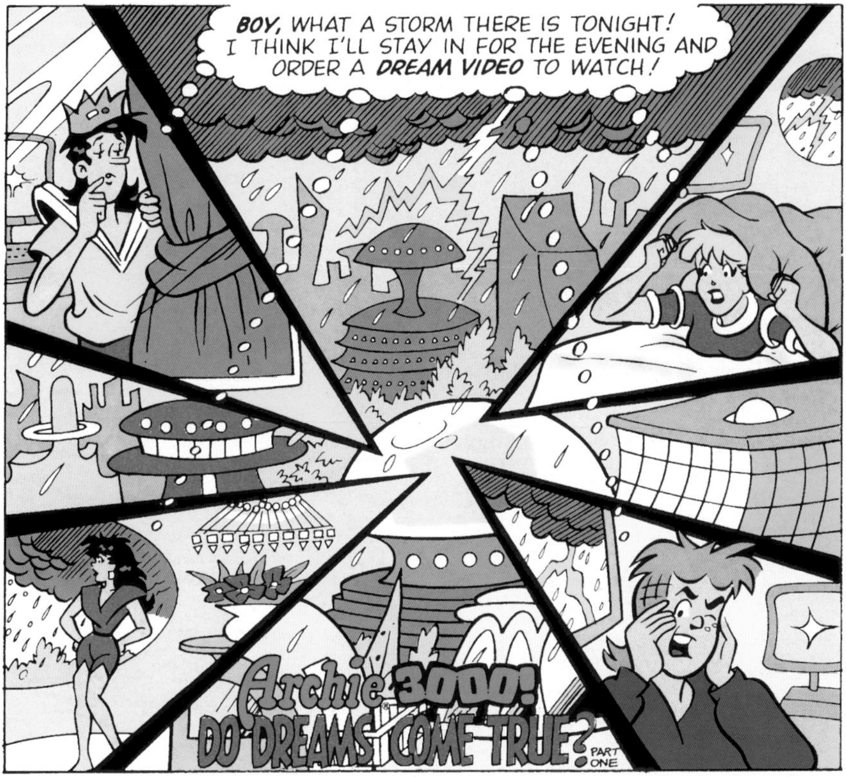
BOY, WHAT A STORM THERE IS TONIGHT! I THINK I'LL STAY IN FOR THE EVENING AND ORDER A DREAM VIDEO TO WATCH!
Archie 3000!
DO DREAMS COME TRUE?
PART ONE

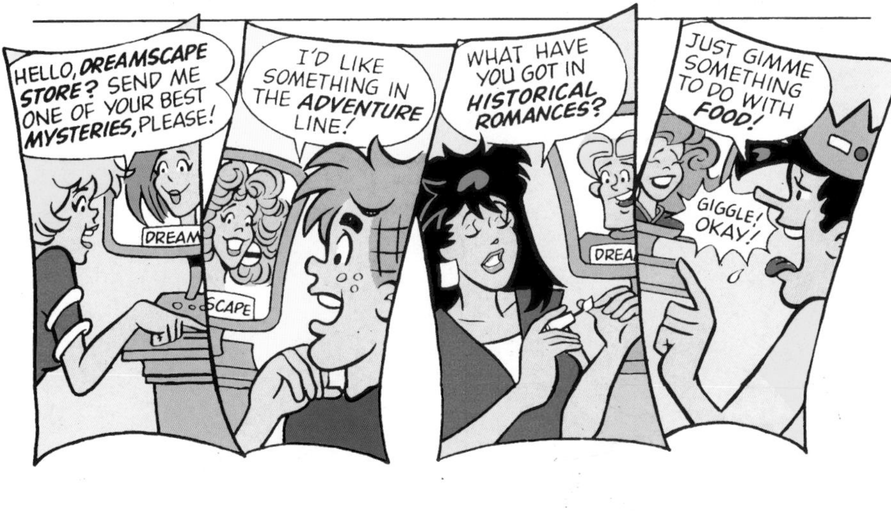
HELLO, DREAMSCAPE STORE? SEND ME ONE OF YOUR BEST MYSTERIES, PLEASE!
DREAM
I'D LIKE SOMETHING IN THE ADVENTURE LINE!
SCAPE
WHAT HAVE YOU GOT IN HISTORICAL ROMANCES?
DREA
JUST GIMME SOMETHING TO DO WITH FOOD!
GIGGLE! OKAY!

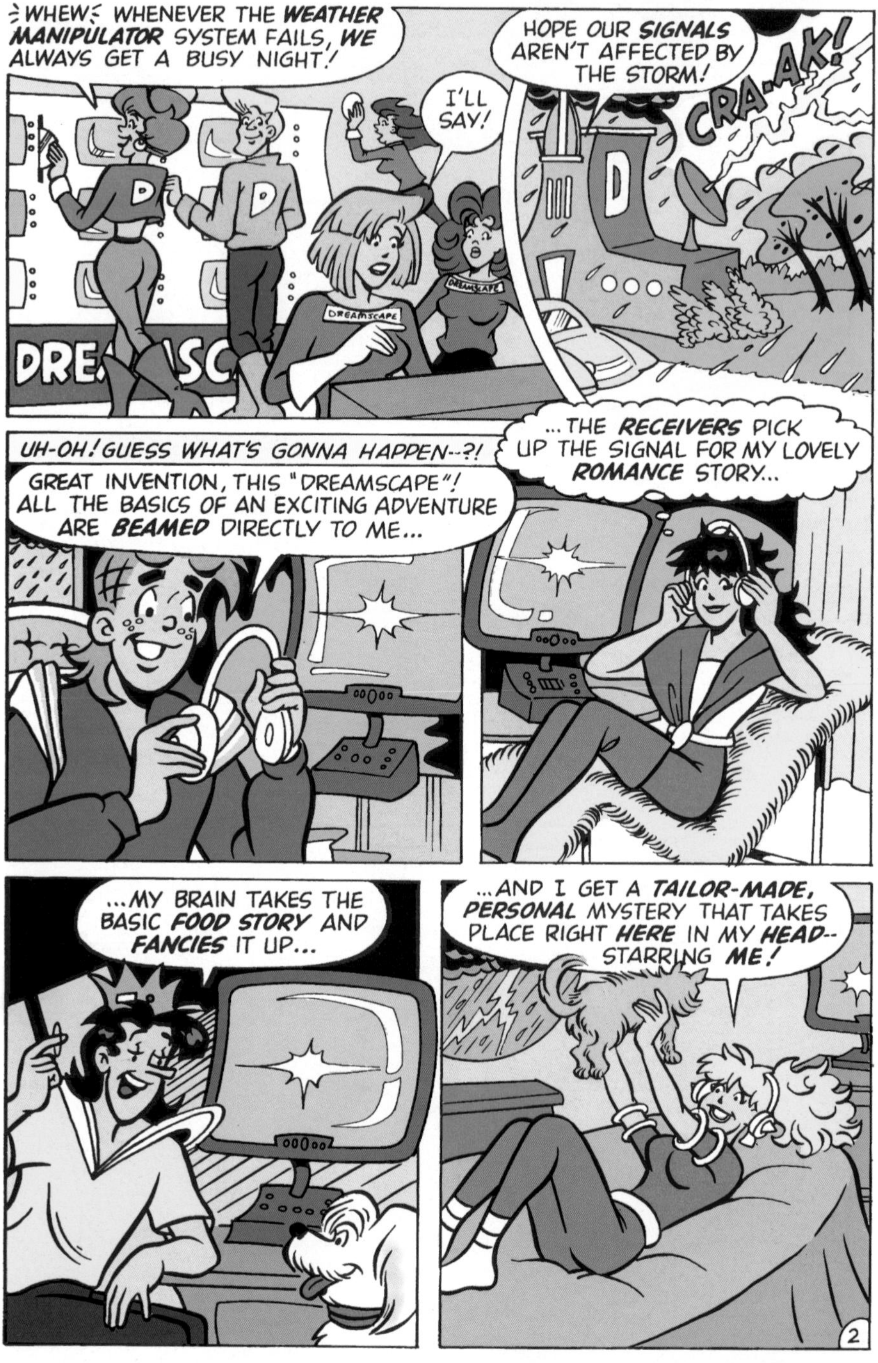
WHEW! WHENEVER THE WEATHER MANIPULATOR SYSTEM FAILS, WE ALWAYS GET A BUSY NIGHT!
I'LL SAY!
HOPE OUR SIGNALS AREN'T AFFECTED BY THE STORM!
CRA-AK!
DREAMSCAPE
DREAMSCAPE
DRE SC
UH-OH! GUESS WHAT'S GONNA HAPPEN--?!
GREAT INVENTION, THIS "DREAMSCAPE"! ALL THE BASICS OF AN EXCITING ADVENTURE ARE BEAMED DIRECTLY TO ME...
...THE RECEIVERS PICK UP THE SIGNAL FOR MY LOVELY ROMANCE STORY...
...MY BRAIN TAKES THE BASIC FOOD STORY AND FANCIES IT UP...
...AND I GET A TAILOR-MADE, PERSONAL MYSTERY THAT TAKES PLACE RIGHT HERE IN MY HEAD-- STARRING ME!
2

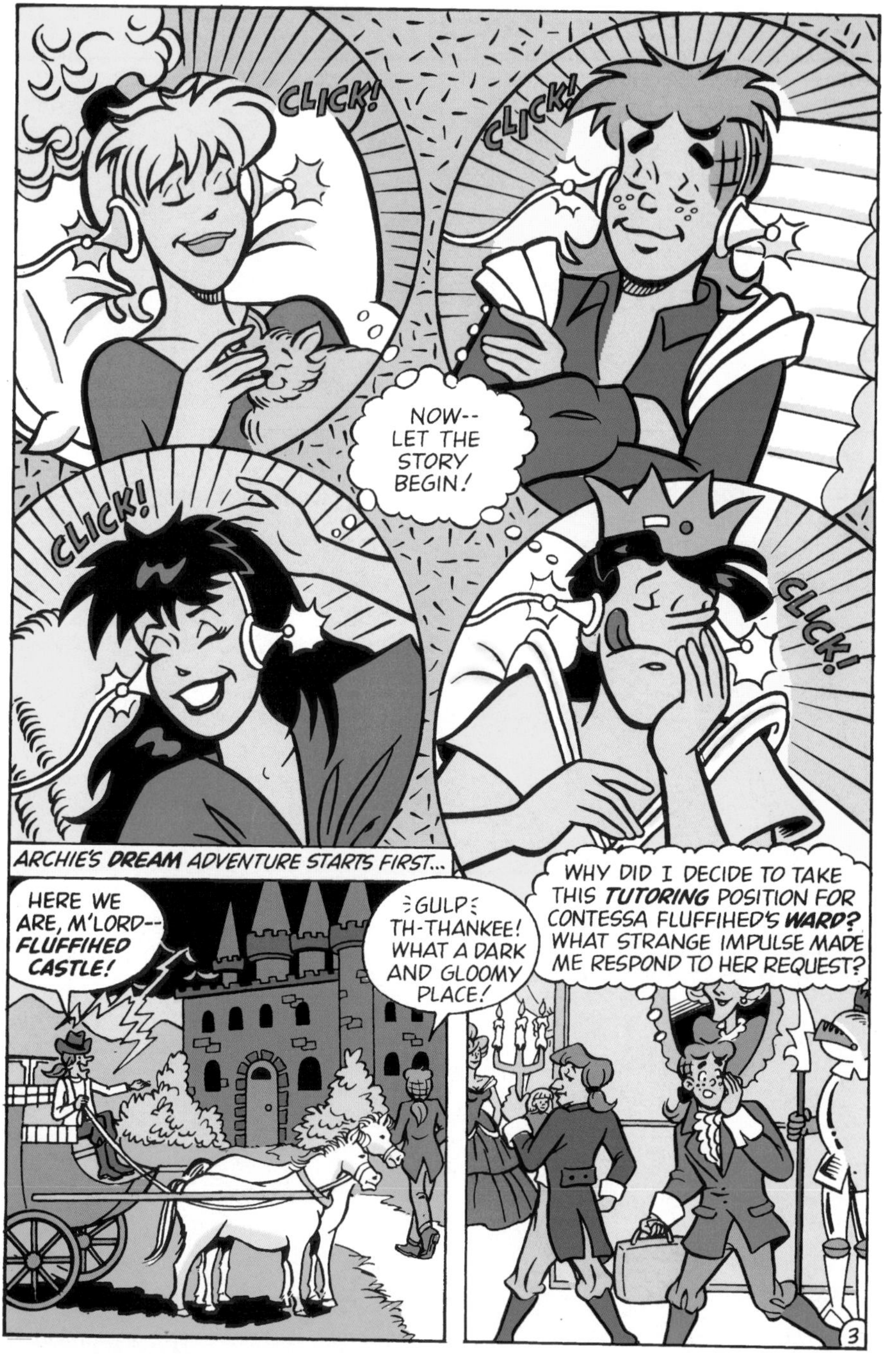
CLICK!
CLICK!
NOW-- LET THE STORY BEGIN!
CLICK!
CLICK!
ARCHIE'S DREAM ADVENTURE STARTS FIRST...
HERE WE ARE, M'LORD-- FLUFFIHED CASTLE!
GULP TH-THANKEE! WHAT A DARK AND GLOOMY PLACE!
WHY DID I DECIDE TO TAKE THIS TUTORING POSITION FOR CONTESSA FLUFFIHED'S WARD? WHAT STRANGE IMPULSE MADE ME RESPOND TO HER REQUEST?
3

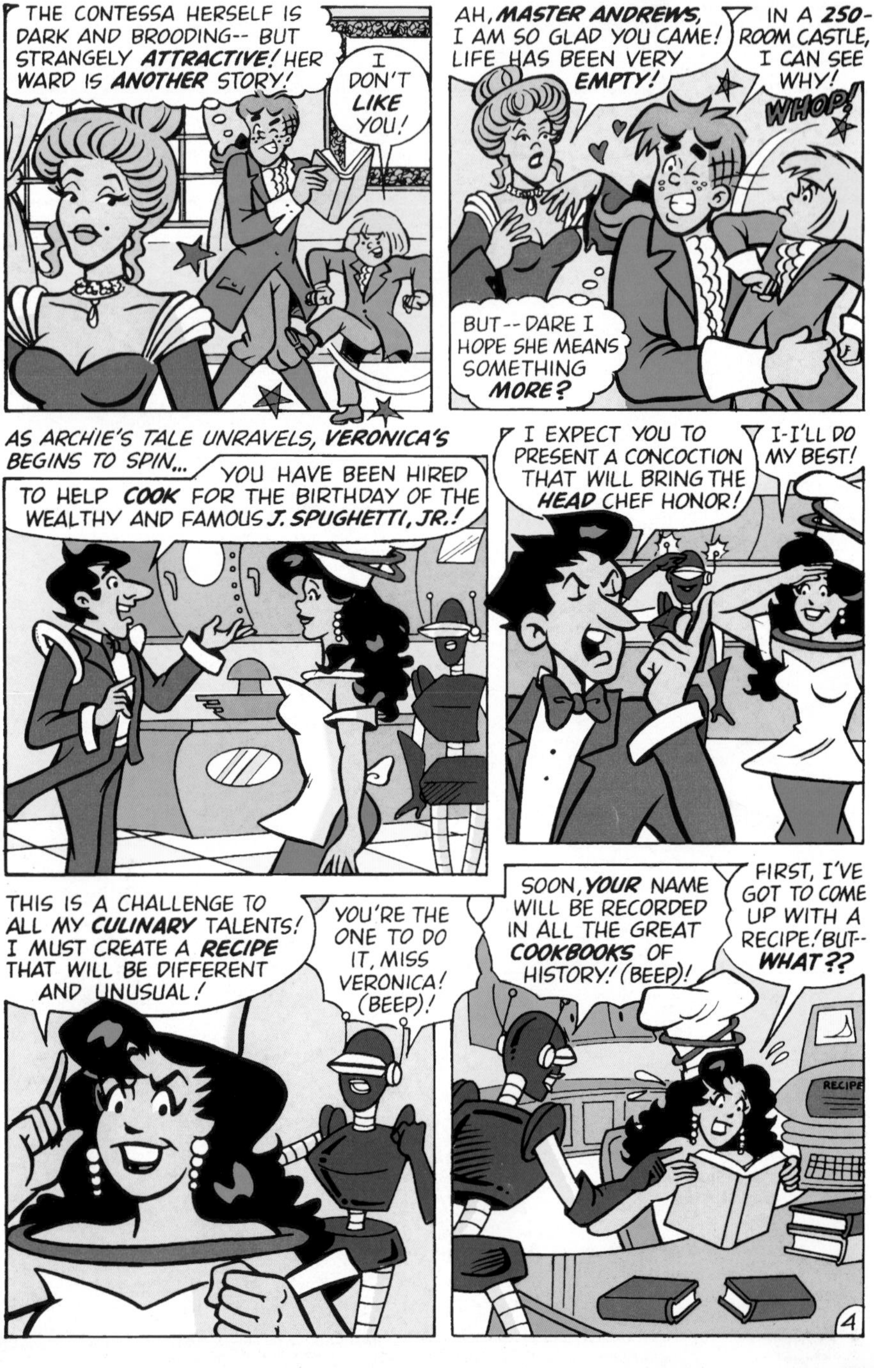
THE CONTESSA HERSELF IS DARK AND BROODING-- BUT STRANGELY ATTRACTIVE! HER WARD IS ANOTHER STORY!
I DON'T LIKE YOU!
AH, MASTER ANDREWS, I AM SO GLAD YOU CAME! LIFE HAS BEEN VERY EMPTY!
IN A 250-ROOM CASTLE, I CAN SEE WHY!
WHOP!
BUT--DARE I HOPE SHE MEANS SOMETHING MORE?
AS ARCHIE'S TALE UNRAVELS, VERONICA'S BEGINS TO SPIN...
YOU HAVE BEEN HIRED TO HELP COOK FOR THE BIRTHDAY OF THE WEALTHY AND FAMOUS J. SPUGHETTI, JR.!
I EXPECT YOU TO PRESENT A CONCOCTION THAT WILL BRING THE HEAD CHEF HONOR!
I-I'LL DO MY BEST!
THIS IS A CHALLENGE TO ALL MY CULINARY TALENTS! I MUST CREATE A RECIPE THAT WILL BE DIFFERENT AND UNUSUAL!
YOU'RE THE ONE TO DO IT, MISS VERONICA! (BEEP)!
SOON, YOUR NAME WILL BE RECORDED IN ALL THE GREAT COOKBOOKS OF HISTORY! (BEEP)!
FIRST, I'VE GOT TO COME UP WITH A RECIPE! BUT-- WHAT??
RECIPE
4

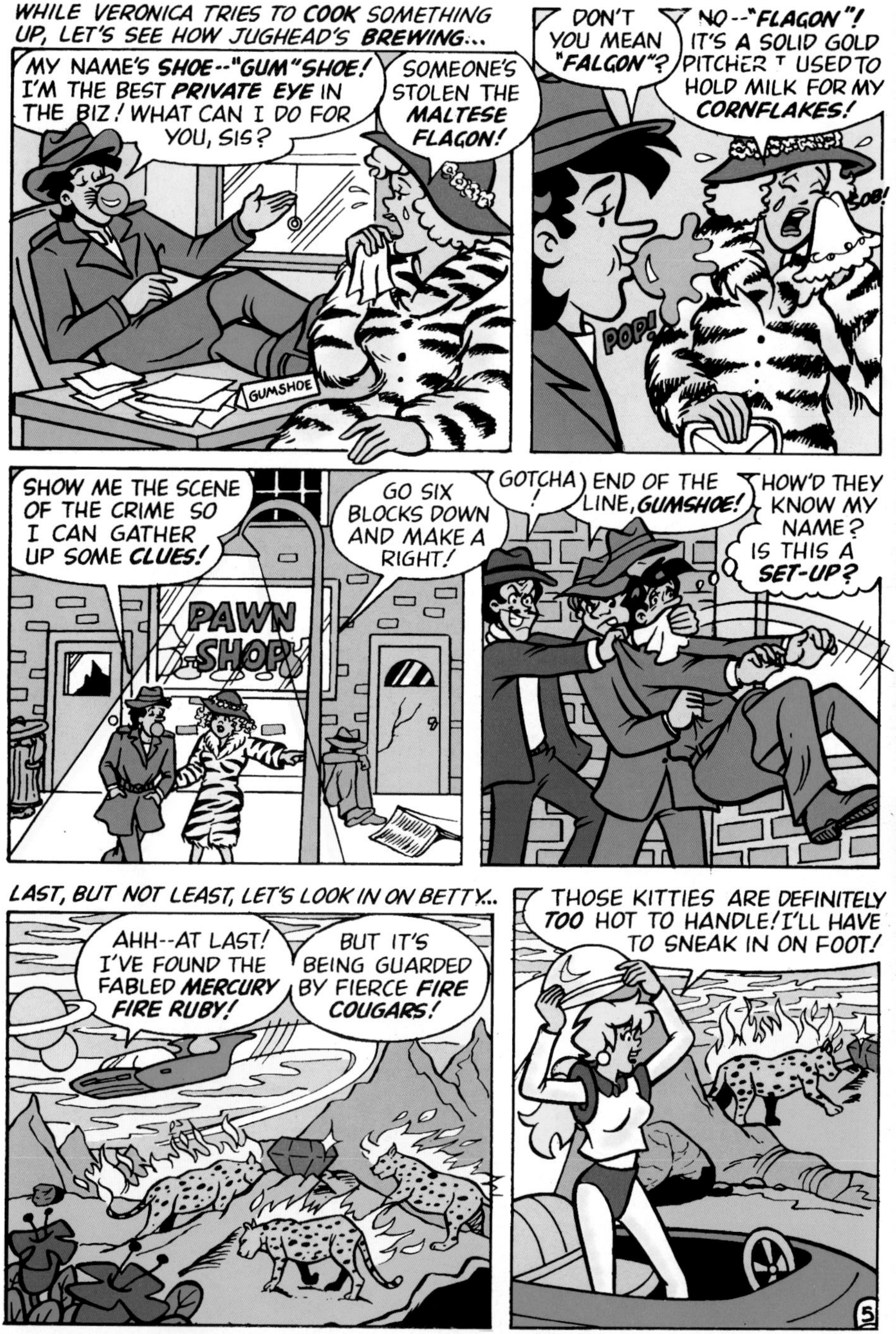
WHILE VERONICA TRIES TO COOK SOMETHING UP, LET'S SEE HOW JUGHEAD'S BREWING...
MY NAME'S SHOE--"GUM"SHOE! I'M THE BEST PRIVATE EYE IN THE BIZ! WHAT CAN I DO FOR YOU, SIS?
SOMEONE'S STOLEN THE MALTESE FLAGON!
GUMSHOE
DON'T YOU MEAN "FALGON"?
NO--"FLAGON"! IT'S A SOLID GOLD PITCHER I USED TO HOLD MILK FOR MY CORNFLAKES!
SOB!
POP!
SHOW ME THE SCENE OF THE CRIME SO I CAN GATHER UP SOME CLUES!
GO SIX BLOCKS DOWN AND MAKE A RIGHT!
PAWN SHOP
GOTCHA!
END OF THE LINE, GUMSHOE!
HOW'D THEY KNOW MY NAME? IS THIS A SET-UP?
LAST, BUT NOT LEAST, LET'S LOOK IN ON BETTY...
AHH--AT LAST! I'VE FOUND THE FABLED MERCURY FIRE RUBY!
BUT IT'S BEING GUARDED BY FIERCE FIRE COUGARS!
THOSE KITTIES ARE DEFINITELY TOO HOT TO HANDLE! I'LL HAVE TO SNEAK IN ON FOOT!
5

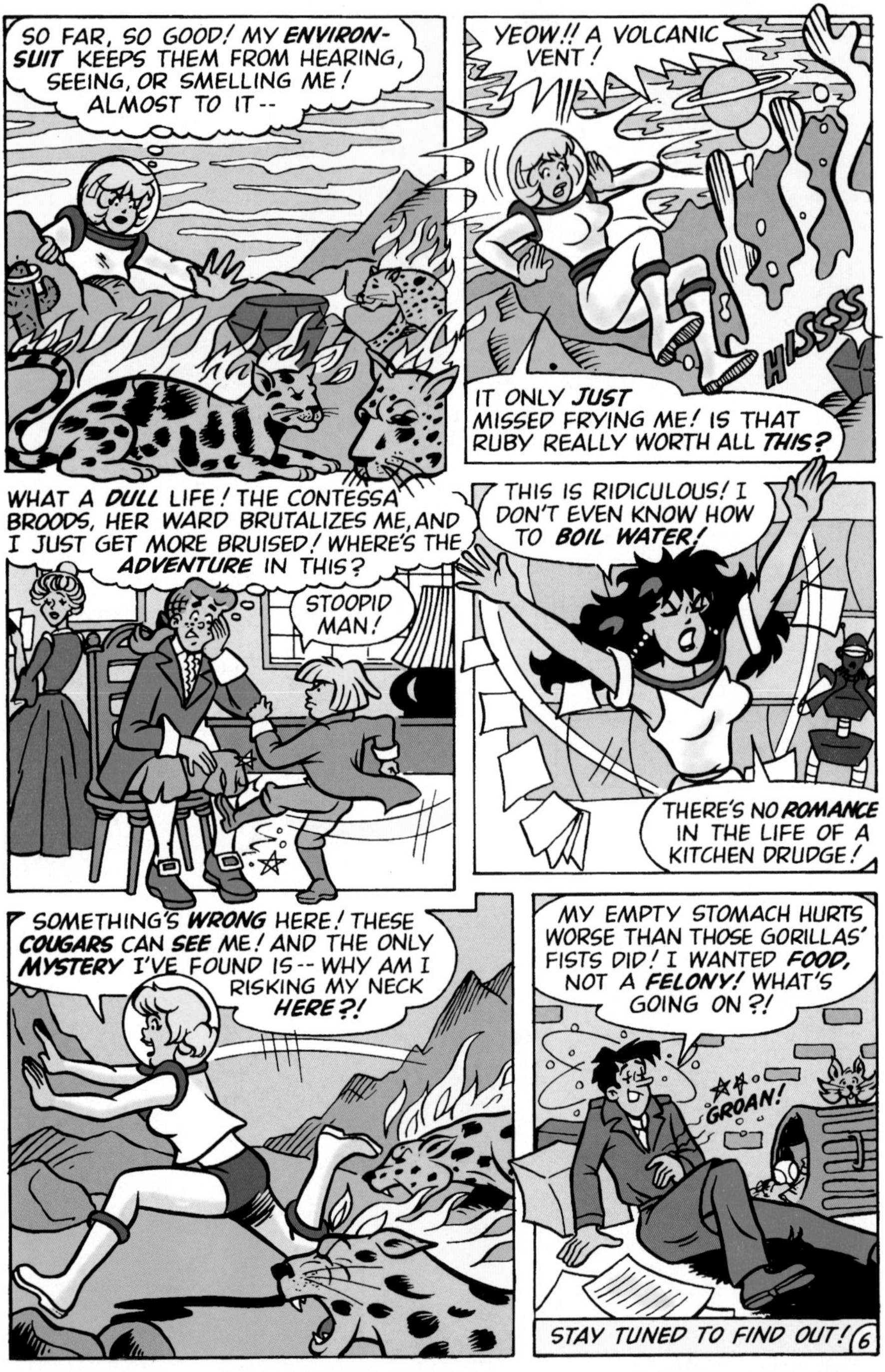
SO FAR, SO GOOD! MY ENVIRON-SUIT KEEPS THEM FROM HEARING, SEEING, OR SMELLING ME! ALMOST TO IT--
YEOW!! A VOLCANIC VENT!
HISSSS
IT ONLY JUST MISSED FRYING ME! IS THAT RUBY REALLY WORTH ALL THIS?
WHAT A DULL LIFE! THE CONTESSA BROODS, HER WARD BRUTALIZES ME, AND I JUST GET MORE BRUISED! WHERE'S THE ADVENTURE IN THIS?
STOOPID MAN!
THIS IS RIDICULOUS! I DON'T EVEN KNOW HOW TO BOIL WATER!
THERE'S NO ROMANCE IN THE LIFE OF A KITCHEN DRUDGE!
SOMETHING'S WRONG HERE! THESE COUGARS CAN SEE ME! AND THE ONLY MYSTERY I'VE FOUND IS--WHY AM I RISKING MY NECK HERE?!
MY EMPTY STOMACH HURTS WORSE THAN THOSE GORILLAS' FISTS DID! I WANTED FOOD, NOT A FELONY! WHAT'S GOING ON?!
GROAN!
STAY TUNED TO FIND OUT!
6

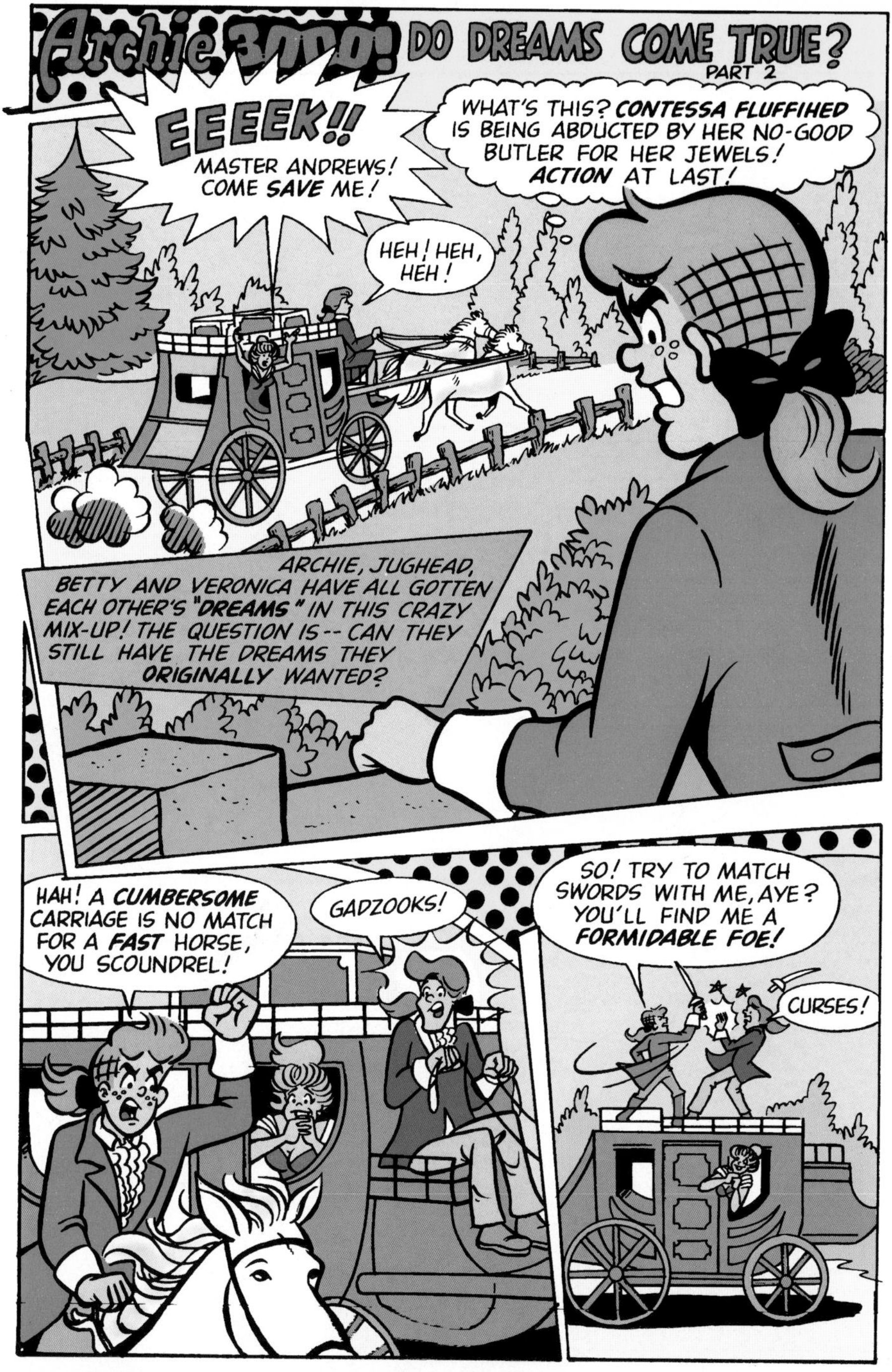
Archie 3000! DO DREAMS COME TRUE?
PART 2
EEEEK!! MASTER ANDREWS! COME SAVE ME!
WHAT'S THIS? CONTESSA FLUFFIHED IS BEING ABDUCTED BY HER NO-GOOD BUTLER FOR HER JEWELS! ACTION AT LAST!
HEH! HEH, HEH!
ARCHIE, JUGHEAD, BETTY AND VERONICA HAVE ALL GOTTEN EACH OTHER'S "DREAMS" IN THIS CRAZY MIX-UP! THE QUESTION IS -- CAN THEY STILL HAVE THE DREAMS THEY ORIGINALLY WANTED?
HAH! A CUMBERSOME CARRIAGE IS NO MATCH FOR A FAST HORSE, YOU SCOUNDREL!
GADZOOKS!
SO! TRY TO MATCH SWORDS WITH ME, AYE? YOU'LL FIND ME A FORMIDABLE FOE!
CURSES!

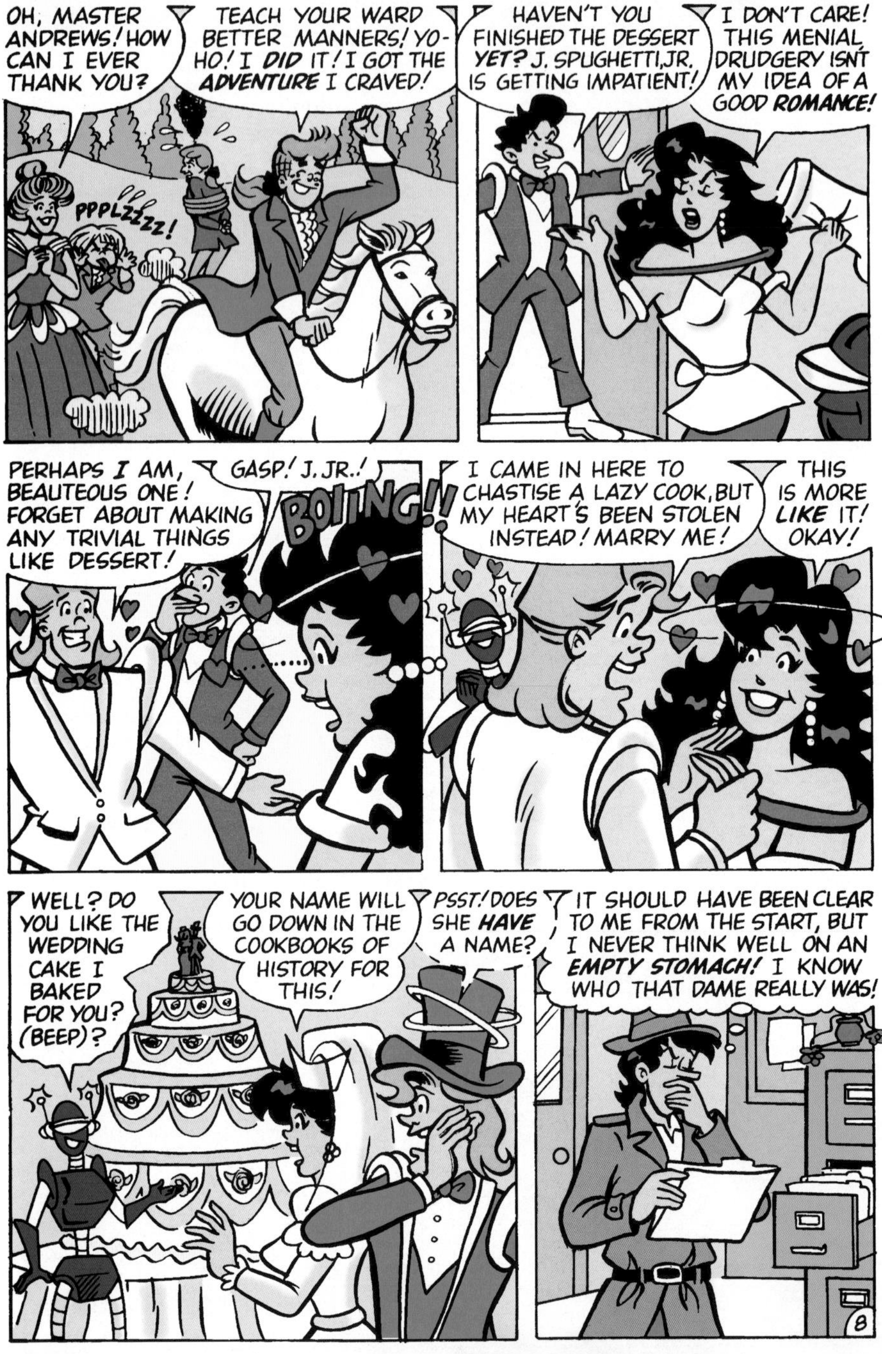
OH, MASTER ANDREWS! HOW CAN I EVER THANK YOU?
TEACH YOUR WARD BETTER MANNERS! YO-HO! I DID IT! I GOT THE ADVENTURE I CRAVED!
PPPLZZZZZ!
HAVEN'T YOU FINISHED THE DESSERT YET? J. SPUGHETTI, JR. IS GETTING IMPATIENT!
I DON'T CARE! THIS MENIAL DRUDGERY ISN'T MY IDEA OF A GOOD ROMANCE!
PERHAPS I AM, BEAUTEOUS ONE! FORGET ABOUT MAKING ANY TRIVIAL THINGS LIKE DESSERT!
GASP! J. JR..!
BOIING!!
I CAME IN HERE TO CHASTISE A LAZY COOK, BUT MY HEART'S BEEN STOLEN INSTEAD! MARRY ME!
THIS IS MORE LIKE IT! OKAY!
WELL? DO YOU LIKE THE WEDDING CAKE I BAKED FOR YOU? (BEEP)?
YOUR NAME WILL GO DOWN IN THE COOKBOOKS OF HISTORY FOR THIS!
PSST! DOES SHE HAVE A NAME?
IT SHOULD HAVE BEEN CLEAR TO ME FROM THE START, BUT I NEVER THINK WELL ON AN EMPTY STOMACH! I KNOW WHO THAT DAME REALLY WAS!
8

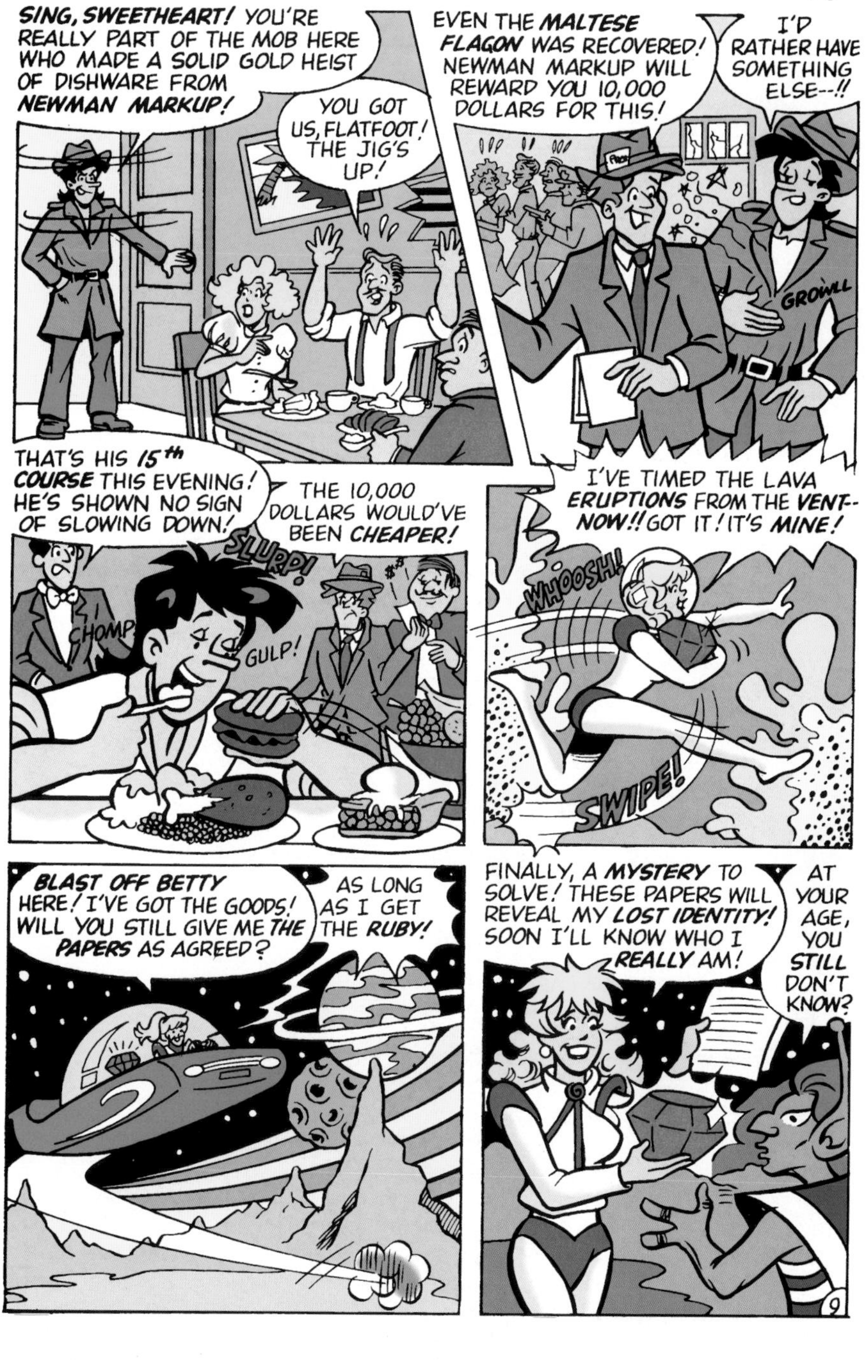
SING, SWEETHEART! YOU'RE REALLY PART OF THE MOB HERE WHO MADE A SOLID GOLD HEIST OF DISHWARE FROM NEWMAN MARKUP!
YOU GOT US, FLATFOOT! THE JIG'S UP!
EVEN THE MALTESE FLAGON WAS RECOVERED! NEWMAN MARKUP WILL REWARD YOU 10,000 DOLLARS FOR THIS!
I'D RATHER HAVE SOMETHING ELSE--!!
GROWL
THAT'S HIS 15th COURSE THIS EVENING! HE'S SHOWN NO SIGN OF SLOWING DOWN!
THE 10,000 DOLLARS WOULD'VE BEEN CHEAPER!
SLURP!
CHOMP!
GULP!
I'VE TIMED THE LAVA ERUPTIONS FROM THE VENT-- NOW!! GOT IT! IT'S MINE!
WHOOSH!
SWIPE!
BLAST OFF BETTY HERE! I'VE GOT THE GOODS! WILL YOU STILL GIVE ME THE PAPERS AS AGREED?
AS LONG AS I GET THE RUBY!
FINALLY, A MYSTERY TO SOLVE! THESE PAPERS WILL REVEAL MY LOST IDENTITY! SOON I'LL KNOW WHO I REALLY AM!
AT YOUR AGE, YOU STILL DON'T KNOW?
9

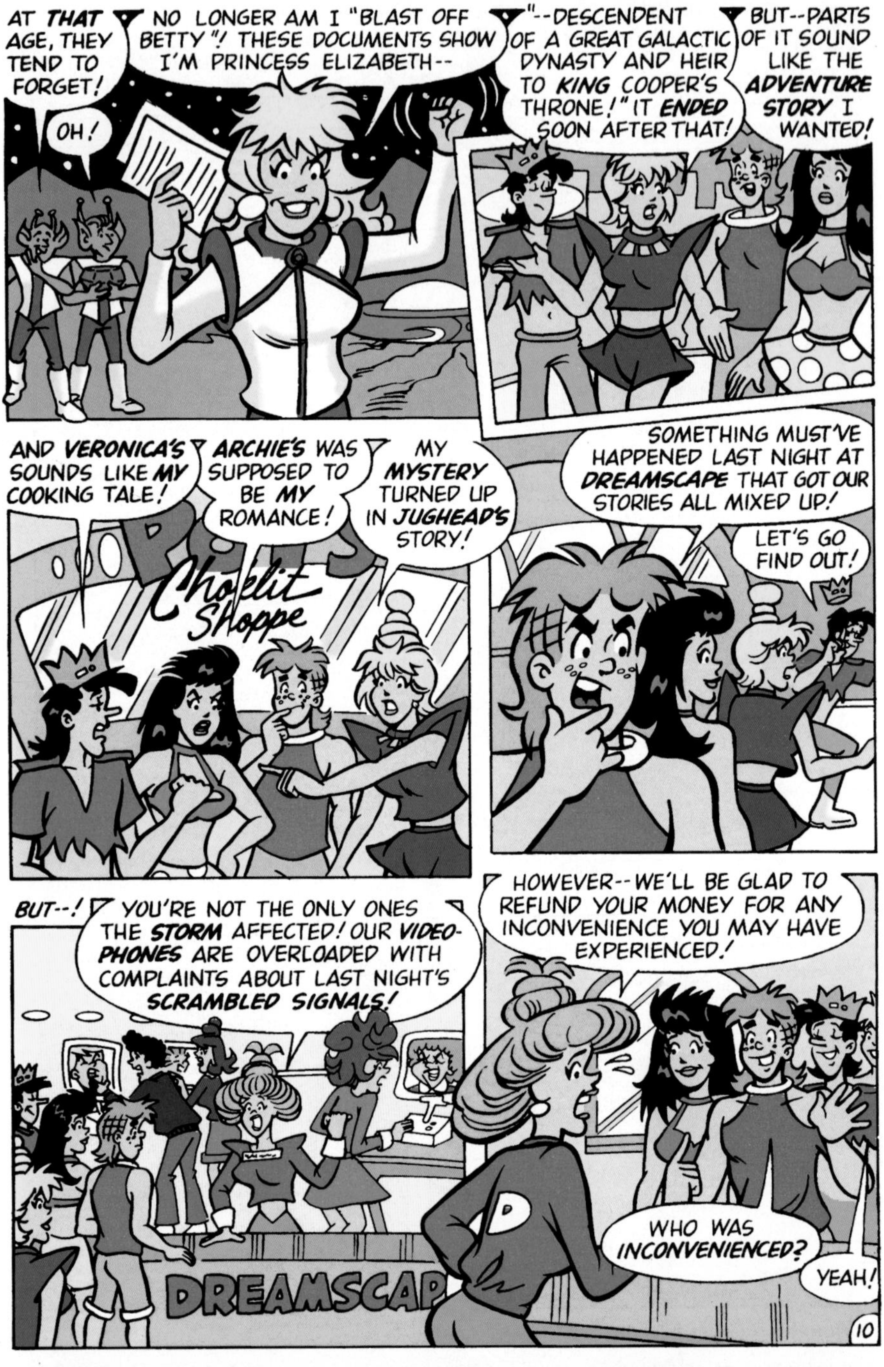
AT THAT AGE, THEY TEND TO FORGET!
NO LONGER AM I "BLAST OFF BETTY"! THESE DOCUMENTS SHOW I'M PRINCESS ELIZABETH--
"--DESCENDENT OF A GREAT GALACTIC DYNASTY AND HEIR TO KING COOPER'S THRONE!" IT ENDED SOON AFTER THAT!
BUT--PARTS OF IT SOUND LIKE THE ADVENTURE STORY I WANTED!
OH!
AND VERONICA'S SOUNDS LIKE MY COOKING TALE!
ARCHIE'S WAS SUPPOSED TO BE MY ROMANCE!
MY MYSTERY TURNED UP IN JUGHEAD'S STORY!
Choklit Shoppe
SOMETHING MUST'VE HAPPENED LAST NIGHT AT DREAMSCAPE THAT GOT OUR STORIES ALL MIXED UP!
LET'S GO FIND OUT!
BUT--!
YOU'RE NOT THE ONLY ONES THE STORM AFFECTED! OUR VIDEO-PHONES ARE OVERLOADED WITH COMPLAINTS ABOUT LAST NIGHT'S SCRAMBLED SIGNALS!
DREAMSCAP
HOWEVER--WE'LL BE GLAD TO REFUND YOUR MONEY FOR ANY INCONVENIENCE YOU MAY HAVE EXPERIENCED!
WHO WAS INCONVENIENCED?
YEAH!
10

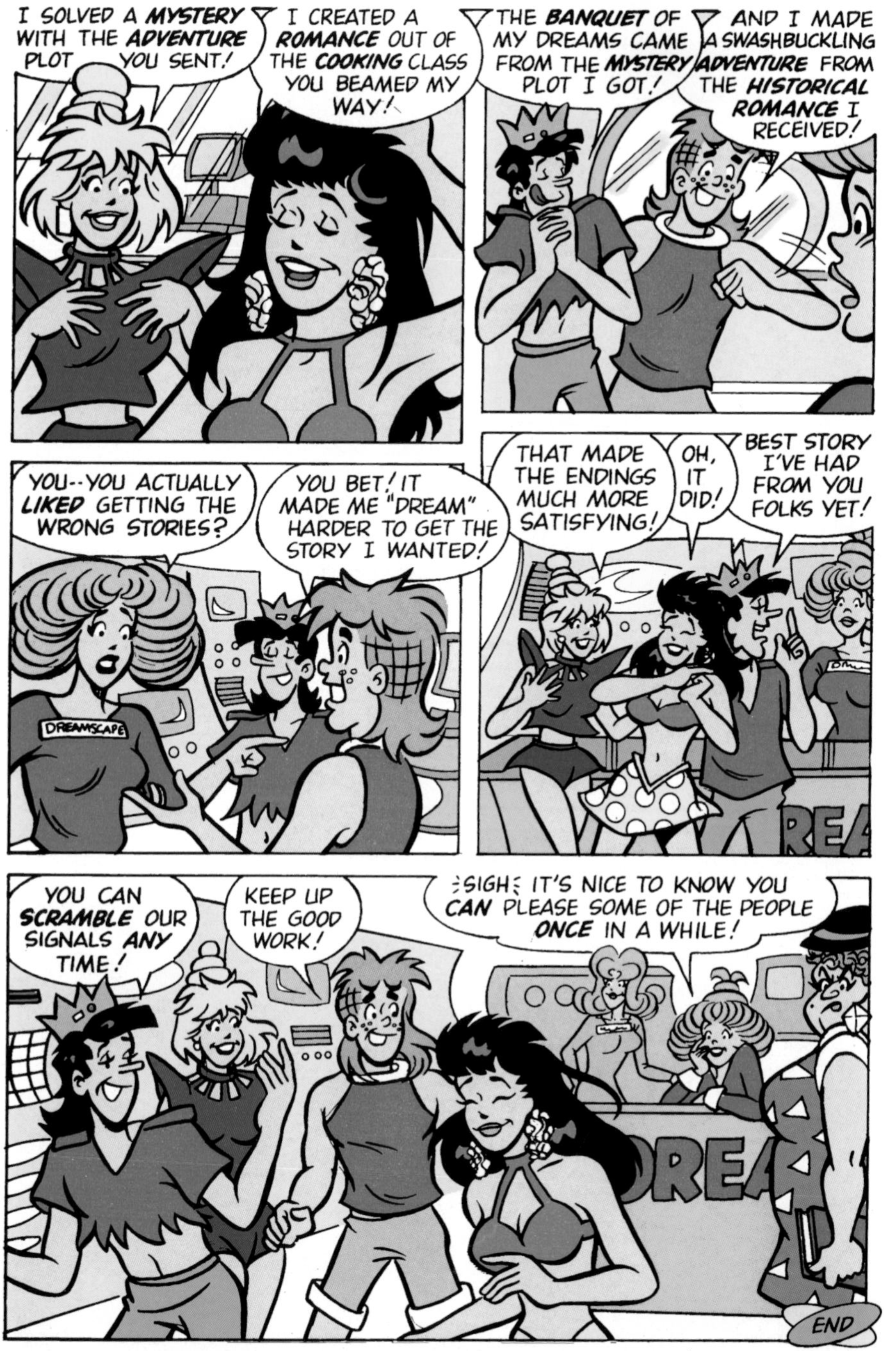
I SOLVED A MYSTERY WITH THE ADVENTURE PLOT YOU SENT!
I CREATED A ROMANCE OUT OF THE COOKING CLASS YOU BEAMED MY WAY!
THE BANQUET OF MY DREAMS CAME FROM THE MYSTERY PLOT I GOT!
AND I MADE A SWASHBUCKLING ADVENTURE FROM THE HISTORICAL ROMANCE I RECEIVED!
YOU--YOU ACTUALLY LIKED GETTING THE WRONG STORIES?
YOU BET! IT MADE ME "DREAM" HARDER TO GET THE STORY I WANTED!
DREAMSCAPE
THAT MADE THE ENDINGS MUCH MORE SATISFYING!
OH, IT DID!
BEST STORY I'VE HAD FROM YOU FOLKS YET!
YOU CAN SCRAMBLE OUR SIGNALS ANY TIME!
KEEP UP THE GOOD WORK!
SIGH IT'S NICE TO KNOW YOU CAN PLEASE SOME OF THE PEOPLE ONCE IN A WHILE!
END

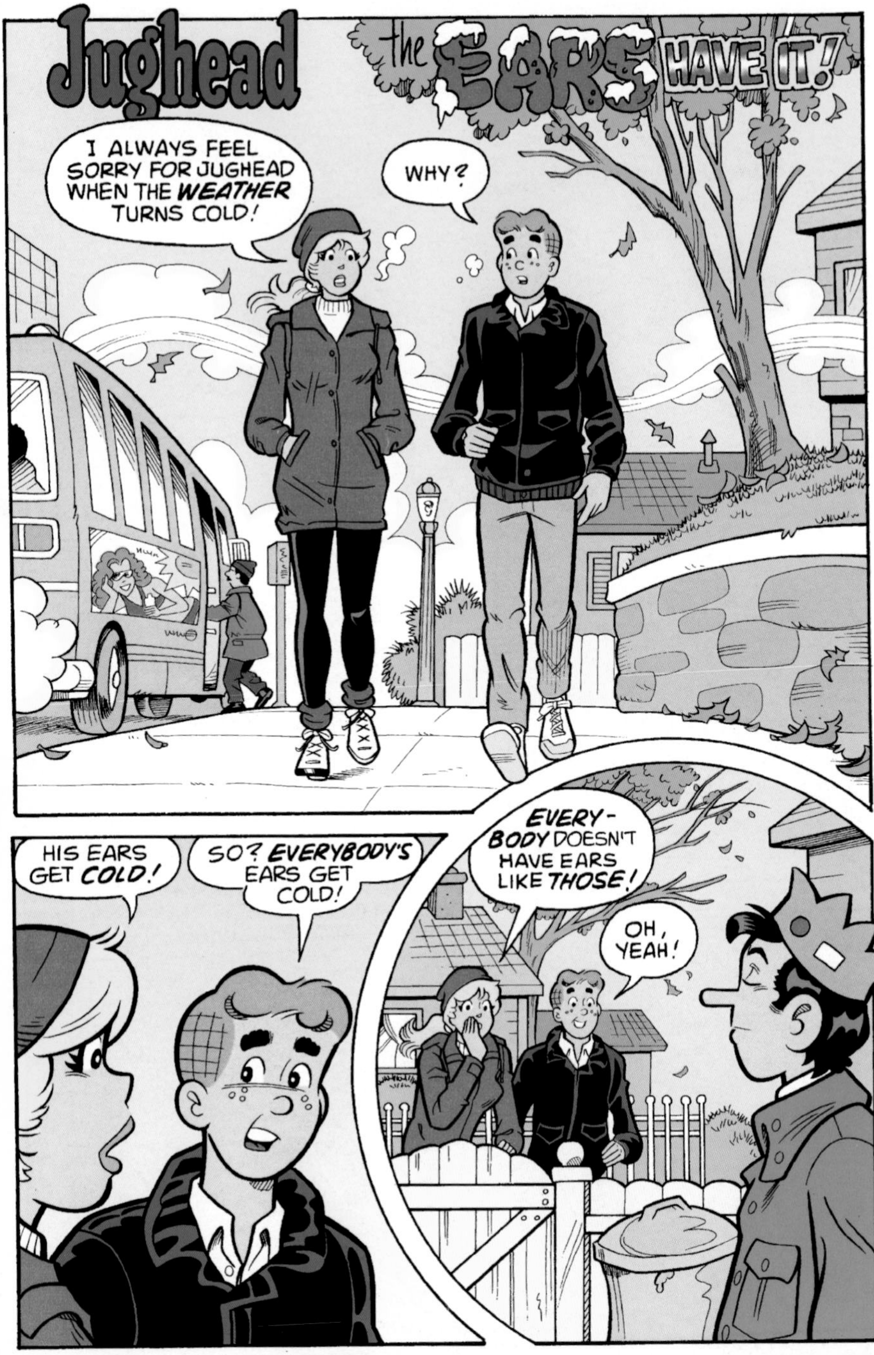
Jughead
the EARS HAVE IT!
I ALWAYS FEEL SORRY FOR JUGHEAD WHEN THE WEATHER TURNS COLD!
WHY?
HIS EARS GET COLD!
SO? EVERYBODY'S EARS GET COLD!
EVERY-BODY DOESN'T HAVE EARS LIKE THOSE!
OH, YEAH!

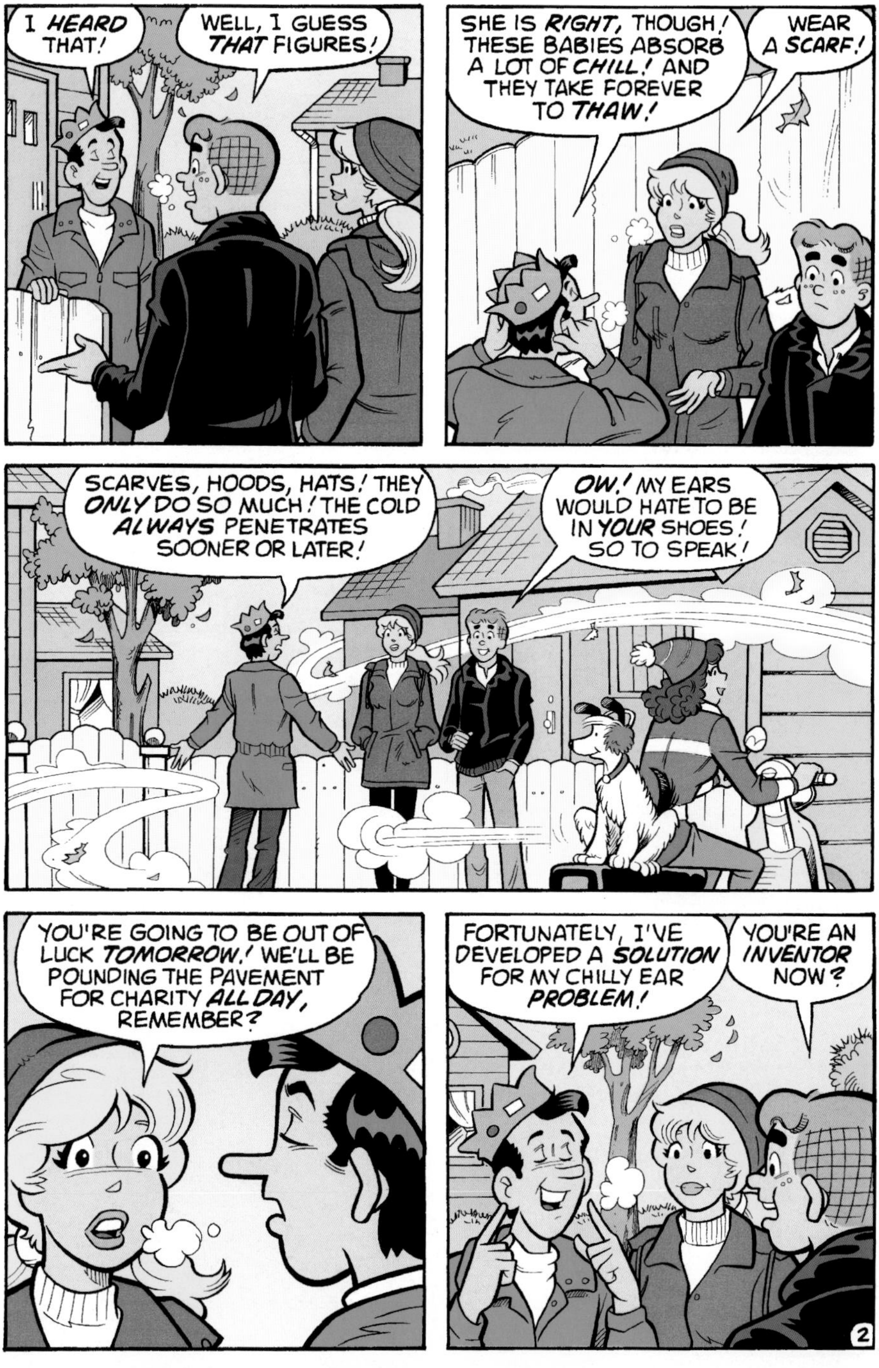
I HEARD THAT!
WELL, I GUESS THAT FIGURES!
SHE IS RIGHT, THOUGH! THESE BABIES ABSORB A LOT OF CHILL! AND THEY TAKE FOREVER TO THAW!
WEAR A SCARF!
SCARVES, HOODS, HATS! THEY ONLY DO SO MUCH! THE COLD ALWAYS PENETRATES SOONER OR LATER!
OW! MY EARS WOULD HATE TO BE IN YOUR SHOES! SO TO SPEAK!
YOU'RE GOING TO BE OUT OF LUCK TOMORROW! WE'LL BE POUNDING THE PAVEMENT FOR CHARITY ALL DAY, REMEMBER?
FORTUNATELY, I'VE DEVELOPED A SOLUTION FOR MY CHILLY EAR PROBLEM!
YOU'RE AN INVENTOR NOW?
2

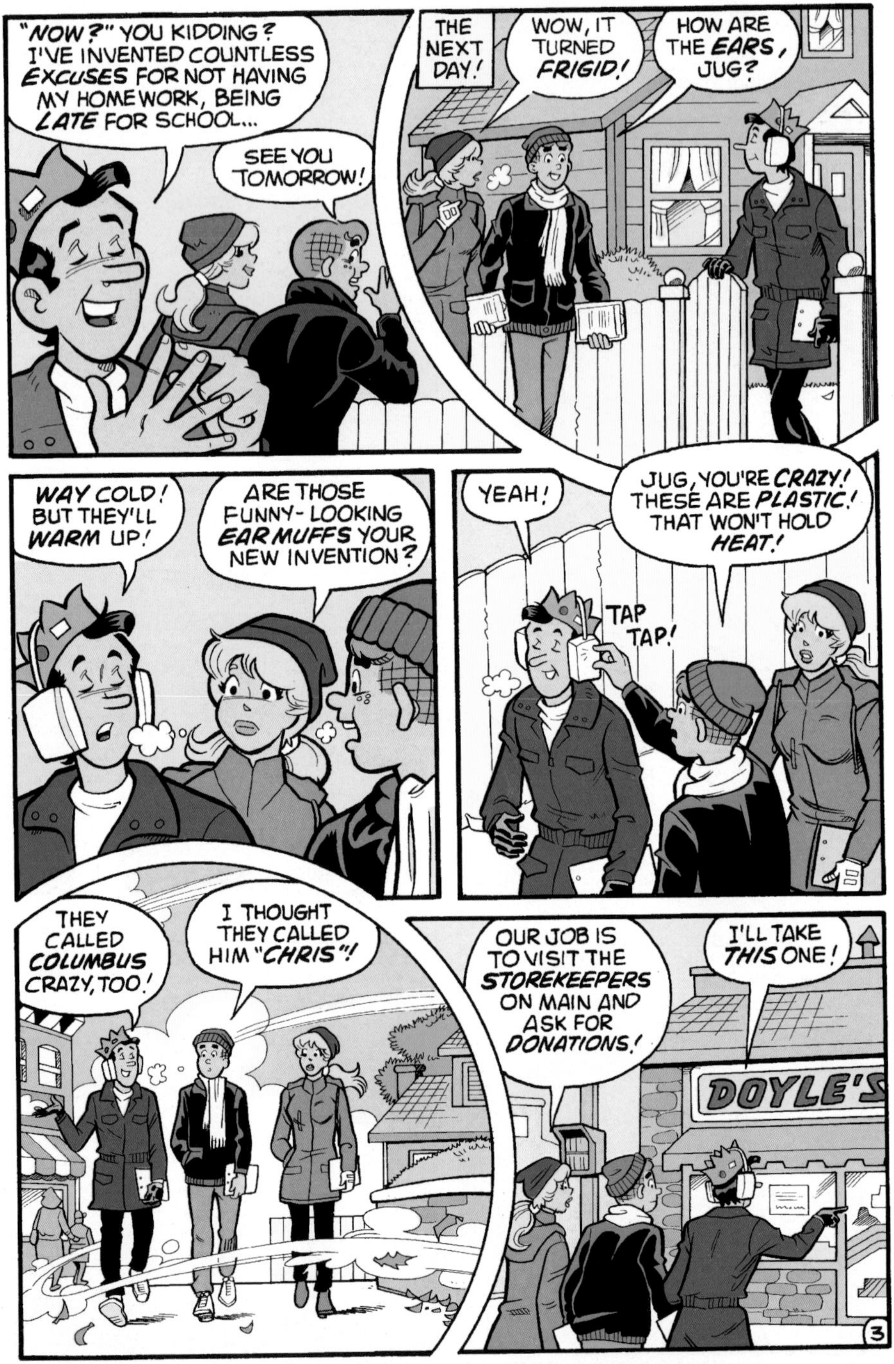
"NOW?" YOU KIDDING? I'VE INVENTED COUNTLESS EXCUSES FOR NOT HAVING MY HOMEWORK, BEING LATE FOR SCHOOL...
SEE YOU TOMORROW!
THE NEXT DAY!
WOW, IT TURNED FRIGID!
HOW ARE THE EARS, JUG?
WAY COLD! BUT THEY'LL WARM UP!
ARE THOSE FUNNY-LOOKING EARMUFFS YOUR NEW INVENTION?
YEAH!
JUG, YOU'RE CRAZY! THESE ARE PLASTIC! THAT WON'T HOLD HEAT!
TAP TAP!
THEY CALLED COLUMBUS CRAZY, TOO!
I THOUGHT THEY CALLED HIM "CHRIS"!
OUR JOB IS TO VISIT THE STOREKEEPERS ON MAIN AND ASK FOR DONATIONS!
I'LL TAKE THIS ONE!
DOYLE'S
3

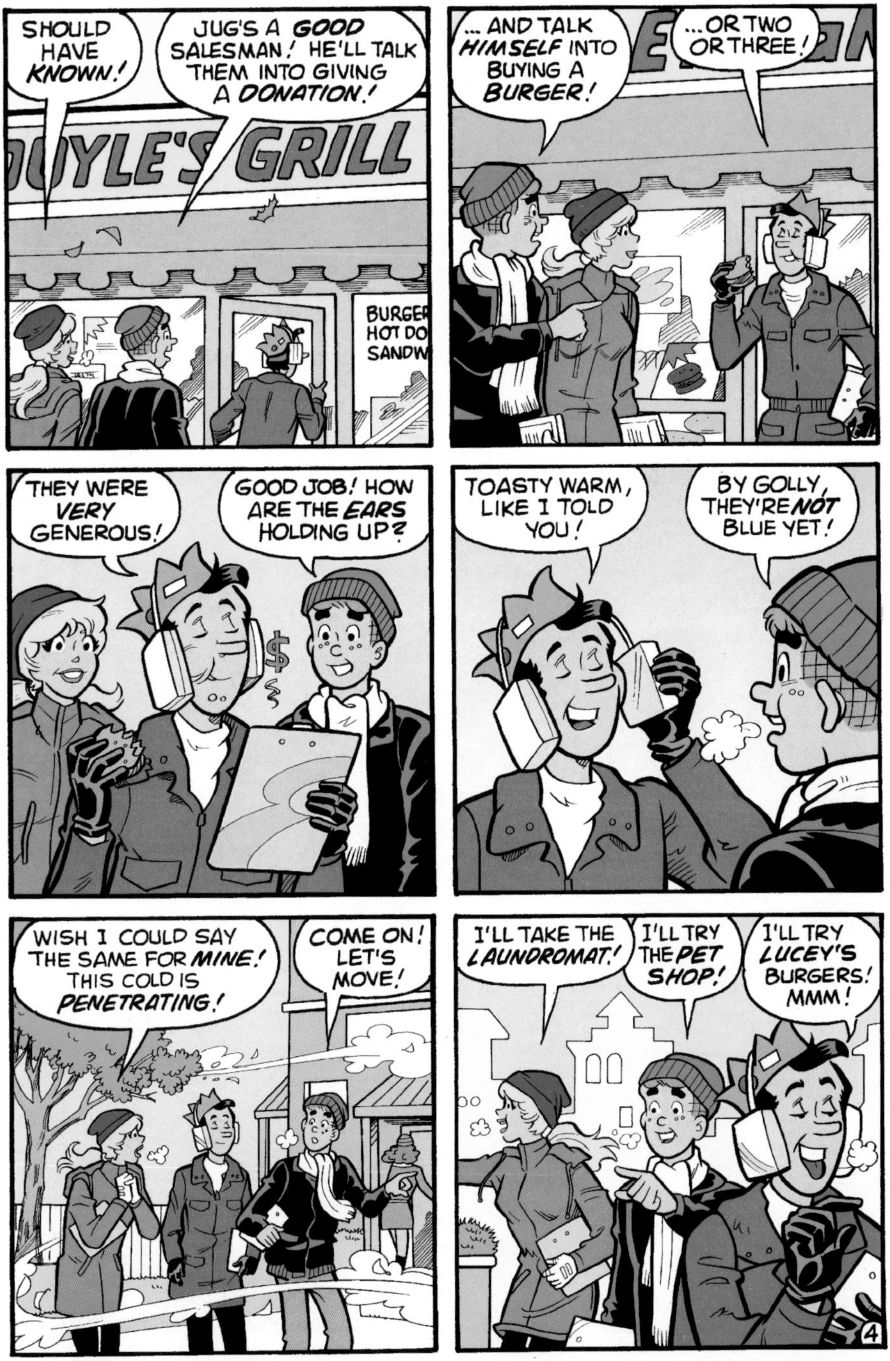
SHOULD HAVE KNOWN!
JUG'S A GOOD SALESMAN! HE'LL TALK THEM INTO GIVING A DONATION!
DOYLE'S GRILL
BURGER HOT DO SANDW
... AND TALK HIMSELF INTO BUYING A BURGER!
...OR TWO OR THREE!
THEY WERE VERY GENEROUS!
GOOD JOB! HOW ARE THE EARS HOLDING UP?
TOASTY WARM, LIKE I TOLD YOU!
BY GOLLY, THEY'RE NOT BLUE YET!
WISH I COULD SAY THE SAME FOR MINE! THIS COLD IS PENETRATING!
COME ON! LET'S MOVE!
I'LL TAKE THE LAUNDROMAT!
I'LL TRY THE PET SHOP!
I'LL TRY LUCEY'S BURGERS! MMM!
4

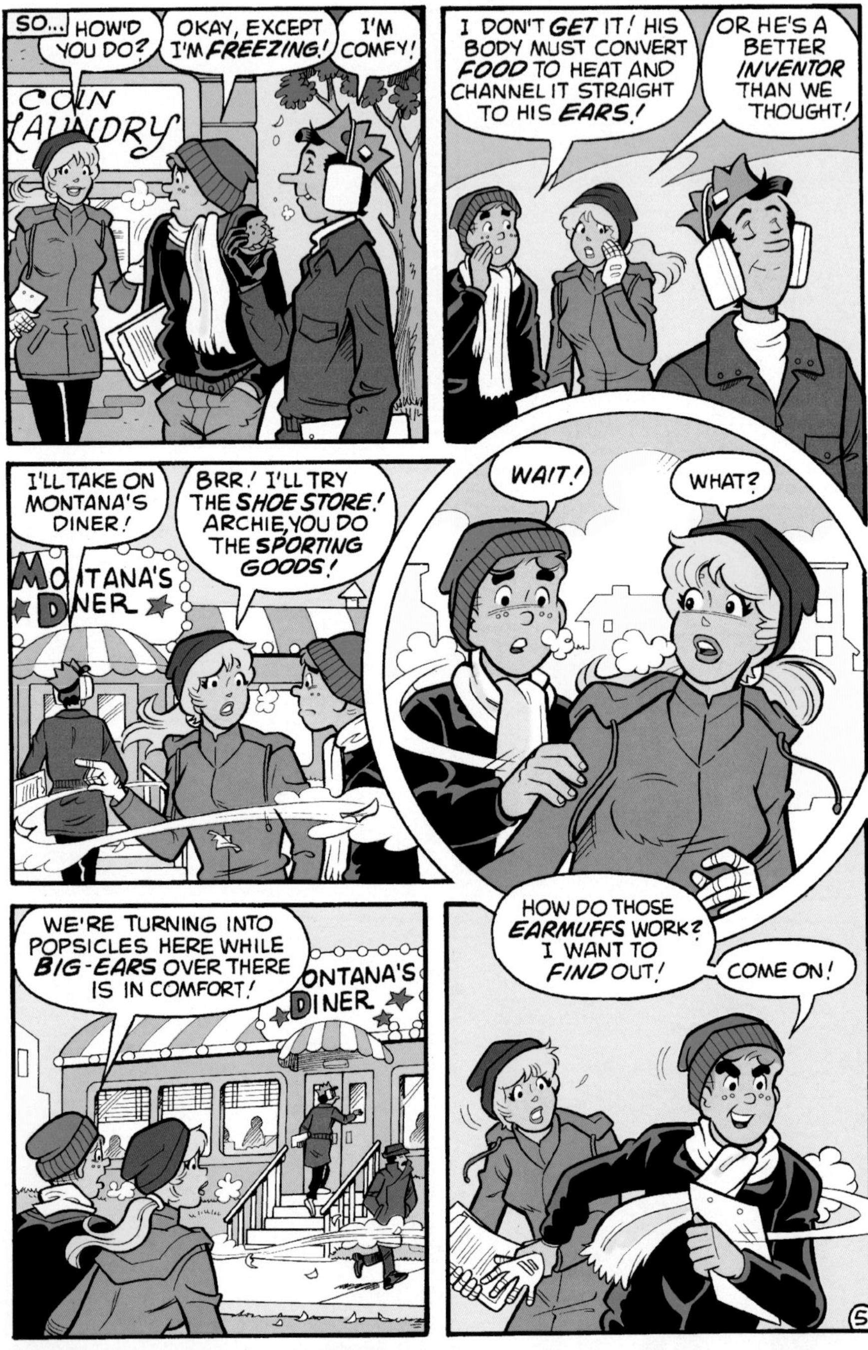
SO...
HOW'D YOU DO?
OKAY, EXCEPT I'M FREEZING!
I'M COMFY!
COIN LAUNDRY
I DON'T GET IT! HIS BODY MUST CONVERT FOOD TO HEAT AND CHANNEL IT STRAIGHT TO HIS EARS!
OR HE'S A BETTER INVENTOR THAN WE THOUGHT!
I'LL TAKE ON MONTANA'S DINER!
BRR! I'LL TRY THE SHOE STORE! ARCHIE, YOU DO THE SPORTING GOODS!
MONTANA'S DINER
WAIT!
WHAT?
WE'RE TURNING INTO POPSICLES HERE WHILE BIG-EARS OVER THERE IS IN COMFORT!
ONTANA'S DINER
HOW DO THOSE EARMUFFS WORK? I WANT TO FIND OUT!
COME ON!
5

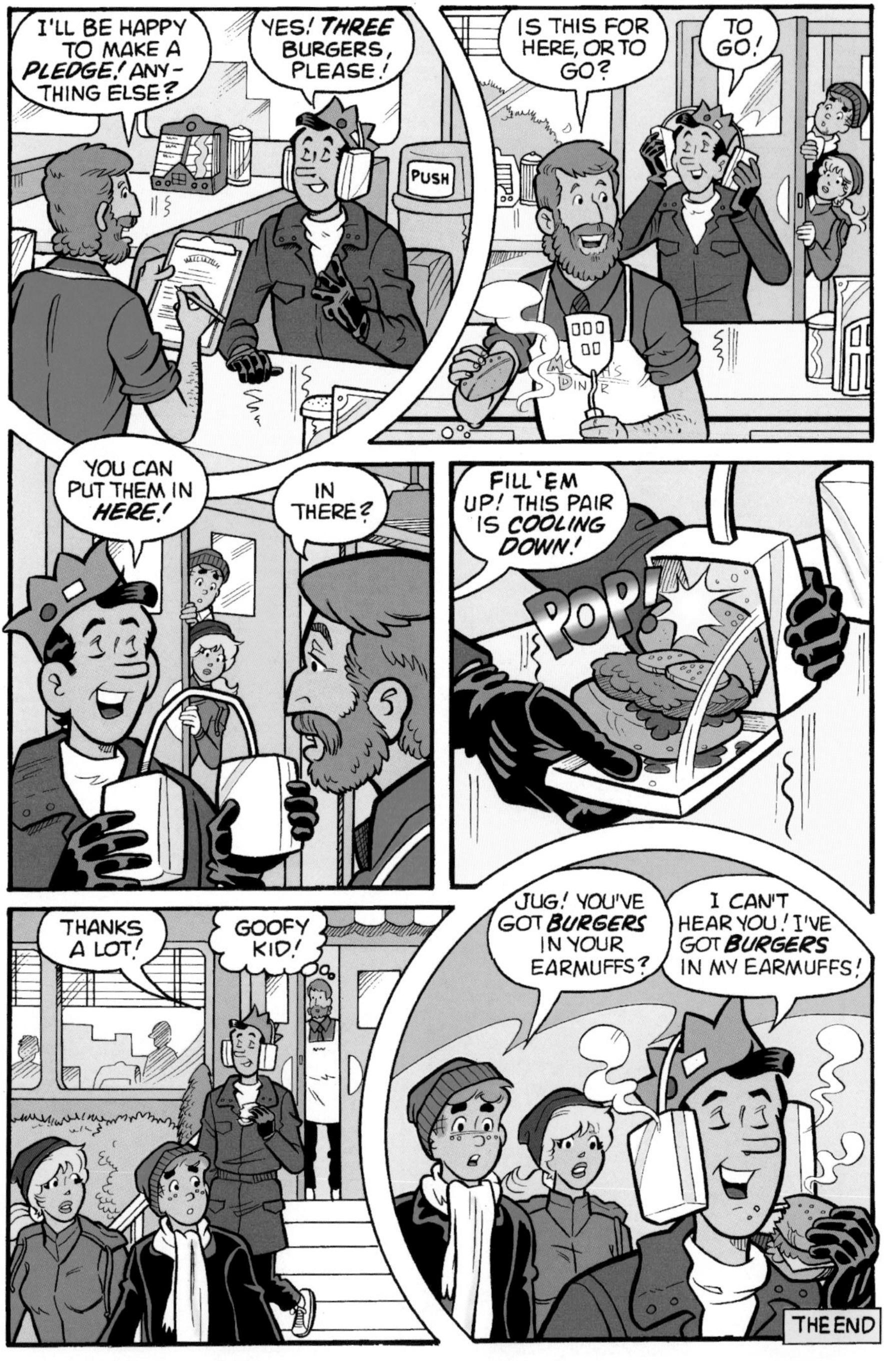
I'LL BE HAPPY TO MAKE A PLEDGE! ANY-THING ELSE?
YES! THREE BURGERS, PLEASE!
IS THIS FOR HERE, OR TO GO?
TO GO!
YOU CAN PUT THEM IN HERE!
IN THERE?
FILL 'EM UP! THIS PAIR IS COOLING DOWN!
POP!
THANKS A LOT!
GOOFY KID!
JUG! YOU'VE GOT BURGERS IN YOUR EARMUFFS?
I CAN'T HEAR YOU! I'VE GOT BURGERS IN MY EARMUFFS!
THE END

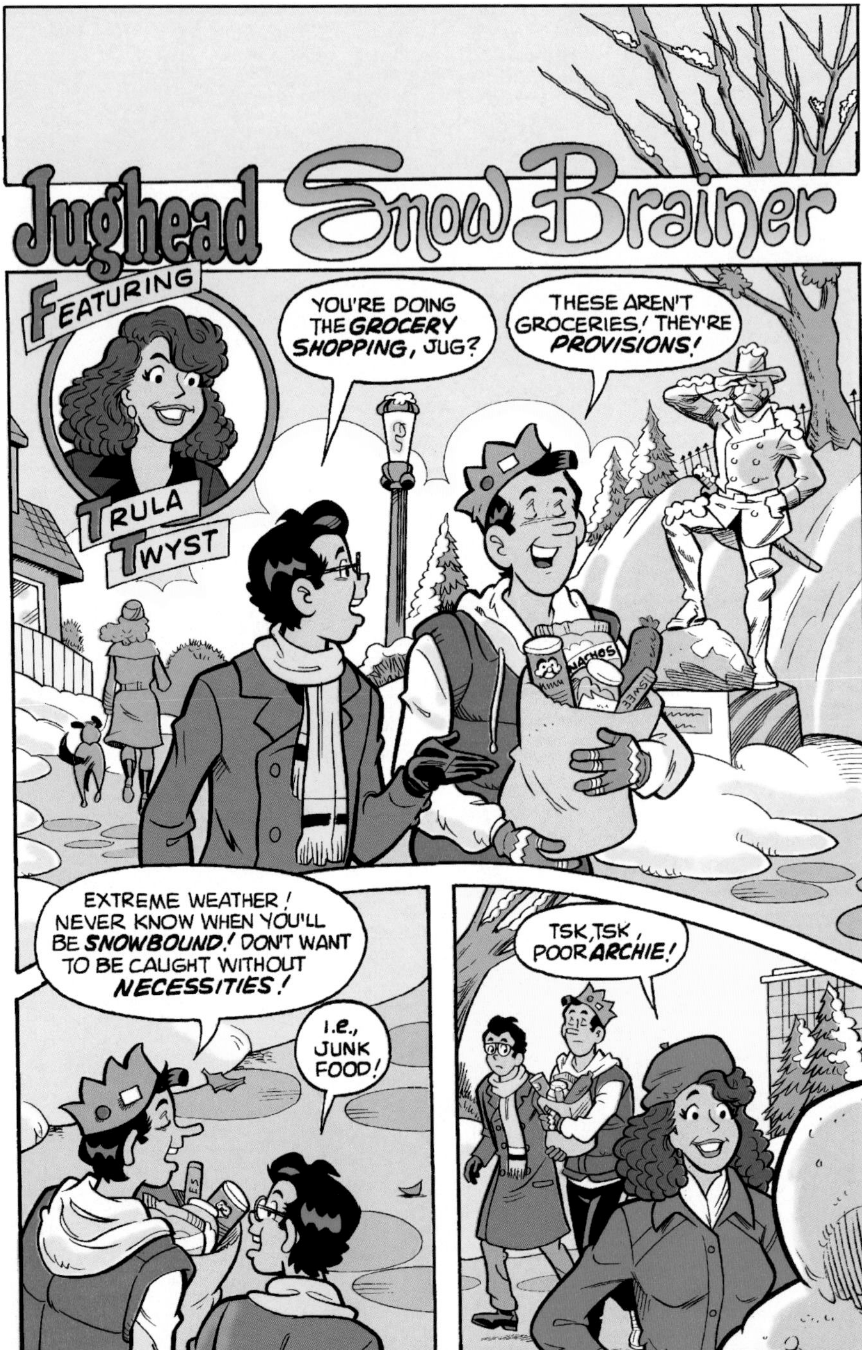
Jughead
Snow Brainer
Featuring
Trula
Twyst
YOU'RE DOING THE GROCERY SHOPPING, JUG?
THESE AREN'T GROCERIES! THEY'RE PROVISIONS!
NACHOS
EXTREME WEATHER! NEVER KNOW WHEN YOU'LL BE SNOWBOUND! DON'T WANT TO BE CAUGHT WITHOUT NECESSITIES!
I.E., JUNK FOOD!
TSK, TSK, POOR ARCHIE!

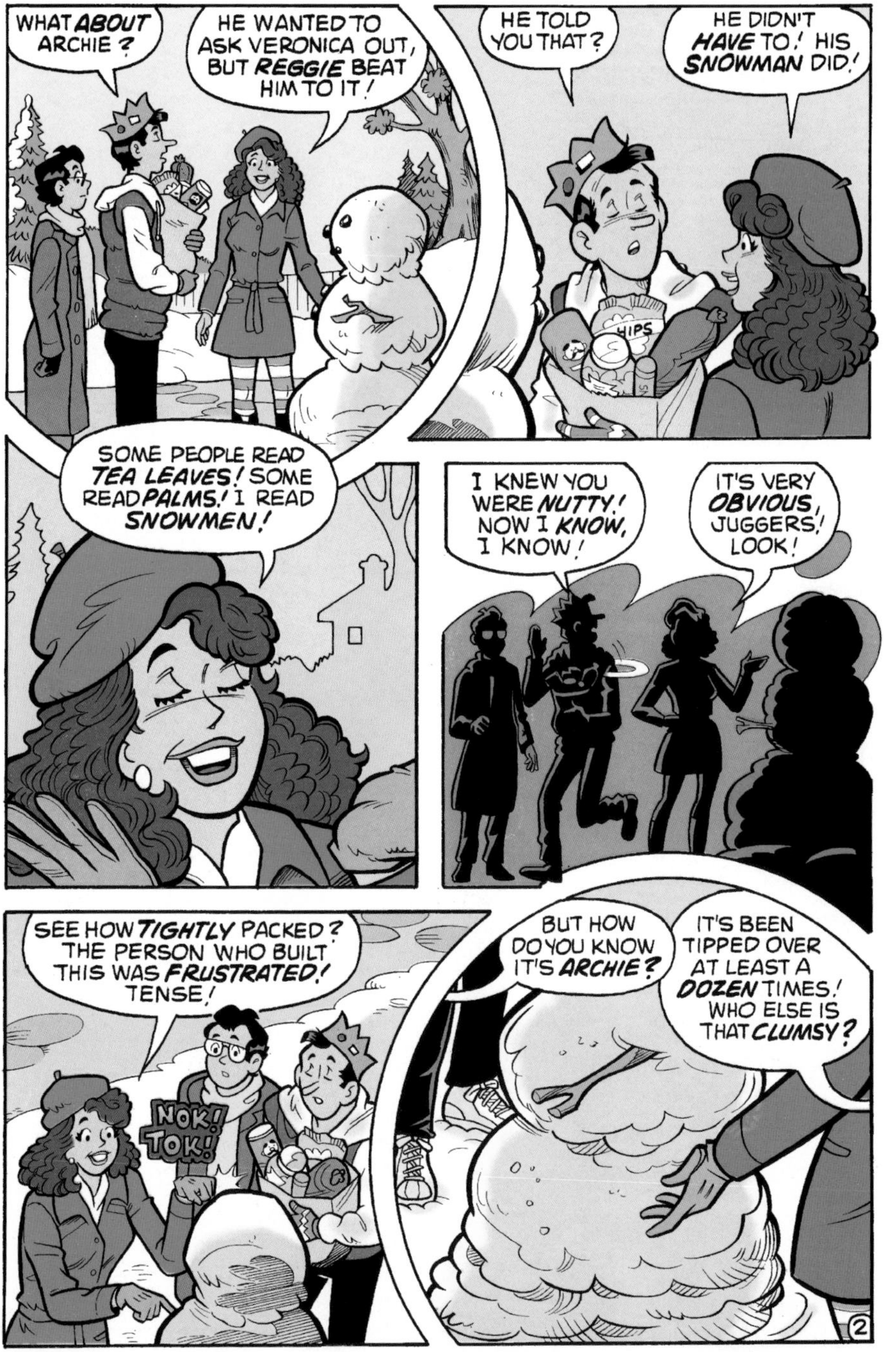
WHAT ABOUT ARCHIE?
HE WANTED TO ASK VERONICA OUT, BUT REGGIE BEAT HIM TO IT!
HE TOLD YOU THAT?
HE DIDN'T HAVE TO! HIS SNOWMAN DID!
HIPS
SOME PEOPLE READ TEA LEAVES! SOME READ PALMS! I READ SNOWMEN!
I KNEW YOU WERE NUTTY! NOW I KNOW, I KNOW!
IT'S VERY OBVIOUS, JUGGERS! LOOK!
SEE HOW TIGHTLY PACKED? THE PERSON WHO BUILT THIS WAS FRUSTRATED! TENSE!
NOK! TOK!
BUT HOW DO YOU KNOW IT'S ARCHIE?
IT'S BEEN TIPPED OVER AT LEAST A DOZEN TIMES! WHO ELSE IS THAT CLUMSY?
2

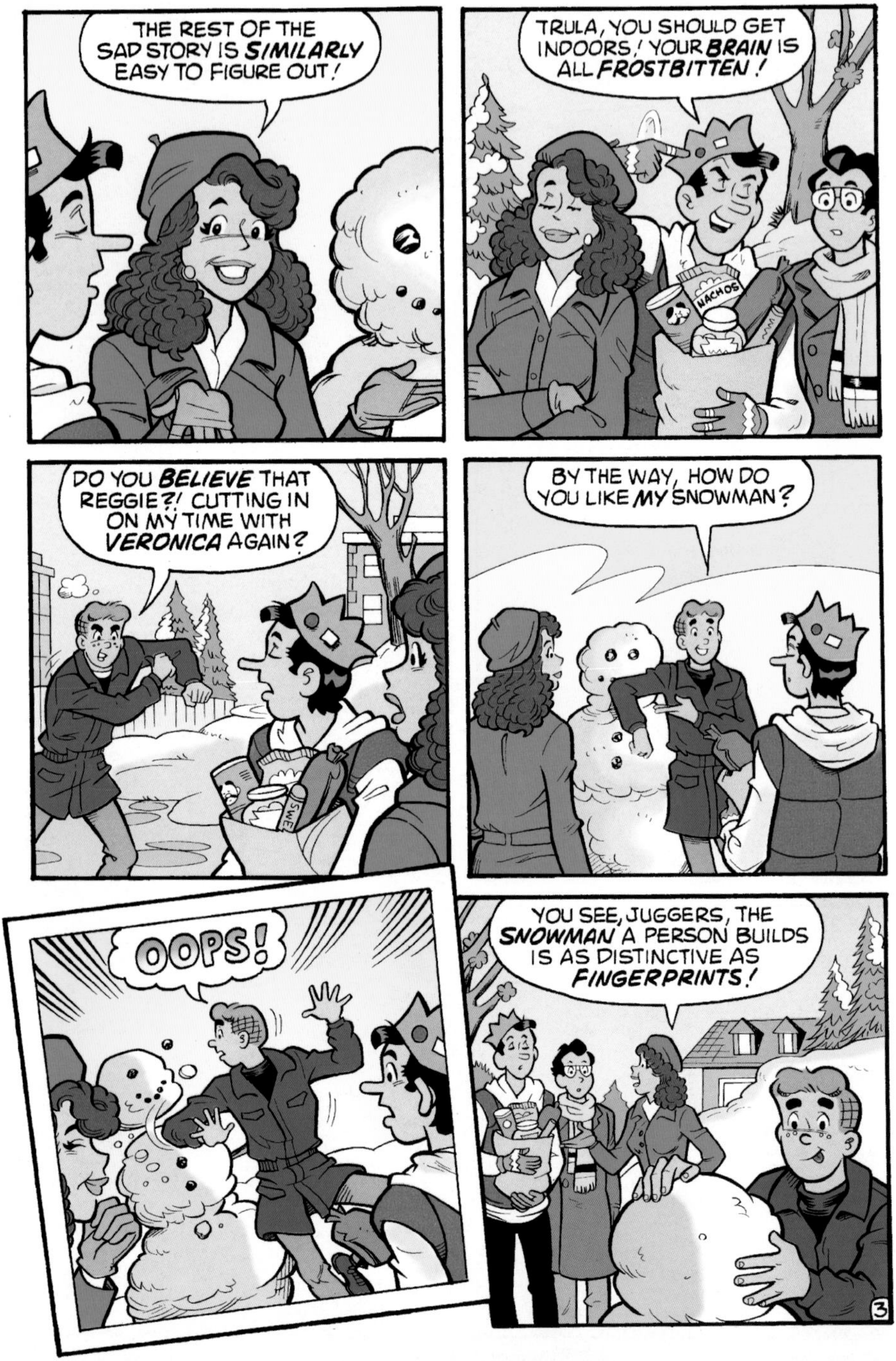
THE REST OF THE SAD STORY IS SIMILARLY EASY TO FIGURE OUT!
TRULA, YOU SHOULD GET INDOORS! YOUR BRAIN IS ALL FROSTBITTEN!
NACHOS
DO YOU BELIEVE THAT REGGIE?! CUTTING IN ON MY TIME WITH VERONICA AGAIN?
BY THE WAY, HOW DO YOU LIKE MY SNOWMAN?
OOPS!
YOU SEE, JUGGERS, THE SNOWMAN A PERSON BUILDS IS AS DISTINCTIVE AS FINGERPRINTS!
3

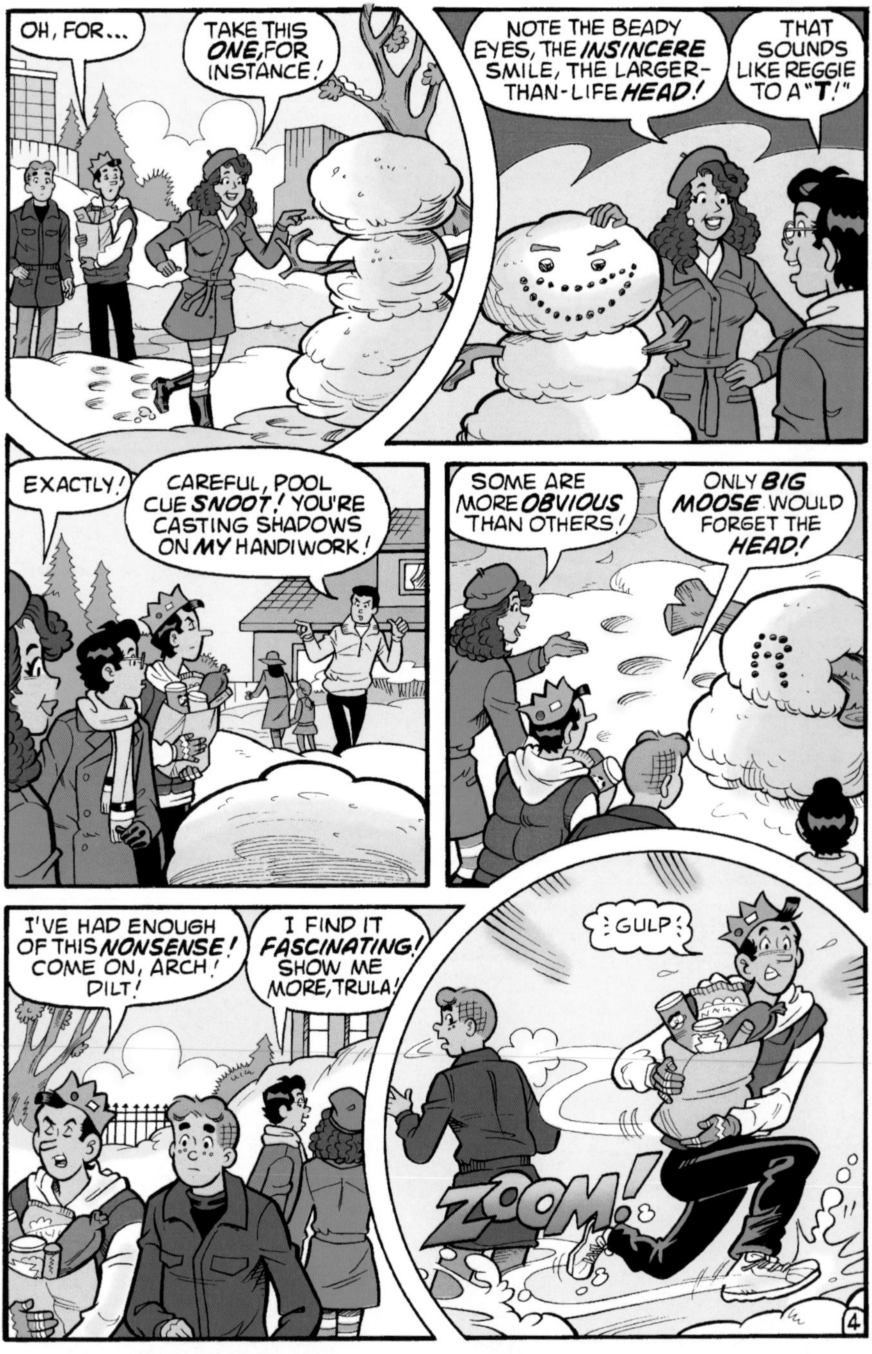
OH, FOR...
TAKE THIS ONE, FOR INSTANCE!
NOTE THE BEADY EYES, THE INSINCERE SMILE, THE LARGER-THAN-LIFE HEAD!
THAT SOUNDS LIKE REGGIE TO A "T!"
EXACTLY!
CAREFUL, POOL CUE SNOOT! YOU'RE CASTING SHADOWS ON MY HANDIWORK!
SOME ARE MORE OBVIOUS THAN OTHERS!
ONLY BIG MOOSE WOULD FORGET THE HEAD!
I'VE HAD ENOUGH OF THIS NONSENSE! COME ON, ARCH! DILT!
I FIND IT FASCINATING! SHOW ME MORE, TRULA!
GULP
ZOOM!
4

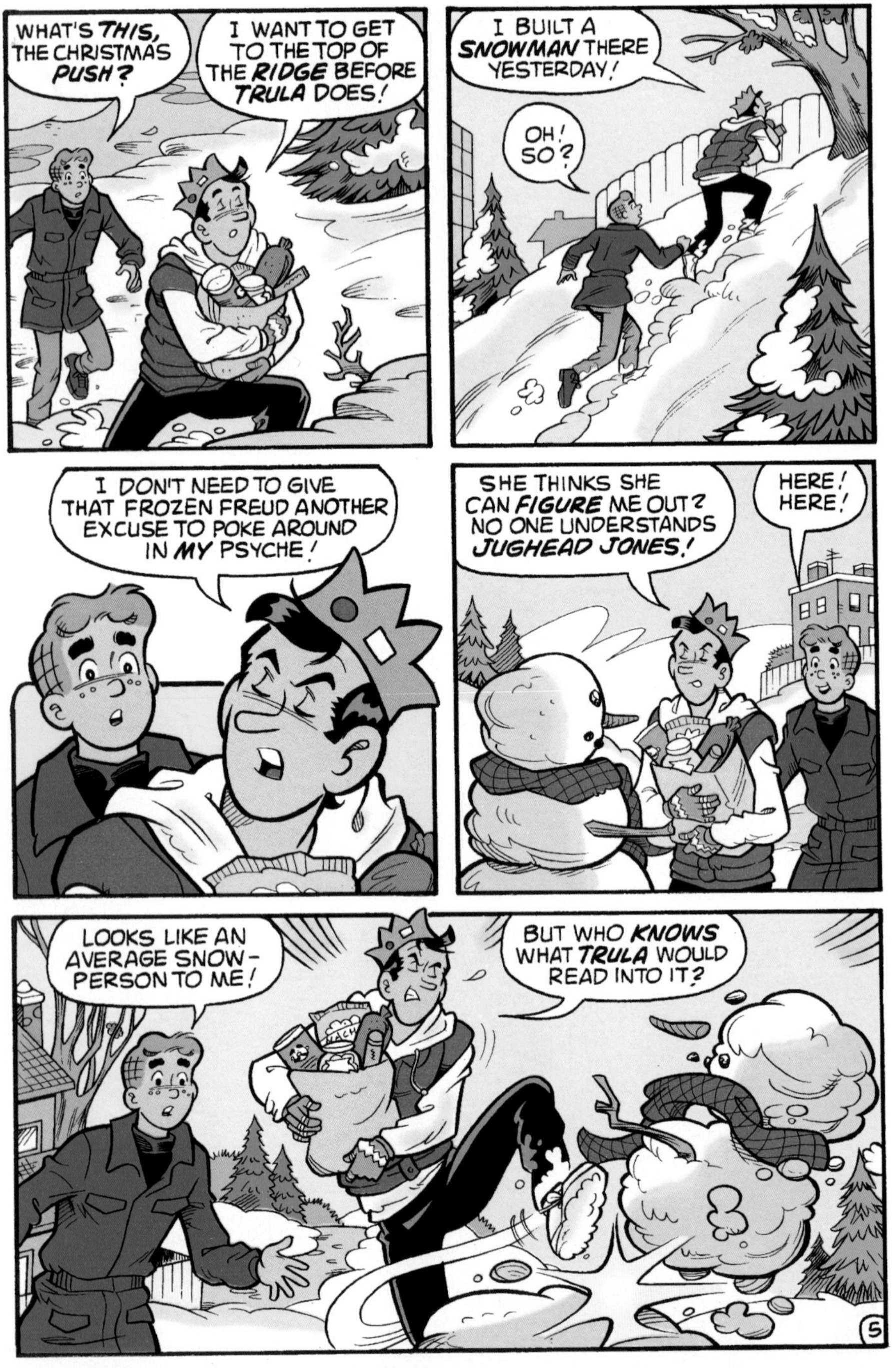
WHAT'S THIS, THE CHRISTMAS PUSH?
I WANT TO GET TO THE TOP OF THE RIDGE BEFORE TRULA DOES!
I BUILT A SNOWMAN THERE YESTERDAY!
OH! SO?
I DON'T NEED TO GIVE THAT FROZEN FREUD ANOTHER EXCUSE TO POKE AROUND IN MY PSYCHE!
SHE THINKS SHE CAN FIGURE ME OUT? NO ONE UNDERSTANDS JUGHEAD JONES!
HERE! HERE!
LOOKS LIKE AN AVERAGE SNOW-PERSON TO ME!
BUT WHO KNOWS WHAT TRULA WOULD READ INTO IT?
5

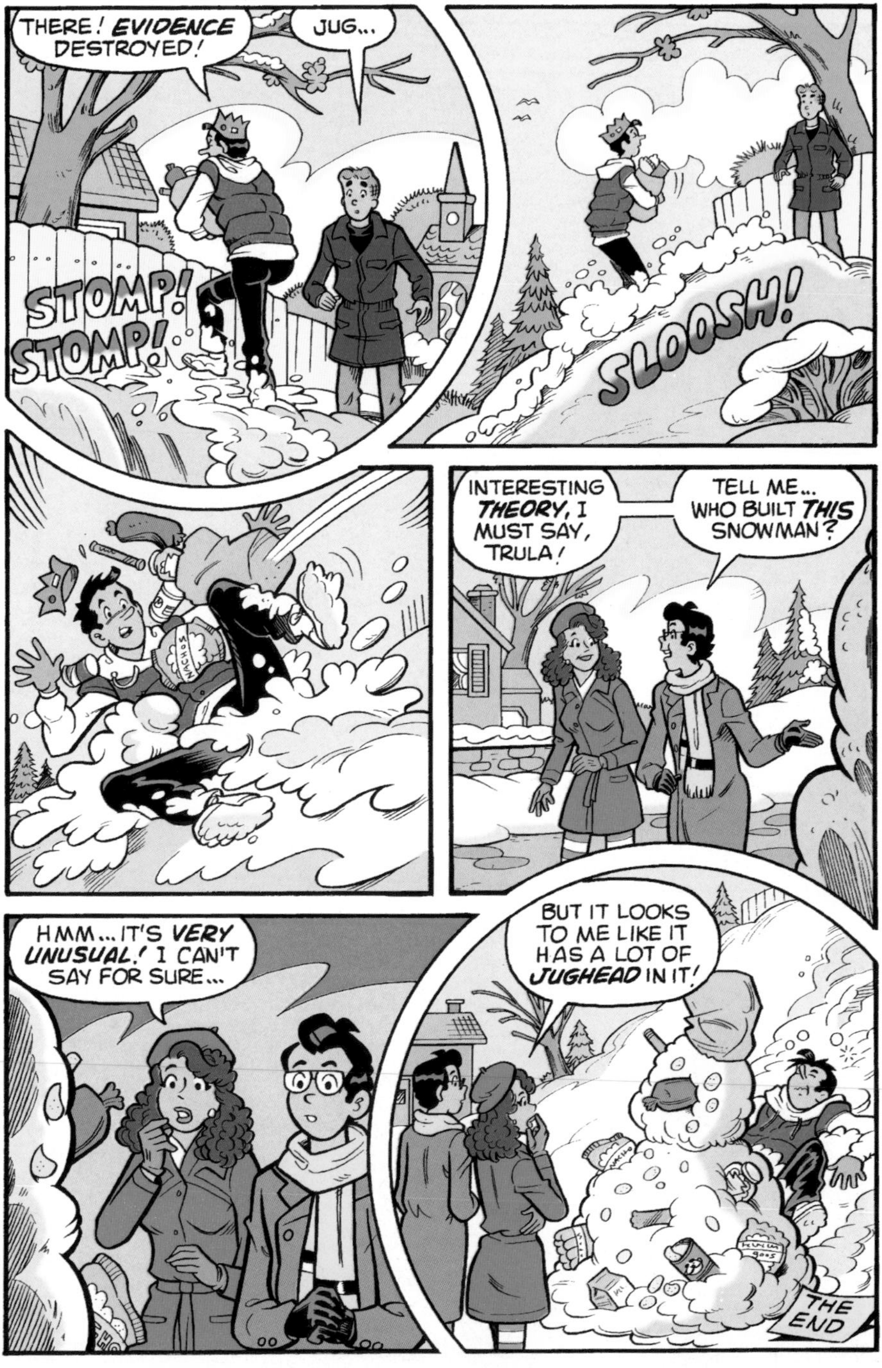
THERE! EVIDENCE DESTROYED!
JUG...
STOMP! STOMP!
SLOOSH!
NACHOS
INTERESTING THEORY, I MUST SAY, TRULA!
TELL ME... WHO BUILT THIS SNOWMAN?
HMM... IT'S VERY UNUSUAL! I CAN'T SAY FOR SURE...
BUT IT LOOKS TO ME LIKE IT HAS A LOT OF JUGHEAD IN IT!
THE END

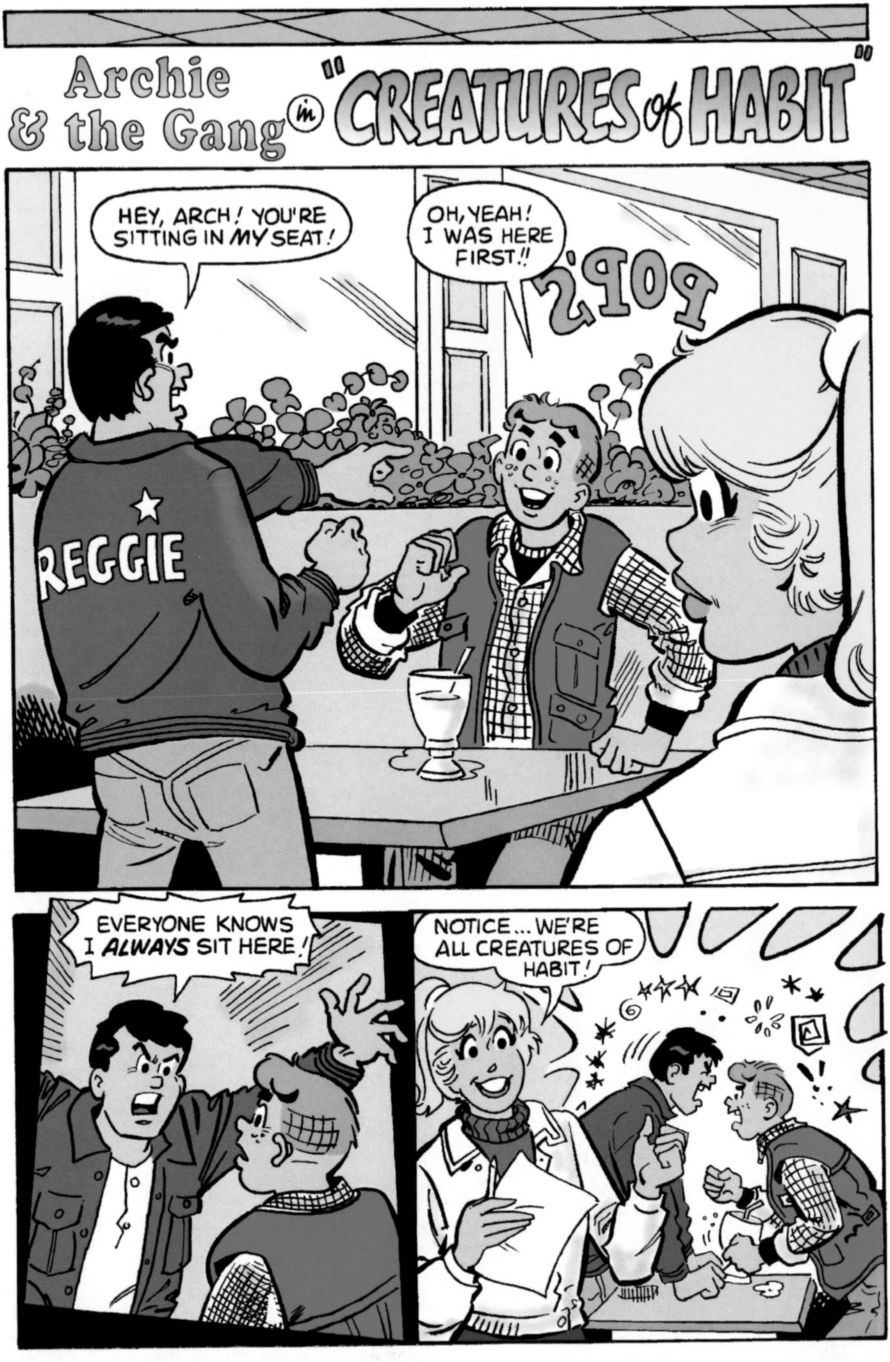
Archie & the Gang in "CREATURES of HABIT"
HEY, ARCH! YOU'RE SITTING IN MY SEAT!
OH, YEAH! I WAS HERE FIRST!!
POP'S
REGGIE
EVERYONE KNOWS I ALWAYS SIT HERE!
NOTICE... WE'RE ALL CREATURES OF HABIT!

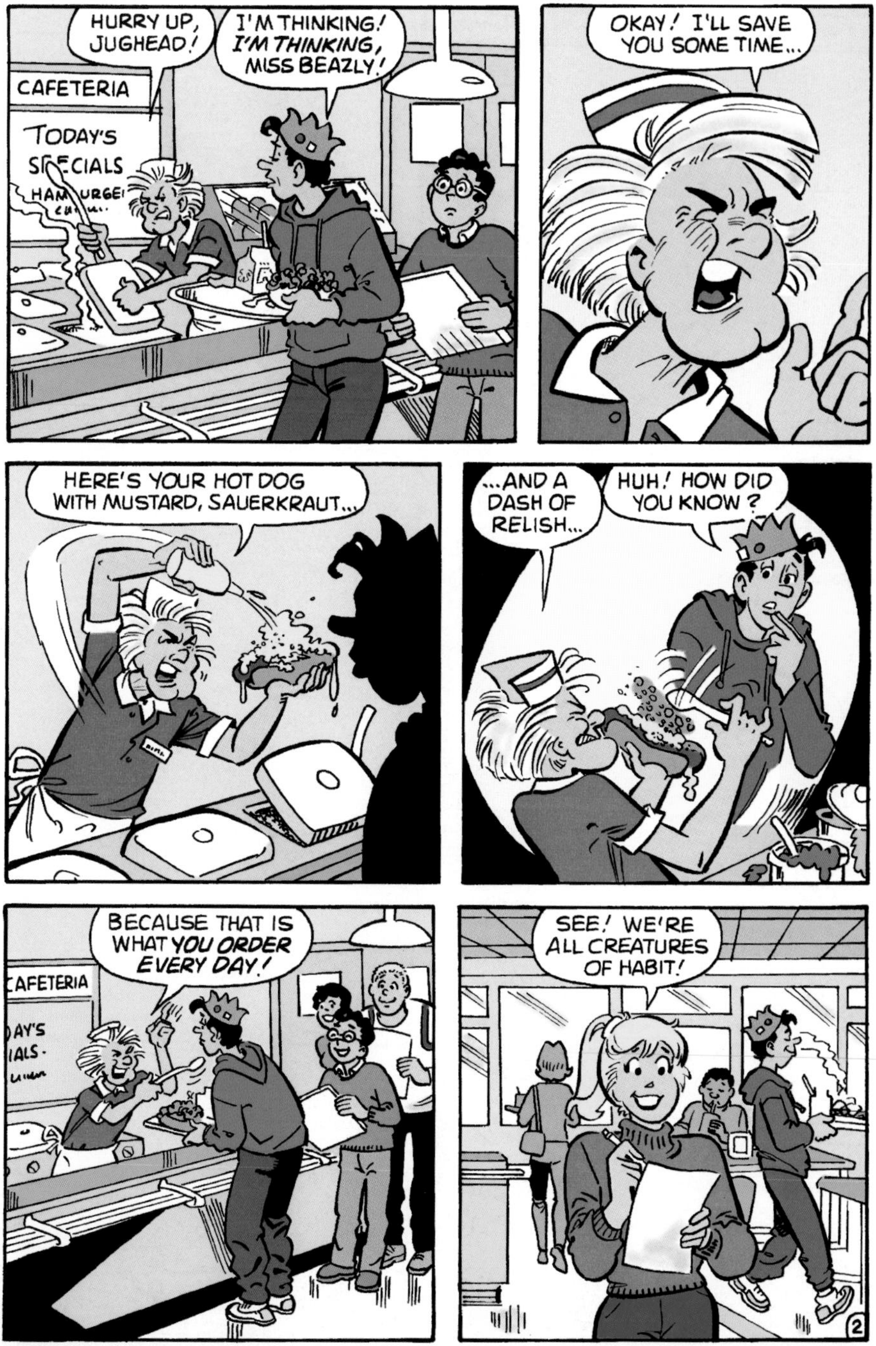
HURRY UP, JUGHEAD!
I'M THINKING! I'M THINKING, MISS BEAZLY!
CAFETERIA
OKAY! I'LL SAVE YOU SOME TIME...
HERE'S YOUR HOT DOG WITH MUSTARD, SAUERKRAUT...
...AND A DASH OF RELISH...
HUH! HOW DID YOU KNOW?
BECAUSE THAT IS WHAT YOU ORDER EVERY DAY!
SEE! WE'RE ALL CREATURES OF HABIT!
2

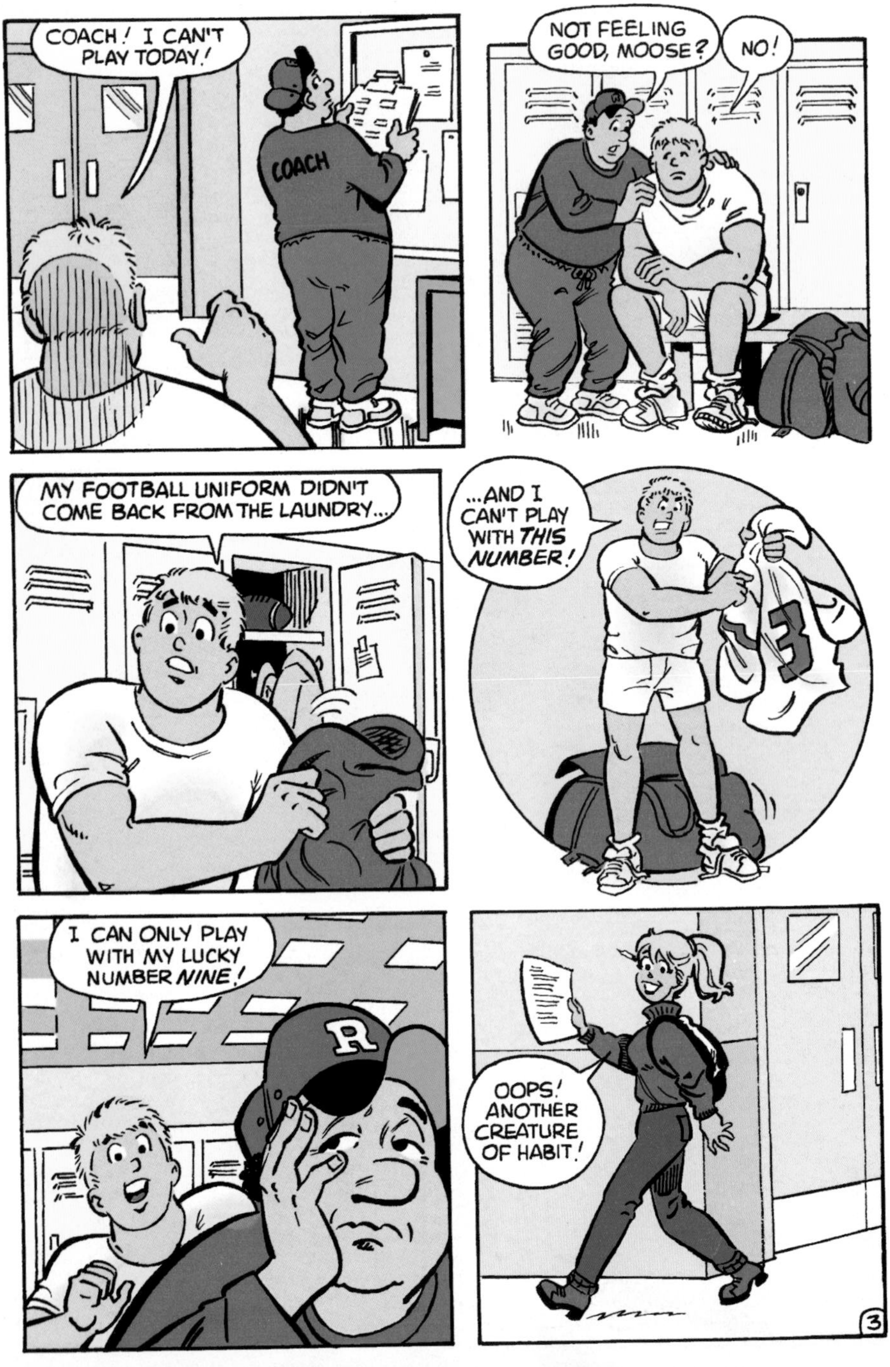
COACH! I CAN'T PLAY TODAY!
COACH
NOT FEELING GOOD, MOOSE?
NO!
MY FOOTBALL UNIFORM DIDN'T COME BACK FROM THE LAUNDRY...
...AND I CAN'T PLAY WITH *THIS NUMBER*!
3
I CAN ONLY PLAY WITH MY LUCKY NUMBER *NINE*!
R
OOPS! ANOTHER CREATURE OF HABIT!
3

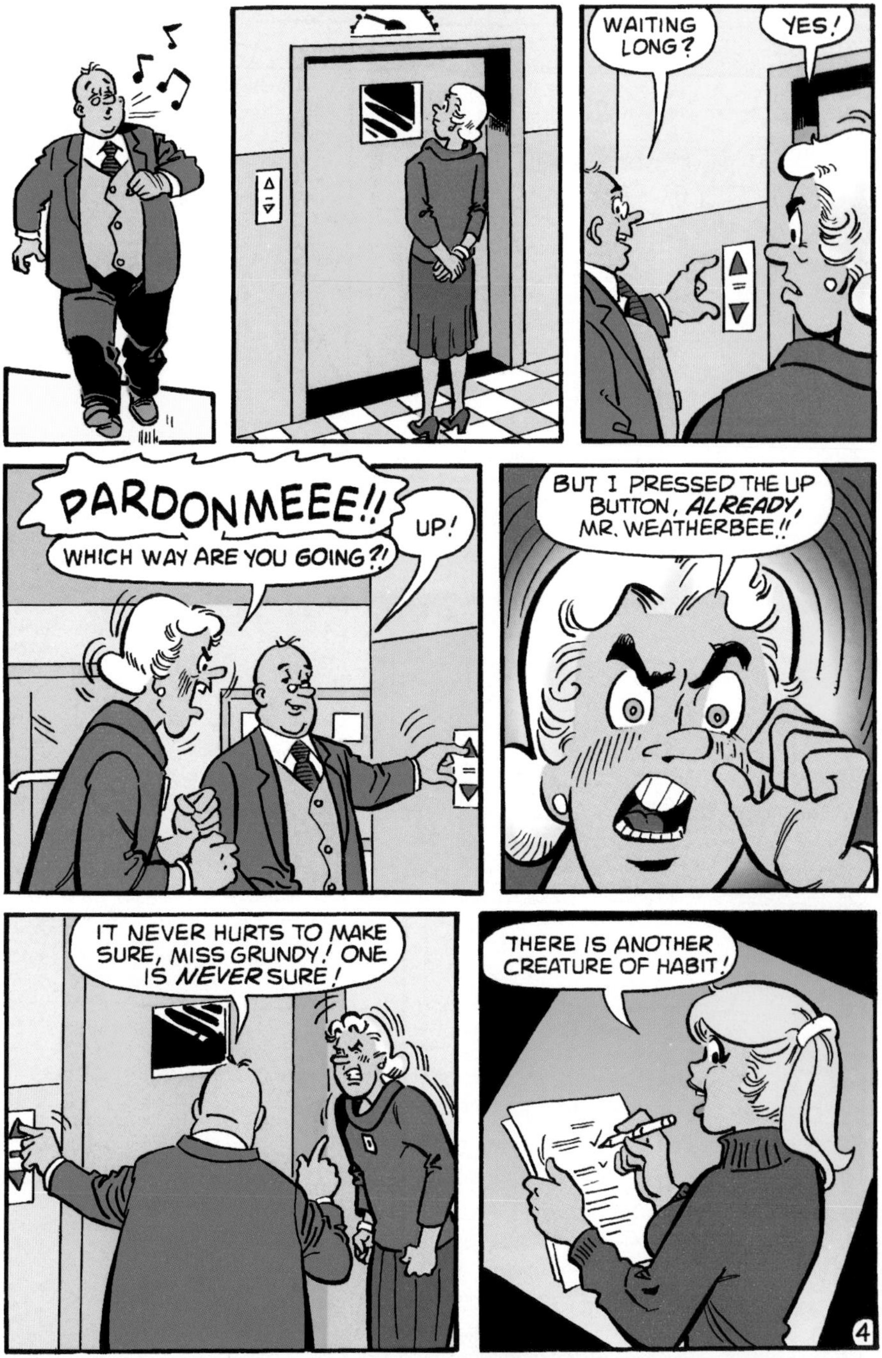
WAITING LONG?
YES!
PARDONMEEE!!
WHICH WAY ARE YOU GOING?!
UP!
BUT I PRESSED THE UP BUTTON, ALREADY, MR. WEATHERBEE!!
IT NEVER HURTS TO MAKE SURE, MISS GRUNDY! ONE IS NEVER SURE!
THERE IS ANOTHER CREATURE OF HABIT!
4

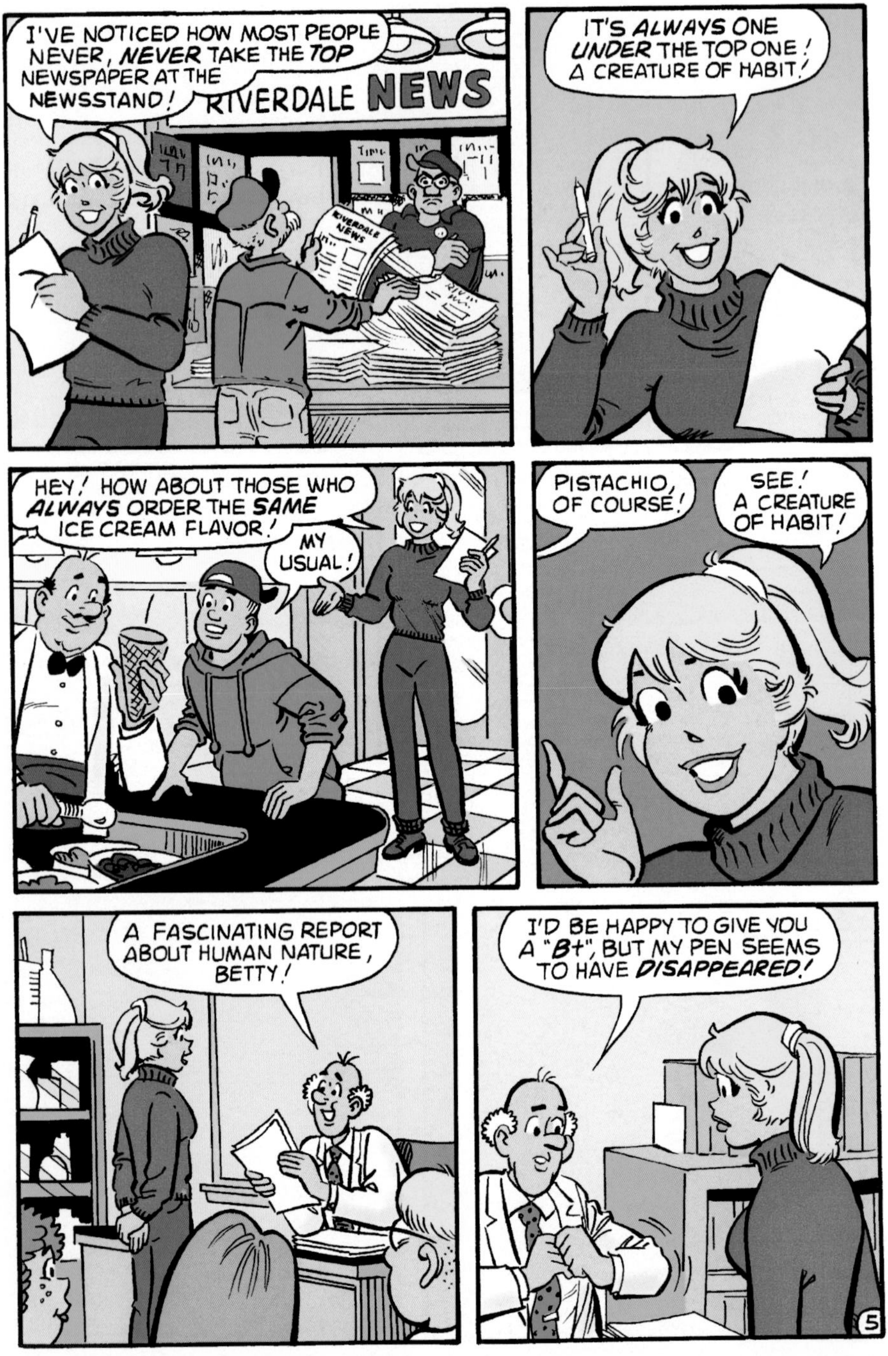
I'VE NOTICED HOW MOST PEOPLE NEVER, NEVER TAKE THE TOP NEWSPAPER AT THE NEWSSTAND!
RIVERDALE NEWS
RIVERDALE NEWS
IT'S ALWAYS ONE UNDER THE TOP ONE! A CREATURE OF HABIT!
HEY! HOW ABOUT THOSE WHO ALWAYS ORDER THE SAME ICE CREAM FLAVOR!
MY USUAL!
PISTACHIO, OF COURSE!
SEE! A CREATURE OF HABIT!
A FASCINATING REPORT ABOUT HUMAN NATURE, BETTY!
I'D BE HAPPY TO GIVE YOU A "B+", BUT MY PEN SEEMS TO HAVE DISAPPEARED!
5

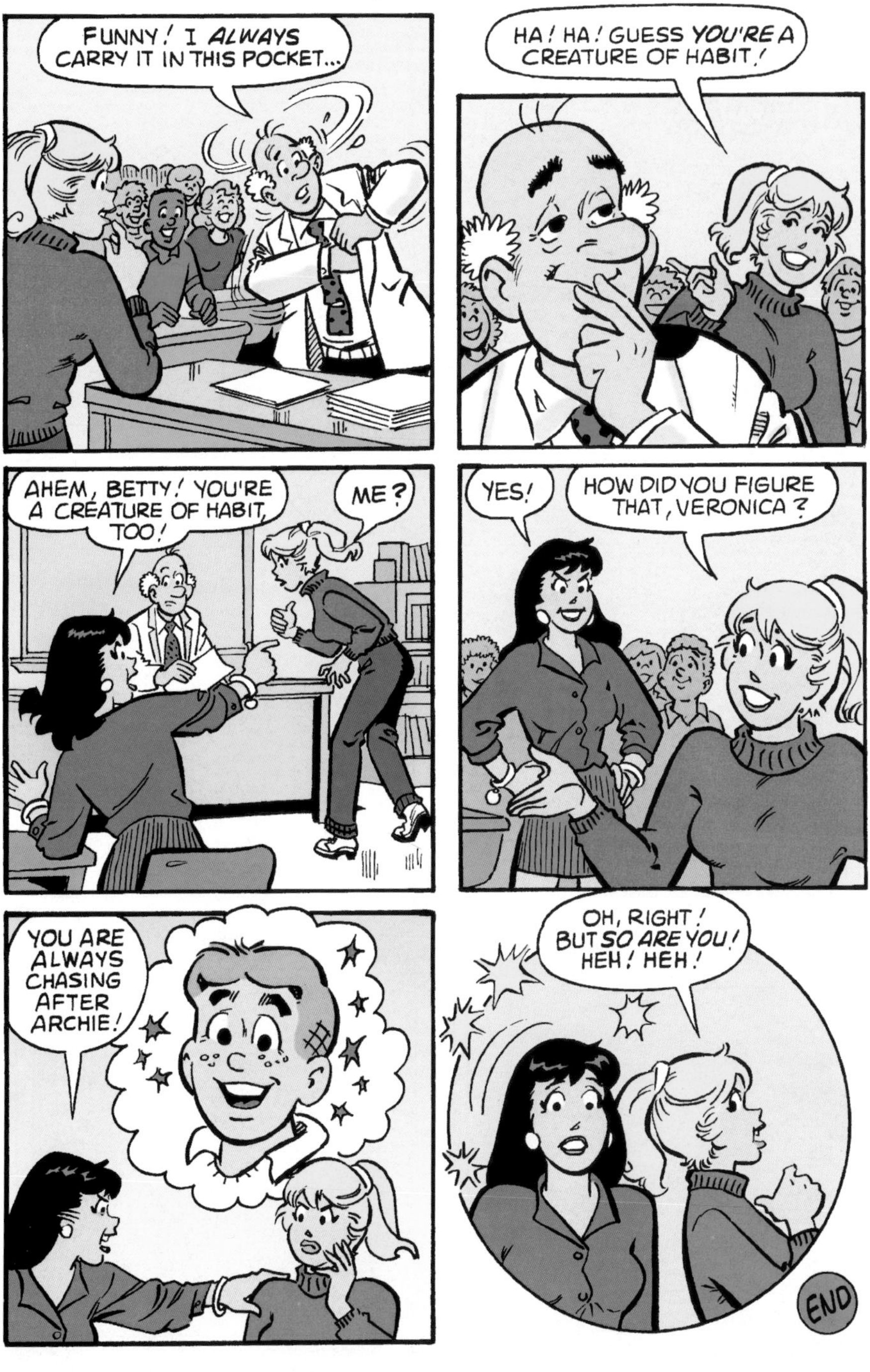
FUNNY! I ALWAYS CARRY IT IN THIS POCKET...
HA! HA! GUESS YOU'RE A CREATURE OF HABIT!
AHEM, BETTY! YOU'RE A CREATURE OF HABIT, TOO!
ME?
YES!
HOW DID YOU FIGURE THAT, VERONICA?
YOU ARE ALWAYS CHASING AFTER ARCHIE!
OH, RIGHT! BUT SO ARE YOU! HEH! HEH!
END

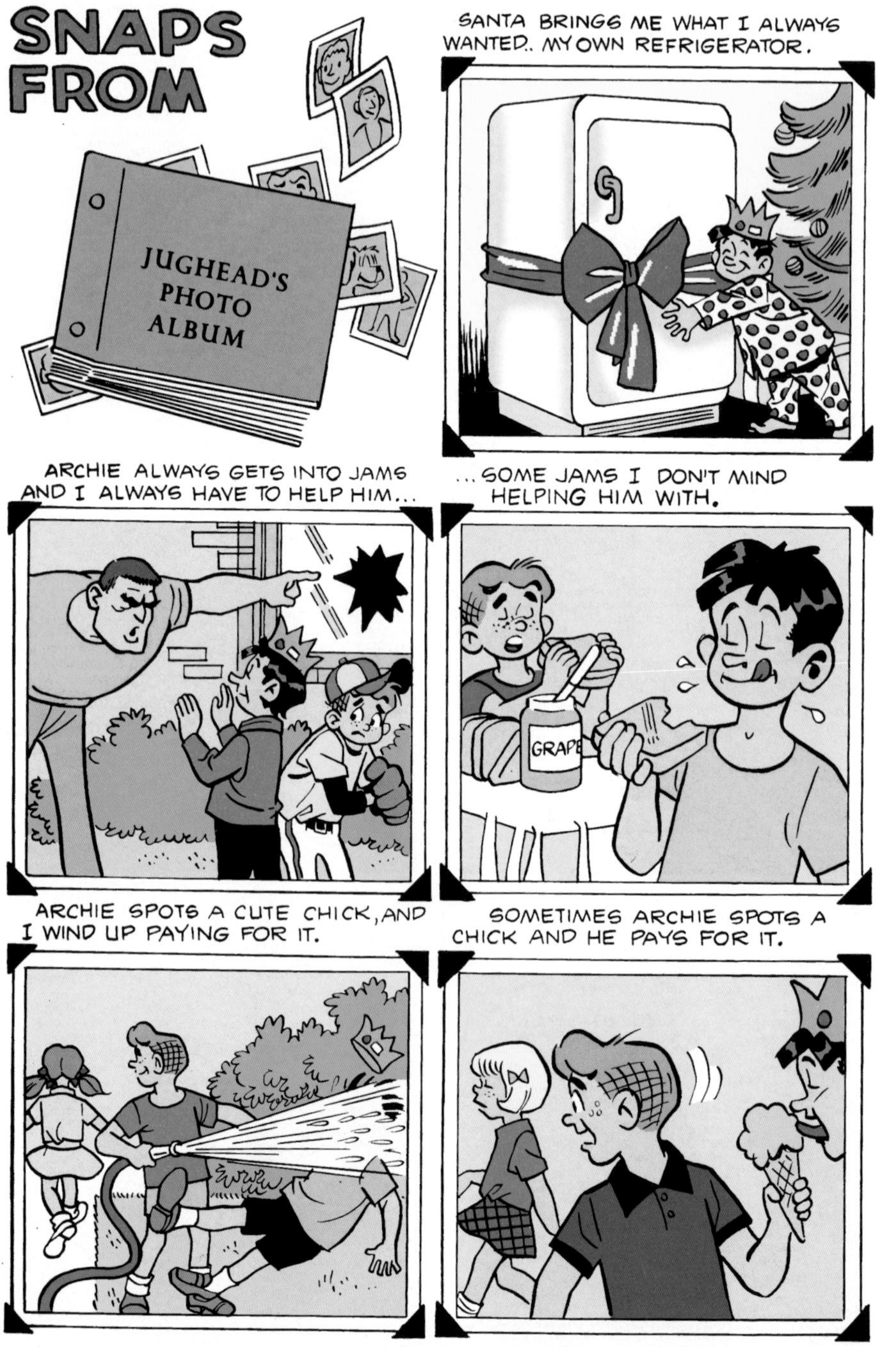
SNAPS FROM
JUGHEAD'S PHOTO ALBUM
SANTA BRINGS ME WHAT I ALWAYS WANTED.. MY OWN REFRIGERATOR.
ARCHIE ALWAYS GETS INTO JAMS AND I ALWAYS HAVE TO HELP HIM...
...SOME JAMS I DON'T MIND HELPING HIM WITH.
GRAPE
ARCHIE SPOTS A CUTE CHICK, AND I WIND UP PAYING FOR IT.
SOMETIMES ARCHIE SPOTS A CHICK AND HE PAYS FOR IT.

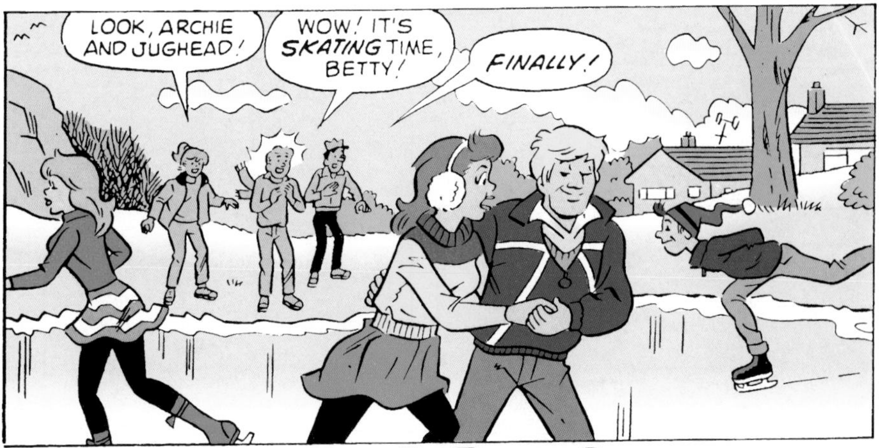
LOOK, ARCHIE AND JUGHEAD!
WOW! IT'S SKATING TIME, BETTY!
FINALLY!

Archie & The Gang in "Christmas Misgivings"

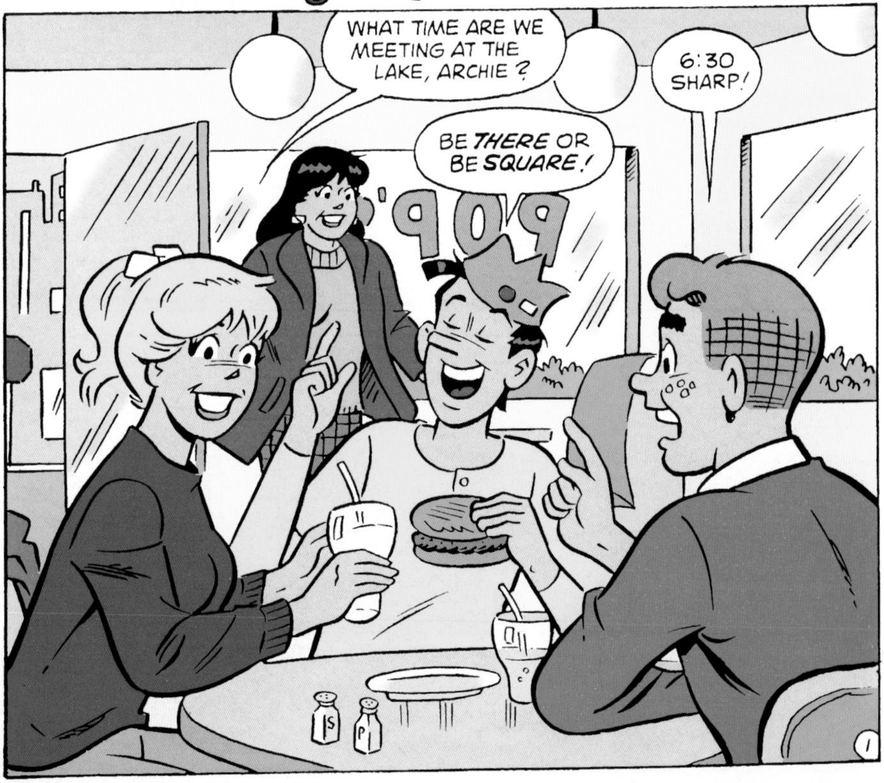
WHAT TIME ARE WE MEETING AT THE LAKE, ARCHIE?
6:30 SHARP!
BE THERE OR BE SQUARE!

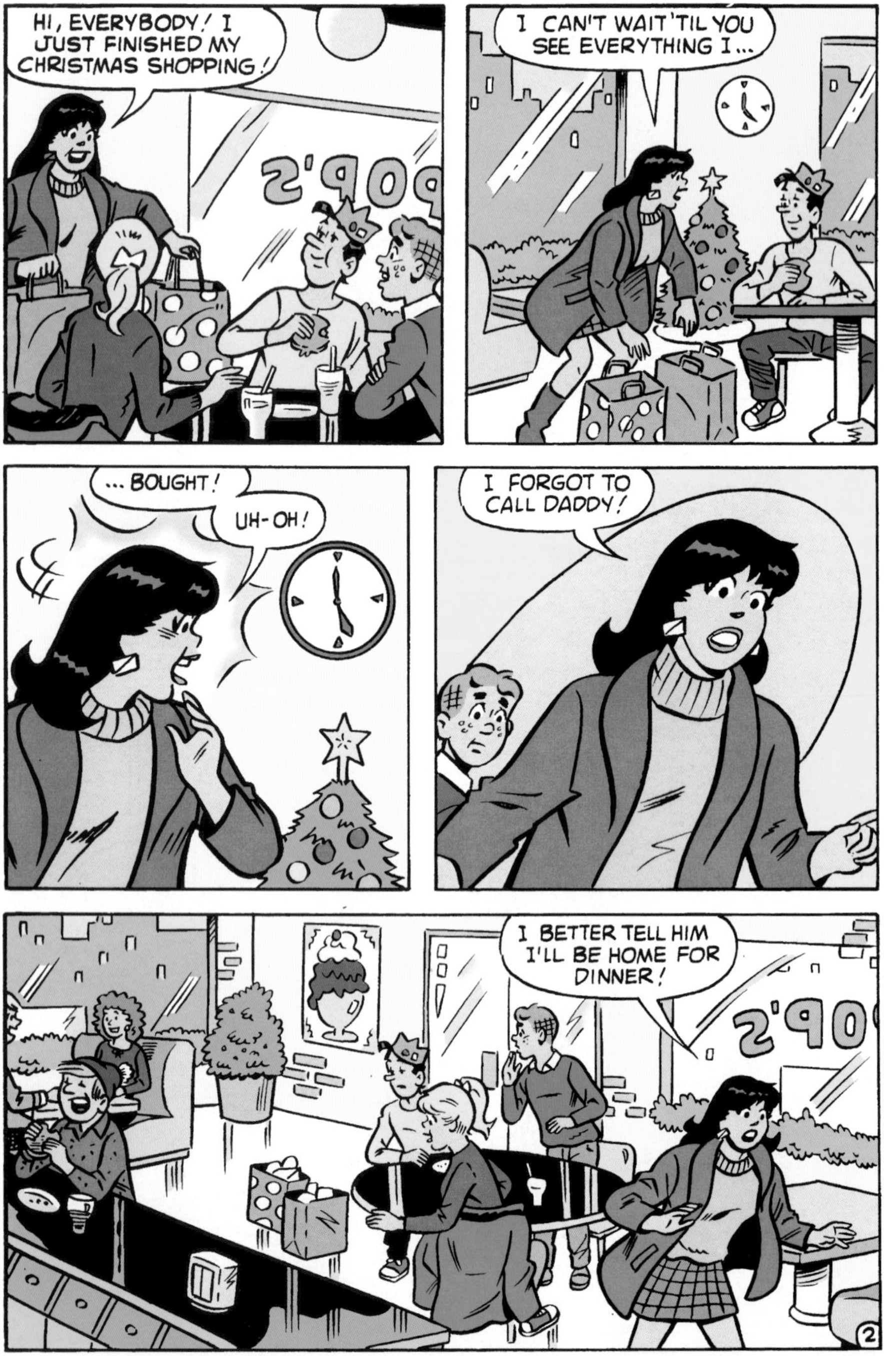
HI, EVERYBODY! I JUST FINISHED MY CHRISTMAS SHOPPING!
POP'S
I CAN'T WAIT 'TIL YOU SEE EVERYTHING I...
... BOUGHT!
UH-OH!
I FORGOT TO CALL DADDY!
I BETTER TELL HIM I'LL BE HOME FOR DINNER!
POP'S
2

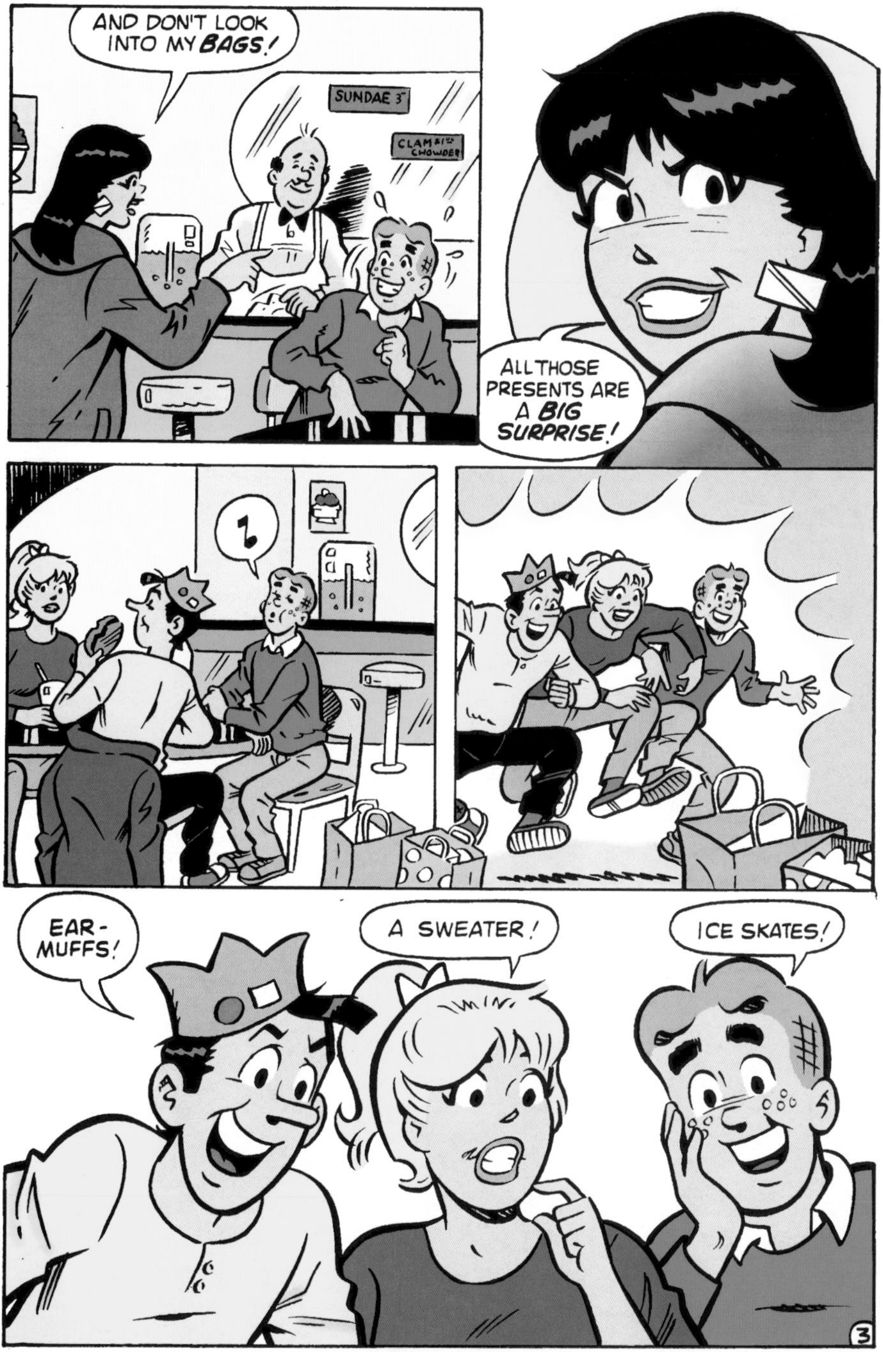
AND DON'T LOOK INTO MY BAGS!
SUNDAE 3¢
CLAM CHOWDER
ALL THOSE PRESENTS ARE A BIG SURPRISE!
EAR-MUFFS!
A SWEATER!
ICE SKATES!
3

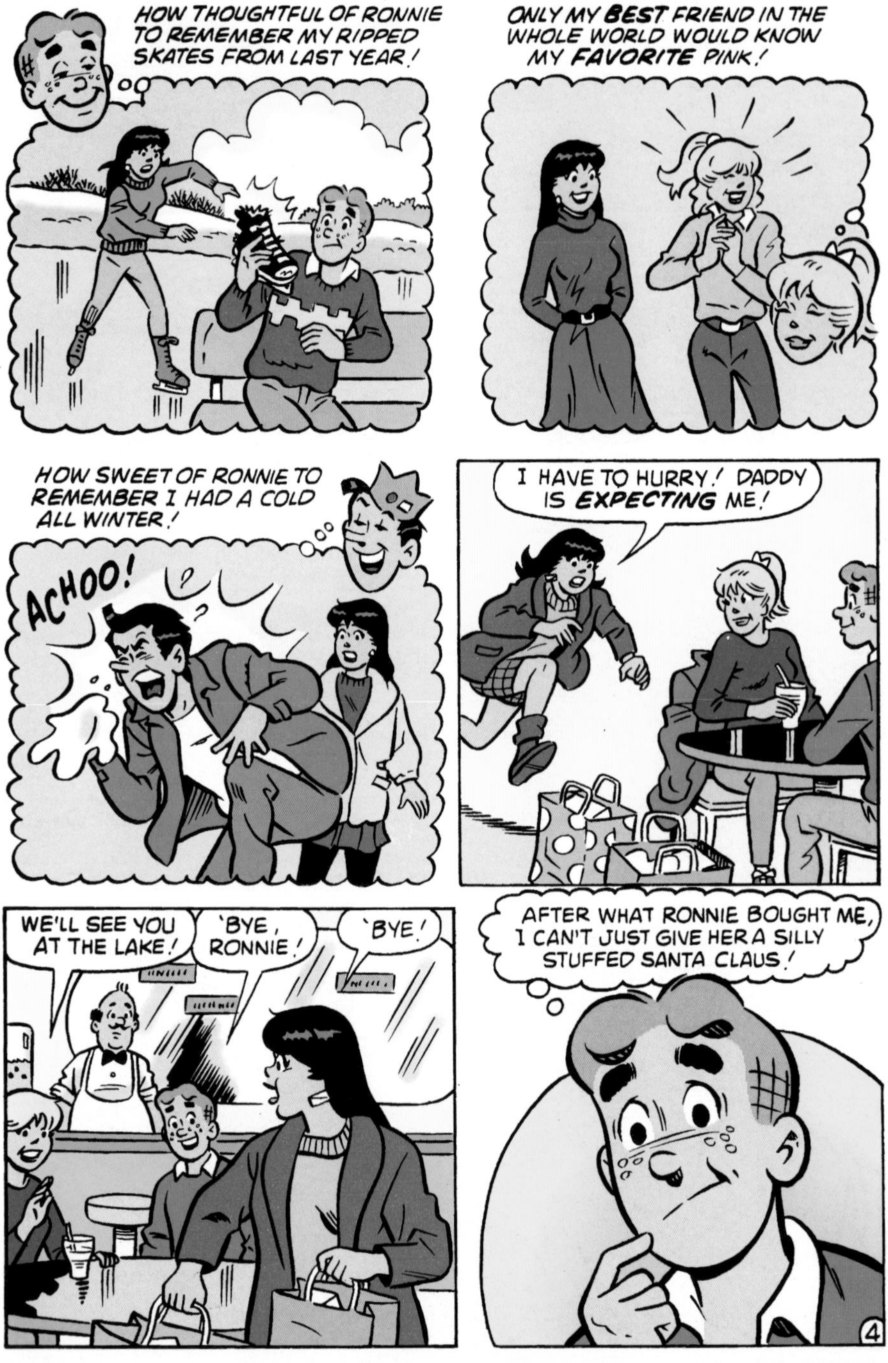
HOW THOUGHTFUL OF RONNIE TO REMEMBER MY RIPPED SKATES FROM LAST YEAR!
ONLY MY BEST FRIEND IN THE WHOLE WORLD WOULD KNOW MY FAVORITE PINK!
HOW SWEET OF RONNIE TO REMEMBER I HAD A COLD ALL WINTER!
ACHOO!
I HAVE TO HURRY! DADDY IS EXPECTING ME!
WE'LL SEE YOU AT THE LAKE!
'BYE, RONNIE!
'BYE!
AFTER WHAT RONNIE BOUGHT ME, I CAN'T JUST GIVE HER A SILLY STUFFED SANTA CLAUS!
4

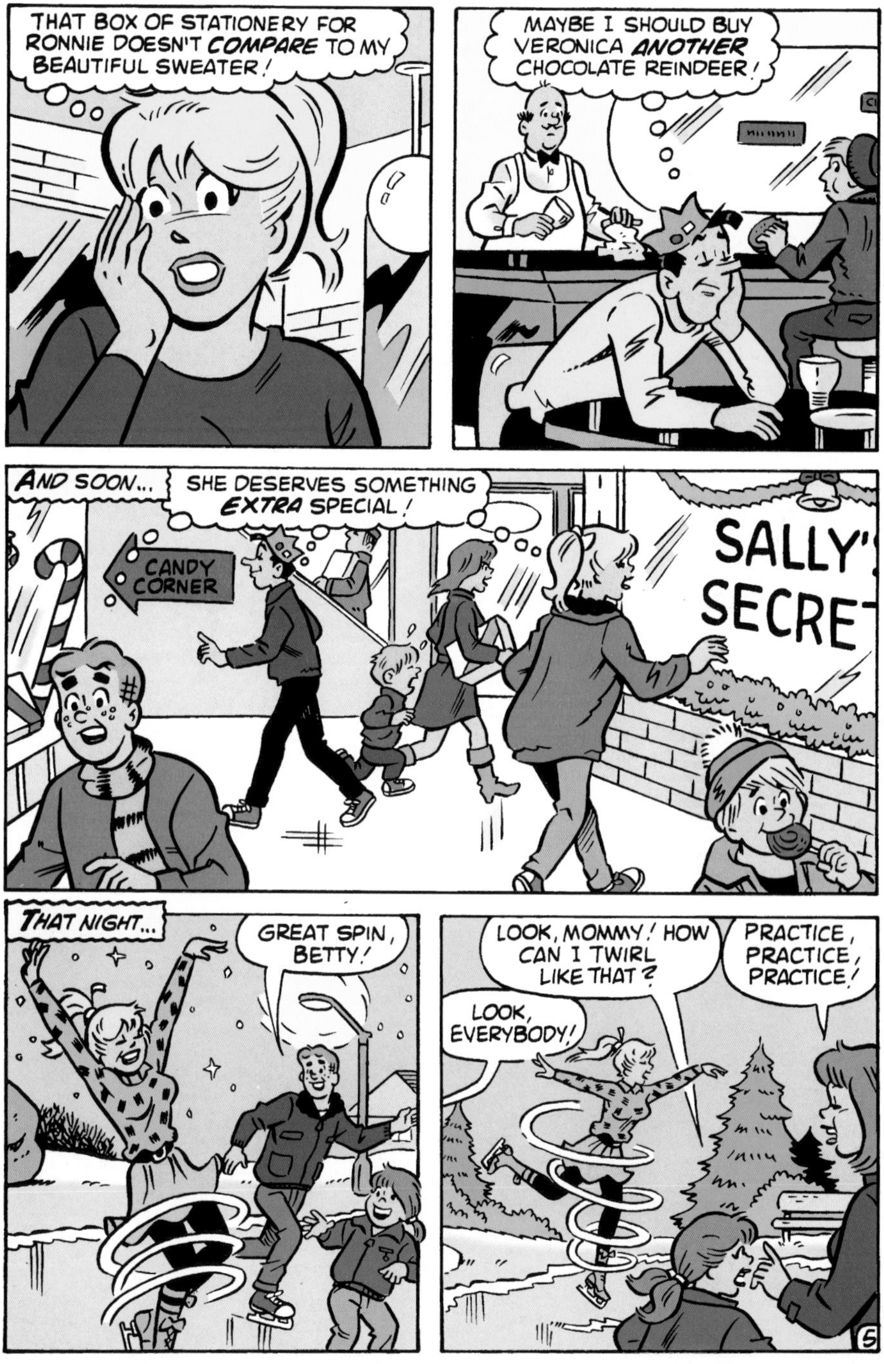
THAT BOX OF STATIONERY FOR RONNIE DOESN'T COMPARE TO MY BEAUTIFUL SWEATER!
MAYBE I SHOULD BUY VERONICA ANOTHER CHOCOLATE REINDEER!
AND SOON...
SHE DESERVES SOMETHING EXTRA SPECIAL!
CANDY CORNER
SALLY'S SECRE
THAT NIGHT...
GREAT SPIN, BETTY!
LOOK, MOMMY! HOW CAN I TWIRL LIKE THAT?
PRACTICE, PRACTICE, PRACTICE!
LOOK, EVERYBODY!
5

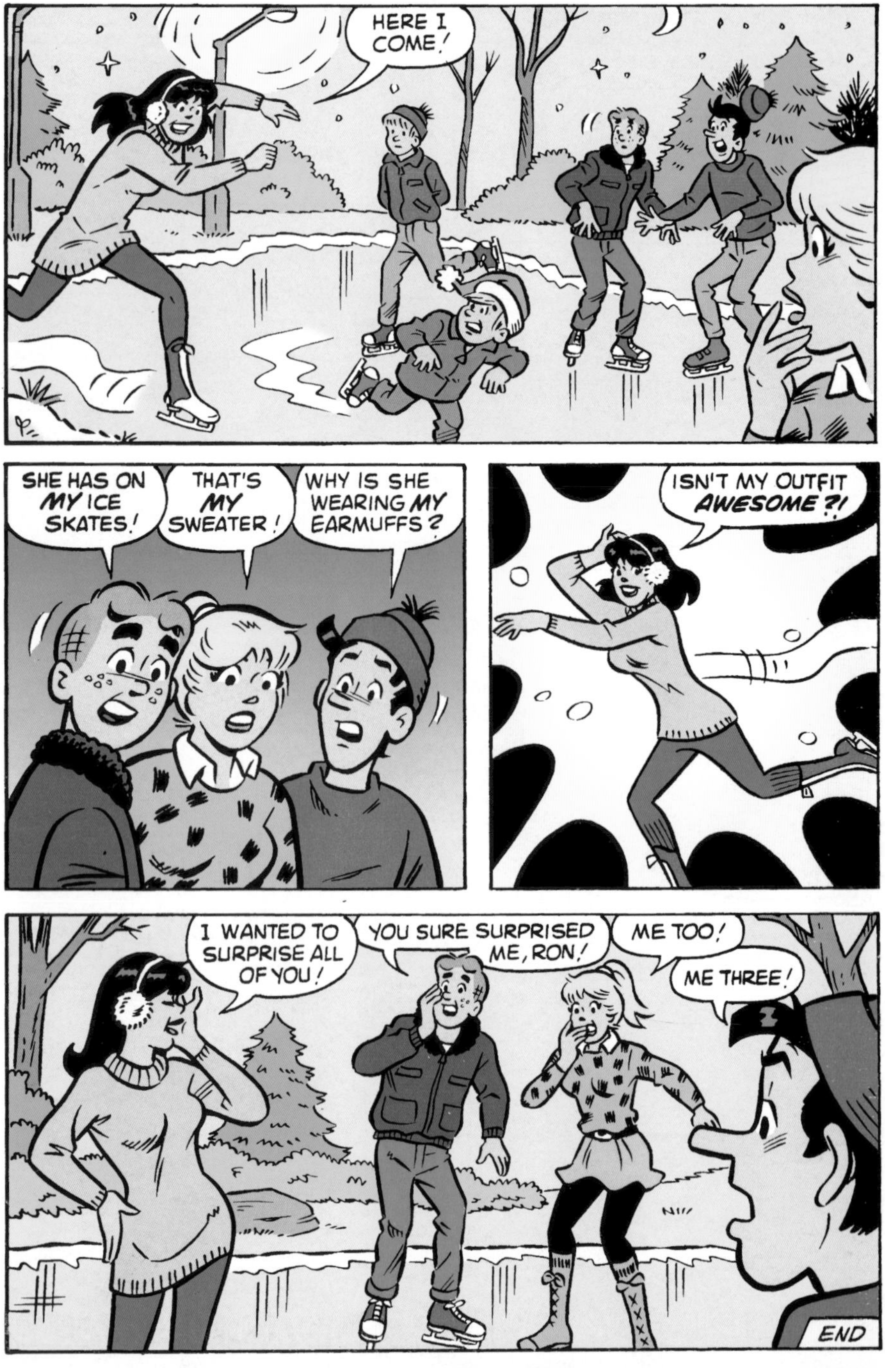
HERE I COME!
SHE HAS ON MY ICE SKATES!
THAT'S MY SWEATER!
WHY IS SHE WEARING MY EARMUFFS?
ISN'T MY OUTFIT AWESOME?!
I WANTED TO SURPRISE ALL OF YOU!
YOU SURE SURPRISED ME, RON!
ME TOO!
ME THREE!
END